Praise for *Someone I Used to Know*

"A beautifully crafted look at the complications of returning to 'regular life' after a devastating sexual assault. Fierce in its unapologetic dissection of rape culture, toxic masculinity, and athletic entitlement, Patty Blount does not hold her punches with respect to how difficult healing can be for an entire family. This book is thoughtful and thought-provoking and ultimately very hopeful for survivors and those around them."

—C. Desir, author of *Bleed Like Me* and *Fault Line*

Praise for *Some Boys*

"A bold and necessary look at an important, and very real, topic. Everyone should read this book."

—Jennifer Brown, author of *Thousand Words* and *The Hate List*

"Blount hits home with this novel… *Some Boys* belongs in every YA collection."

—*School Library Journal*

"A largely sensitive treatment of an emotionally complex topic."

—*Kirkus Reviews*

Praise for *The Way It Hurts*

"This novel illustrates both the good and bad sides of social media, a key player in the plot. Young readers who are immersed in many online sites will enjoy that aspect, and hard rock aficionados, as well as lovers of teen romance, will find enjoyment. This thoroughly modern novel investigates age-old teen problems showing up in new ways."

—*VOYA*

"This book sensitively covers topics such as sexism, handicapping conditions, and ageism. The characters' issues are eventually resolved through hard work and understanding, making this an interesting and informative read."

—*School Library Connection*

Praise for *Nothing Left to Burn*

"An authentic, fast-paced romance with emotional intensity to burn."

—Huntley Fitzpatrick, author of *The Boy Most Likely To* and *My Life Next Door*

"A heartbreaking novel—real and full of hope."

—Miranda Kenneally, author of *Coming up for Air* and *Defending Taylor*

Praise for *Send*

"Blount's debut novel combines authentic voice with compelling moral dilemmas...raise[s] important questions about honesty, forgiveness, the ease of cyberbullying, and the obligation to help others."

—*VOYA*

"A morality play about releasing the past and seizing the present...the ethical debates raised will engage readers."

—*Publishers Weekly*

Praise for *TMI*

"Blount has a good handle on teen culture, especially the importance of social media...realistically expressed...[and] honestly portrayed."

—*School Library Journal*

"[A] tech-driven cautionary tale...Blount addresses the potential perils of online relationships and the sometimes-destructive power of social media without proselytizing."

—*Publishers Weekly*

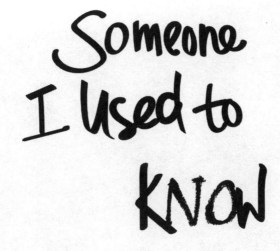

Someone I Used to Know

PATTY BLOUNT

sourcebooks
fire

Published by Sourcebooks Fire, an imprint of Sourcebooks, Inc.
P.O. Box 4410, Naperville, Illinois 60567-4410
(630) 961-3900
Fax: (630) 961-2168
sourcebooks.com

Library of Congress Cataloging-in-Publication Data

Names: Blount, Patty, author.
Title: Someone I used to know / Patty Blount.
Description: Naperville, Illinois : Sourcebooks Fire, [2018]
Identifiers: LCCN 2017061768 | (pbk : alk. paper)
Subjects: | CYAC: Rape--Fiction. | Brothers and sisters--Fiction. | Family
    problems. | High schools--Fiction. | Schools--Fiction.
Classification: LCC PZ7.B6243 Soq 2018 | DDC [Fic]--dc23 LC record available
at https://lccn.loc.gov/2017061768

Printed and bound in Canada.
MBP 10 9 8 7 6 5 4 3 2 1

To the men in my life—Fred, Rob, and Chris—for supporting me on this odyssey, for not being that guy, and for giving me hope.

September

1

ASHLEY

Your Honor, thank you for letting me address this court. The first thing I want to say is that I couldn't wait to start high school. I liked the defendant. I really liked him. And I thought he liked me back. But now I know he never saw me as a person. I was nothing more than an opportunity for him. So now I can't wait until I'm done with high school.

—**Ashley E. Lawrence, victim impact statement**

NOW

BELLFORD, OHIO

The mirror is my enemy.

So is the closet.

There's literally nothing to wear. Clothes litter my room. Several pairs of jeans are balled up on my bed because they hug my butt too tightly. T-shirts lie in piles on the floor because they're too clingy. Shorts and skirts? No. They reveal too much leg. I throw them over my shoulder. Dr. Joyce, my therapist, claims it's normal to have trouble getting dressed after what happened.

I always tell her I don't care what's *normal after what happened*; I just want *normal*—without qualifiers. I want to open my closet, pull on any old outfit, and not obsess about people thinking I'm *asking for it*.

"Ashley?"

I glance up and find Mom in my doorway, looking me over. I'm wearing a robe even though it's about ninety degrees outside.

"You okay?"

"Fine," I lie and dive back into my closet, mopping sweat from the back of my neck. We'd agreed that I'd go to school on my own today. It's time.

"Ashley, look at me."

I pull my head out of my closet and meet her eyes.

"Honey, I know you're upset. We all are, but I promise you, it's going to be okay."

At those words, I clench my jaw and shoot up a hand. Then I just turn away because, honestly, I don't know which part pisses me off more…the colossal understatement implied by a wimpy word like *upset* or the addition of the pronoun *we*, suggesting everybody else in this family knows exactly how I feel when they don't have the slightest clue.

She sighs but nods and then steps over to the closet, rehanging the discarded clothes I dumped on my bed. "We haven't

SOMEONE I USED TO KNOW

looked west yet. California is truly beautiful. You know I've never been there?"

I roll my eyes. We haven't looked anywhere. All we've done is *talk* about it, so I say the same thing I always say when this comes up. "Mom, I don't want to move away."

"But it could be a fresh new start for all of us, Ashley. No one would even have to know you were—"

"Mom." I cut her off, forcefully this time. "I really have to get dressed."

Her blue eyes, the eyes both of my brothers inherited, fill with the look that's become way too common over the last two years. It's disappointment. Is it directed at me or what happened to me? I don't know anymore, and I don't think it even matters. All I know is it's so acute, I can't bear to see it and have to look away. Once again, I return my attention to the closet to find something to wear.

"Okay. Have a great first day. Call if…if you need me." She turns and heads downstairs.

I don't answer because great days are yet another myth I've discovered in a long series of them, starting with the concept of justice. I roll my eyes. *California.* Like it would be no problem to just shut down Dad's auto repair shop and move a family of five across the country where there are no grandparents, no aunts, no uncles or cousins.

As the front door closes and the engine starts in the driveway, my phone buzzes. It hardly ever does that anymore. I glance at the display, annoyed when some stupid tiny seed of hope blooms because there's a text message from Derek.

Derek: Good luck today.

Rage ignites inside me like a match held to dry leaves. Cursing, I kick over my hamper, swipe every last book and paper off my desk, and come perilously close to hurling my cell phone at the wall. *Good luck.* Could he be this clueless?

As this is my brother, yes. He could be and often is this clueless…and worse.

Ashley: Yeah. Sure. Luck. That'll help.

The phone buzzes again.

Derek: I'm sorry. I swear I am.

Sorry? I almost laugh. Derek doesn't do apologies.

"Derek, tell Ashley you're sorry," Mom would order him after he'd made me cry for some thing or another.

And he'd say, "Sorry, Ash." Mom would walk away or turn her back, and he'd stick out his tongue or roll his eyes and smile that Derek smile, and I'd *know*. I'd know he wasn't really sorry. He was only saying it to make Mom happy. Apologies happen when you own up to having been wrong, and Derek has never been wrong in his life.

I stare at the words I'd have given anything to hear my brother say two years ago, but they're too little, too late, and knowing Derek as I do, false.

I toss the phone to my bed and go back to pawing through every drawer in my dresser and every hanger in my closet for something to wear and finally spy something. It's this old maxi dress Mom bought for me years ago. The tags are still on it. I grab it and hold it up. It probably doesn't fit. I think I was twelve or thirteen when she bought it.

There's a little pang in my chest. *Twelve or thirteen.*

Before everything changed.

I swallow hard, trying to hold on to the pain because if it gets loose—

Deep breath. Hold it in. Okay. Dress. Right.

I hold the dress up to my body, considering it. Yeah, it might work. I slip it on, smooth it out. It's actually a bit big. And ugly. Shades of dull beige and brown in a paisley print that hangs all the way to my ankles. I grab a sweater to hide my shoulders revealed by this outfit and smooth down a cowlick in my hair, which has finally reached shoulder length again.

Above the shelf on my wall, there's a mirror Mom bought so I could get ready for the new school year. I'd smashed the old mirror in another fit of rage not long after I'd hacked off my long hair. Yeah, this outfit *does* work. It hides pretty much everything.

I grab my phone and try to visualize the day ahead. Tara, my best friend, will meet me at school. She always has my back. The rest of the school is a different story.

Derek's words rattle around inside my head like some kind of curse. *Good luck, Ash Tray. You'll need it.*

Deep breaths. Breathe in, hold for one…two…three…four,

breathe out. In, hold, out. In, hold, out. I hate doing these breath-ing exercises because I feel like a total loser. I mean, who has to concentrate on breathing?

Traumatized people like me, that's who.

Two years. It's been two years. I'm fine. I'm absolutely fine. I roll my eyes because that's another thing I must do. Tell myself complete and total lies. It's supposed to help me believe them, turning them into what my therapist claims are *self-fulfilling prophecies*. I get it. The power of positive thinking and all that crap. But the truth is, I'm still waiting to feel fulfilled, yet I keep doing the same stupid breathing exercise, and I keep repeating the same stupid lies until finally my heart stops trying to beat out of my chest.

This is it—the first day of school. Junior year. I can do this. I can. I *will* do this.

I do something else...something my therapist never told me about. I visualize. I imagine building a dam...a little beaver dam of logs and twigs and dried mud to keep all of the triggers and memories and rage and...pain from leaking out into my life. I spend some time shoring up my dam, and with one last deep breath, I head downstairs, pretending the dread that's still climbing up my rib cage is anticipation for the first day of my junior year.

I see two coffee cups in the sink and dishes from my parents' breakfast. It's normal and typical, and it gives me something to hang on to while I wrestle all that dread back behind the dam.

I glance at the clock to make sure I have time and discover it's after 8:00 a.m.

No, that can't be right. I woke up extra early.

My shoulders sag while I stare at the clock blinking on the microwave over the stove and then pull the phone from my pocket. It shows the same time. How? How is this possible? They're wrong. They're both wrong. They have to be. I run to the family room, but the cable box is blinking the same time.

I've not only missed the bus, but I've missed the start of first period.

I shoulder my bag and start walking.

I thought I was past this. I thought the days when I'd lost huge chunks of time doing nothing except breathing were behind me.

......

School is terminally irritating.

I missed first period entirely, and by the time the old bat in the front office gives me my pass, I've missed half of second, too.

"Ashley. Hey," Tara whispers when I finally take my seat in lit class, her face split in a huge smile. "What took you so long?" And then she looks at my outfit. "What *are* you wearing?"

I shake my head. "Don't even."

She puts up both hands in apology—or maybe surrender—and turns back to her notebook. Mrs. Kaplan is reading us the class rules and information about homework, exams, and class participation. I know this drill so I zone out. I take a look around the class, see who's here, who's not, and spot Sebastian Valenti over by the window at the same second he jerks his eyes away from me.

7

They're really amazing eyes. *Hazel.* I used to think hazel was a color but found out it actually means eyes that change colors. Sebastian's eyes look green sometimes, and other times, they look brown, and I've even seen them look practically yellow. Sebastian's a good guy. The best. He saved me when my stupid brother didn't. Wouldn't. He keeps asking how I'm doing, and I keep saying *fine.* And that's about as deep as our conversations ever get, so I just don't bother anymore. I haven't talked to him all summer. But he's still a really good guy.

"May I have your attention please?"

The PA system cracks into life, and Mrs. Kaplan takes a seat at her desk while the principal welcomes us back to the new school year and tells us about some after-school clubs. And then, right after an announcement about several new teachers, Principal McCloskey ruins what's left of my life.

"We'd like to welcome our new calculus teacher, Mr. Davidson, to Bellford High. In addition to teaching calculus, Mr. Davidson has agreed to help us start a new and improved football program. Tryouts for this year's Bengals team will be held after school."

A cheer goes up around the classroom.

I sit in my seat, frozen. *I'm fine. I'm absolutely fine.* I lie to myself, but my brain knows better, and I can feel that old pressure spinning inside my chest.

A hand squeezes mine, and I jolt like I've been struck by lightning. I look up into the concerned eyes of Tara. That's when I discover everybody in the entire class has swiveled around to see how I'm taking this news. Most people look concerned, like Tara.

But others are triumphant, like Andre, sitting at the front of the classroom, and Bruce, over by the windows next to Sebastian. I can't stand it, can't deal with it. Suddenly, I'm on my feet, running for the door. "Ashley! Ashley, come back here!" Mrs. Kaplan shouts after me.

I dart across the hall into the girls' bathroom and lock myself into a stall. *I'm fine I'm fine I'm fine I'm fine.*

I repeat the words over and over so fast, they morph into percussion that syncs to the pounding of my heart. It's bad enough seeing everybody stare at me. Everybody blames me for canceling football.

Derek blames me.

My brother blames me for what happened two years ago. I can never forget that…or forgive it.

It doesn't matter how many lies I tell myself or how deep I bury those memories, how strong the dam is. Those memories—the pain they cause—they keep finding ways to break out, and I'm just not strong enough to hold them back.

I don't think I ever will be.

TWO YEARS AGO
BELLFORD, OHIO

It's raining, but I don't care. I love the way the air smells when it rains. Earthy. Clean and fresh and—so *alive*. I'm totally psyched to start high school and don't care if there's a hurricane. Armed with my bright pink umbrella, I'm ready to head to the bus stop, but Mom says Derek could have the car if he drives *both* of us to school. I squeal and clap. I love riding shotgun with Derek... when he lets me, that is.

Derek's been treating me like crap for ages. We're only a year and a half apart, so we shared a stroller, took baths together, went to gymnastics and soccer together. We were on different teams, though. That always bugged me. I wanted to play on *his* team. We're a unit, a combo special, a *team*. Justin, our brother, is a lot older. He has his own separate life. But Derek and I are best friends. Nobody knows it but me, but Derek wants to make video games when we grow up. He has a ton of cool ideas, too.

At least, he used to. He never talks about that kind of stuff with me anymore. Now he's all about football and girls and driving and avoids me as much as he can. I *annoy* him. I don't see how that's even possible. I try to do all the things he always liked doing with me like movie nights and epic game battles. Now he just rolls his eyes and says I should get a life.

But this is my first day of high school. So that means we can hang out again. I'm older and not so annoying. Derek doesn't argue with Mom about driving me to school, so I kind of assume that means he's finally outgrown his problems with me. Mom said he would...eventually. I also kind of assume that driving us to school also means driving us home. He has other ideas.

"Take the bus home. I'm hanging with my friends later."

"Oh," I say, smile fading. "Yeah. Sure."

My first day of high school is awesome in every possible way. I have lunch with Donna Jennings, a girl I know from middle school, who got her hair cut in this really cool undershaved style *and* got a boyfriend over the summer. She showed everybody the gold heart necklace he'd given her, and my heart sighed. It had stopped raining by the afternoon, so I take my time heading to the parking lot to ride home with Derek, but the space where he'd parked Mom's car is empty.

Darn. I was supposed to take the bus home. I totally forgot.

"You look lost." A boy with messy hair and blue eyes says. He is seriously cute and standing with three other boys against a blue car.

"Must be a freshman," another says.

"Just looking for my brother."

"Who is he?"

"Um. Derek Lawrence."

They exchange glances and laugh. "Oh, you're *Ash Tray*. Sorry, you just missed him."

"Cut it out," the cute one says. "I'm Vic. Victor Patton." He smiles at me. Dimples. Wow.

"Hey, that's what Derek calls her." The boy laughs.

Oh my God. Derek told them that? My face bursts into flames, and I turn away.

"Leave her alone." Vic straightens up and walks toward me. He's tall, taller than Derek. "Derek left. He might be back. Why don't you call him?"

Yeah. Good idea. I pull out my phone and hit his name. It rings, but he never picks up. Next, I try texting him. Meanwhile, the boys pile into the blue car and take off, splashing water all over me.

11

I brush muddy splotches from my clothes, choking back tears, and call Mom's cell phone, but it goes straight to voicemail. I try calling Dad too. Same thing.

What am I supposed to do? I head back to the main entrance, sink down on one of the steps, and drop my chin into my hands. I sit there, quietly crying, until the steel doors burst open and a bunch of laughing girls jog past me. Quickly, I fluff my waist-long hair in front of my face to hide the tears. All but one of the five girls wear warm-up suits bearing the word *Fusion* in bright red letters down one leg.

One crouches down to get a look at me. "Hey. You okay?"

I nod vigorously. "Yeah. Fine."

"You're crying. Can I help?" She takes a step closer, and I scrub at my face with the back of my hand, like that has even a remote chance at erasing my complete embarrassment.

"Not unless you have a magic potion that works on stupid brothers," I blurt. Oh my God! I slap a hand over my mouth. I need to die. Right now. Where's a lightning bolt when you need one?

"Oh, a stupid brother. I have one of those." She smiles. She's so pretty. Long, dark, and lean, she looks like one of the models in my *Teen Vogue* magazines.

I'm suddenly interested in hearing her story. "Older or younger?"

"Younger. Takes annoying to whole new levels, like it's some kind of vow he took. Do you know he actually put my retainer in the toilet? My mother nearly burst a blood vessel after that." She giggles. "Oh! I'm Candace Ladd."

"Hey." This time, my smile is bigger. "Ashley. Ashley Lawrence."

"You must be a freshman."

I wince, face burning all over again. "Does it show?"

She laughs, revealing perfectly straight, bright white teeth that somehow remained impervious to her little brother ruining her retainer. "Nah. I've just never seen you before, and I know pretty much everybody. I'm a junior." She studies me, her head angled to one side. "Lawrence, huh?" And then her dark eyes open wide. "Oh my God. Is that stupid brother you mentioned *Derek* Lawrence?"

"You know him?"

She nods. "Yeah, we're in the same homeroom. Oh, wow. Brittany is gonna *hate* hearing he's a jerk. She's really into him." Candace points to the field on the other side of the small parking lot. The pretty blond with the great smile is doing ballet pliés.

I stare and swallow hard. Brittany is everything I'm not. Beautiful. Skinny. She even looks like Derek with perfect blond hair and blue eyes. They could be Ken and Barbie. I have dark hair and dark eyes. "Maybe he'll be nicer to her."

"Come on." Candace Ladd grabs my hand, tugging me off the step where I'd been sitting, crying. "You know what's great for getting over the stupid stuff brothers do?"

I have no idea, but I follow her anyway, making my way across the lot to the field that's empty except for these girls.

"Dancing."

I plant my feet in the grass at that. I *love* dancing. I'd taken dance classes for years when I was little. But I stopped about two years ago and now have a roll of fat bulging from the top of my jeans. I'd stick out like one of those old *Sesame Street* games— one of these things is *so* not like the others.

"Everybody, this is Ashley Lawrence. She's Derek's sister."

The really pretty blond snaps her head up at that. Her smooth hair is pulled back in a ponytail, and her blue eyes are so blue, I wonder if she wears contacts. "I'm Brittany," she says with a smile. "And this is Tara, Marlena, and Deanne."

"Hi," I manage to squeak out while the girls each smile and greet me.

Oh God, they're all so beautiful. Next to them, I feel like a freak.

I *am* a freak.

"Ashley's gonna dance with us today. She's got some brother crap to work out of her system," Candace explains to her friends, and Tara's face instantly breaks into an expression of total understanding.

"Oh, honey. I got two of them. Is Derek what caused all this?" She waves a hand with pink-striped fingernails at my new back-to-school outfit, currently splattered in mud thanks to the boys in the blue car.

"Um, indirectly," I admit.

"Jerk."

"What an asshole!"

One by one, they all give their opinion of Derek while adjusting hairstyles, retying shoes, and stretching leg muscles. I'm entranced.

"You a freshman?" Marlena asks, and my face heats up again.

I nod, expecting her to make a disgusted face, but she just says, "I'm a sophomore. Candace and Brittany are juniors. And Tara's a freshman, like you."

I perk up at this news. Finally, somebody my own age.

Brittany pulls a small wireless speaker from her backpack, turns it on, and sets it on a bench at the edge of the athletic field. "It's nice having the field to ourselves for once."

"Hey, let's teach her the routine," Deanne suggests. "Then she can try out for Ms. Pasmore."

Wait, what? Try out?

Holy crap, I can't. But the rest of the girls agree. Candace crosses her arms and studies me. "Can you do basic moves like pirouettes and leaps?"

I shake my head. "I haven't done those in a long time."

"But you know how?" Candace prods. I can only shrug. "Oh, come on. Just try." She urges me with a smile.

"Come on, Ashley. It would be great if we both make it on to the team," Tara adds.

Tara's words shoot straight into my heart and sort of plant roots. Suddenly, I want this. I want to dance and be on the team and have friends who understand all of my Derek problems.

"It's okay, Ashley. You can do this," Tara says, and that spot inside my heart warms up again.

I swallow hard, rub my damp palms down my legs, and get into fourth position…or is it fifth? I perform a slow, shaky pirouette. The girls applaud, and my face feels hot.

"That's seriously not bad for someone who hasn't danced in a couple of years." Candace lifts her palm for a high five that I happily give her.

Derek would freak out if I do this.

So I should totally do it.

"That's really great, Ashley. Okay, now strut!" She calls out, and the girls line up with me, everybody moving left, pumping their arms. I follow along, astounded by my efforts. "Other way. That's good, Ashley! Now make it bigger."

We strut back and march in place, and then Brittany takes over, leading us in a series of big, bold movements—kicks, leaps, shoulder shimmies, and pirouettes. They were right. This is fun. We dance for over an hour. The girls teach me their entire routine, and I do it all and have no time to be mad about Derek.

When we finally stop, Brittany angles her head, studying me.

"You know, you should cut some of that. It's way too long for you." She waves a hand over my hair.

My hair reaches my waist. "I, um, don't look good with short hair. I mean, no offense," I quickly say to Tara, whose jaw-length bob looks totally awesome.

"No, not that short," Brittany says. "Maybe about here." She indicates the middle of my back with her hand. "Take some of it off. I think it'll have more volume."

"Yeah," Candace agrees. "When you do those snap turns, you won't whip us in the face."

Deanne hands me some forms. "Here. After you try out, you'll need to order these."

I stare down the sheet of papers, see the various items, each bearing the team name, Fusion.

"What do you say, Ashley? Are you in?" Candace grins, those bright white teeth gleaming at me.

I scan the group of them, all of them perfect and pretty and good at dancing. "Aren't you worried I'll make you look bad? I don't…look like you all."

"Oh, honey," Tara says, putting an arm around me. "All you need is some practice to build up your confidence." She looks around the group for verification.

"Hell, yeah. In freshman year, I had braces on my teeth, a terrible haircut, and I was six inches shorter than I am now. I could barely talk to anyone," Brittany admits. "But you have something I didn't have in freshman year."

I did? "What's that?"

"Boobs." The other girls crack up as my face bursts into flames. "The boys won't see anything else. Trust me."

Brittany and Candace hop into a car and are gone after a honk and a wave. Deanne and Marlena stand with me until a minivan pulls up, and then it's just me and Tara. We start walking toward the school's main exit.

"So how are you getting home?" I ask her, and she shrugs.

"Walk. I live pretty much next door." She points down the road.

"Handy."

"Well, see you tomorrow. It was nice meeting you."

"You too," I call back.

I start walking toward town, where my dad's garage is, wishing

I had a bottle of water with me. My legs are like noodles after all that dancing, and a two-mile walk does not appeal to me. Like a wish granted, a horn honks, and a shiny black Chevy slows down beside me.

"Hey, Derek's sister! Need a ride?"

Oh. Em. Gee.

It's *him*. The boy with the cute smile and the dimples.

My voice gets stuck in my throat, so I only nod.

"What's your name? Your real name, I mean," he asks through the open passenger side window, smiling and making my wobbly legs even weaker. He isn't going to call me Ash Tray? *Swoon.*

"Um. Ashley." My voice is all squeaky.

"I'm Vic."

"Yeah, I remember." Vic. What a cool name. The coolest name in the world. I want to name a baby Vic.

He laughs. "Good. So where are you heading?"

"Oh, um. To my dad's garage. Over on Blaine."

"Right, right. I know where it is. Hop in," he invites with a jerk of his head. "I'll give you a lift."

It never occurs to me to say no. He has such a great smile. His hair is somewhere between blond and brown and so messy I itch to touch it and smooth it. He's really tall but lean. And his eyes are so blue, they look like pools you never want to get out of. But it's that smile, the one with the dimple at the corner, that makes me forget my name.

"So, Ashley. You're what? A freshman?"

Is there a sign hanging over my head or something? Wincing, I nod. "It must show."

"Just a little." He looks over and winks. "I'm a senior."

A senior is driving me home. Ohmygodohmygodohmygod.

"Did you join a club or something?"

I nod, and suddenly remember I am probably in urgent need of a shower or a can of deodorant or a wet wipe, and I try to shrivel up against the passenger door and hope he doesn't get close enough to sniff me. "Yeah. The dance team."

"Fusion? That's awesome! The dance team performs at all the Bengals games. I'll probably see you at practice. Our coach had a meeting today, otherwise we'd have been on the field." He slows down for a traffic light.

Can he hear my heart pounding?

"How do you like Bellford High?"

"I like the girls on the dance team. And I like my science teacher."

"Who did you get?"

"Mr. Wilder."

"Oh, yeah, he's great. I had him. He likes to give pop quizzes every week, so be ready."

"Oh. Yeah. I will."

"Nothing terrible. Just read ahead and you'll be fine."

Read ahead. I can do totally do that.

Vic puts on his turn signal and waits for a left turn. "So your brother's kind of a jerk to you, huh?"

My heart sinks, and I slide a little lower in my seat.

"Don't worry about it. I'll say something to him tomorrow."

Suddenly, I'm grinning like a maniac. There's probably a circle of cartoon birds and butterflies flying around the heart that just floated out of my body. Vic laughs and shakes his head as he pulls to the curb.

"We're here. It was nice to meet you, Ashley Lawrence." Vic hands me my bag as I pretty much fall out of the car on legs I can no longer feel. "See you tomorrow."

"Yeah. Tomorrow."

He honks and waves as he pulls away. I'm halfway in love.

"Ashley? Who was that?" Dad asks. He just stepped out of one of the garage bay doors.

"Hmm?"

"Ashley!"

I turn and see Mom in the entrance to Dad's garage. "Mom! Can we get my hair cut? Please? I'm gonna try out for the dance team, and my hair is too long, and it's in the way, and I met a senior named Vic, and I need to buy these if I make the team." I finally pause for air, and Mom takes the Fusion gear order form I have clutched in my hand.

"A haircut. And a uniform. Well, okay. But a senior? No. I don't know about that."

"I'm with you on that," Dad says, grabbing Mom in a hug and tickling her until she squeals.

2

DEREK

NOW

LONG ISLAND, NEW YORK

My sister hates me.

Ashley's hated me for a couple of years now, and it's okay. I *wanted* her to hate me, and I did whatever I could to make that happen. Of course, that was before I knew what *hate* really meant. Now that I get it, I can't change it, can't undo all the shit I did, can't fix what went wrong. So I *suffer*.

See, *hate* is a meaningless word. Everybody tosses the word around like it's confetti, diluting it, rendering it about as effective as a Band-Aid over a gushing wound to describe how they feel about every little thing that annoys them. They hate this song, that food, that person, or this movie. They hate homework, hate their teachers, hate their parents. They hate this team and that game. They *hate* every damn thing, but nobody has even the smallest clue what *hate* really means unless they're the object of it.

The *focus* of it.

Hating somebody is more than you stop caring about them, and it's more than not wanting to see that person ever again. It's this need—an urge you can barely control—to make that person suffer. True hate goes all the way down to your bone marrow. Sometimes, it's glacier cold and infinitely patient; other times, it's surface-of-the-sun hot and bullet fast.

Ashley hates me in that glacier-cold, slow-moving kind of way. It leaves me permanently frostbitten and has this really annoying habit of shadowing me even when she's not around.

Like right now—I can't get away from these damn flyers. One was slipped under my dorm room door, another was stuck on the exit door of my building, the third was stuffed into my hand when I ordered some breakfast, and now dozens of them are folded into little tent cards and placed on top of every single table in the dining hall.

I've been on campus at Rocky Hill University—several states and hundreds of miles away from my sister—for a few weeks, relieved to be away, to be anonymous, to be on my own. Mom and Dad wanted to come with me, set up my dorm room, and have the big sloppy farewell like they did when Justin left for college four years before, but I wanted no part of that. I just wanted to be gone. Free. When Dad got the last of my crap into the car and asked if I'd said my goodbyes to everybody, I'd said yes.

But I hadn't.

I tried to say goodbye to Ashley. She held up a hand and said, "Just go."

It had cut deeply, but I knew I deserved it, so I climbed into the passenger seat. Mom came to the front door and waved as Dad pulled the car out of the driveway. Ashley stood behind her, freezing me with that same cold, dead stare she'd been using on me since the trial. I adjusted my seat and settled back, happy to be rid of her for the next four years.

And what happens?

Everywhere I look, I see reminders of her.

The flyers announce You Can Stop Campus Sexual Assault! The white text on the blue paper proclaims they're gonna Take Back the Night.

Great.

There's a huge rally being planned for the week of homecoming—it's called *Rock Stock* here. Because we're the *Rockets*.

Of course, it would be homecoming week, because, like I said, I must suffer.

Homecoming week is when Ashley was…when she was assaulted. Like I could forget.

There will be guest speakers and live music and a candlelight vigil for all the survivors of sexual assault. I flip it over to read my favorite part: *Are you a guy against rape? Join GAR today!*

GAR. I wonder if people say it with a rolling *R*, like a pirate. *Garrrrrrr.*

Oh, and my coach informed us the entire football team would don special uniforms for that game to show our support.

Awesome. I was already planning on being sick, injured, or maybe both that day.

I crumple up the collection of flyers into a single giant ball and shove my breakfast aside, my stomach churning up acid.

"Hey, Derek."

I glance up into the smiling face of Brittany Meyers, my girlfriend. We actually met in high school but didn't hook up until we both arrived here. "Hey, Britt." I sit up a little straighter and shove thoughts of my sister the hell out of my brain. Brittany's hot in that girl-next-door way. Her long blond hair's tied up in a loose knot with strands hanging loose. She's wearing a tank top, shorts, and flip-flops, and her toenails are painted an electric green. My mouth goes suddenly sandpaper dry. Happens every time I see her.

Quickly, I take a sip of orange juice. A big one.

"What's this?" She indicates my balled-up collection of flyers, and I shrug. Understanding dawns a second later. "Oh. The rally."

"Yeah. That." I rub the side of my face and scratch at the scar near my temple.

"You're gonna go, right?"

Hell no. I shake my head. "No way. I'm the last person who should be there."

She slides into the chair opposite mine and covers my hand with hers, and my whole body heats up. "Derek, you're the *best* person to be at that rally. You get it. A lot of guys claim they get it and have no clue. But you do."

I look into her big blue eyes for a minute and finally decide she believes her own bullshit. And then I decide she's right. I *do* have a clue. In fact, I have the whole mystery solved. And because I do, there's no way in hell I'm going anywhere near that rally because I don't need the entire university knowing I'm Derek Lawrence, the guy whose sister is the *Bellford High School Rape Victim.*

That's what the media called her.

Ashley was barely fourteen when it happened. A minor. So her identity was protected. But she took her story public, posting a detailed account to her blog. And she included my role in it. Now everybody from feminist bloggers to Ellen DeGeneres knows our names.

So, yeah. I don't want my whole school saying, "Oh! You're *that* Derek Lawrence."

Yep. The Derek Lawrence who played a stupid game that got his sister raped and then told a court of law to go easy on her rapist. The same Derek Lawrence who drove away and left her standing alone in an empty parking lot, putting the whole fucking ordeal into motion.

Self-hatred runs another ice-cold finger across my bare skin, and I shiver, reminding myself I deserve this…deserve every second of it.

Ashley was a surprise baby, born just a year and a half after me and close to six years after Justin. Mom was *so* happy to finally get a girl, I think she went a little bit nuts. She got a kick out of raising us like we were twins with the whole matching outfits thing. Maybe it was cute when we were toddlers. But the fake twin thing was epically annoying when I hit middle school.

Ashley was spoiled rotten, got away with absolutely any damn thing she wanted, and grew up to be a real pain. By the time I hit sixth grade, I'd had enough.

SIXTH GRADE
BELLFORD, OHIO

Martin's got this ancient issue of *Playboy*. We're not really friends. He's just a kid at school. But this old magazine is awesome, so when he invites me to his house, I can't wait to go because he claims there's a whole box of them in his basement.

It's an issue from way back in the eighties, and the pictures show women of every type you can imagine. Blonds, brunettes, redheads—each more beautiful and sexier than the last. Blue eyes, brown eyes, green eyes, and they all have these big, beautiful, and bare breasts. I can't stop staring. I don't want to stop staring.

It's the first time I see a girl as, well—a *girl*, and not a sister or a mother.

I like it. A lot.

But next thing I know, Ashley's coming with me to Martin's house to play with his little sister, which not only means no *Playboy*, it means *two* sisters bugging us every minute of the day. We whine to his mother, who does nothing, which, in my experience, is what all mothers do when little sisters annoy big brothers. So we start teasing the girls and make it into a contest to see who we can make them cry first.

I win.

I call my sister *Ash Tray* instead of Ashley.

Martin high-fives me.

I just want to do some guy things. Why do I have to spend every single moment of every single day with my sister?

I ask Dad that question when I get home one day.

"Because she's your sister," he says, as if that explains everything.

Yeah, duh. That's the entire problem!

I ask Mom next.

"Derek, there are three of you and two of us. When Dad's working in the garage all day, I have to take Justin to soccer practice, baseball practice, basketball practice, and take you to Martin's house, not to mention go grocery shopping and run all my other errands. And then I have to meet Dad at the garage so I can do the bookkeeping. What's the big deal if Ashley stays with you at Martin's house and gives me one tiny little break?"

Whoa, I'm not the one who decided to have three kids. Jeez.

So I back off. I may be dumb, but I'm not dumb enough to keep pushing Mom when she's pissed off.

I ask Justin as he's heading out why I have to spend all of my time with Ashley and he gets off free and clear.

"D, come on, she's a kid. She looks up to you."

"I can't take it anymore, J. You don't know what it's like. She's a friggin' barnacle on my ass. Can I come with you? Please?"

"You don't even know where I'm going."

"I don't care. Anywhere. As long as Ashley's not there."

Justin pushes his glasses up on his nose and snorts. "Yeah. I have no idea how annoying siblings are. None at all."

I punch his arm. Justin's in tenth grade—way cool—but I'm pretty strong for a sixth-grader. "I'm not annoying."

"Yeah, you *are*." He rubs his arm. "It's just a phase. Soon, Ashley will be hanging out with girls, getting her nails done, and whatever. You can hang on until then, right?"

"No, man. I really can't." My voice cracks.

Justin rolls his eyes. "Jeez, Derek, it's not difficult. Sit down and talk to her. Tell her you need some space. Give her a little, too. If she bugs you, offer to play a game with her and put a clock on it. After that time, you're outta there."

Okay. Maybe that'll work. "So where are you going, anyway?"

"Chess club." He grins at my look of horror and walks out.

When the door shuts behind him, I sigh heavily. Well, at least he gave me actual advice. Mom and Dad don't even see the problem.

I try what he suggested. I tell Ashley I'm not—repeat *not*—taking the bus home from school anymore. I'm taking my bike like all the other guys do.

She waits for me at the bicycle stand—actually expects to ride on the back of my bike all the way home. I'm so mad, I leave her there. Why can't she tell when she isn't wanted? Why does she have to make this so hard?

"Derek, wait!" she calls, running after me as fast as her chubby legs will allow her.

I don't wait. I pedal faster.

It's worth the week without my PlayStation when she makes it home way later than I do, her long hair knotted in one huge tangle and tear streaks down her face.

"Derek, she's in fourth grade! She is way too young to come home alone. You're older. You should have known better." Mom is so mad, her face is purple.

Yeah, yeah.

When she hits sixth grade, I finally get a reprieve.

Ashley makes some new friends. She's invited to sleepovers and to birthday parties and to mall trips. Those are the best days of my eighth-grade life. But, like most things, they don't last long.

If I go to the family room to watch a monster movie, Ashley comes too—and we end up watching some Disney princess shit. If I go out on my bike to race with some guys, she grabs hers too, and we end up circling the block like we still have training wheels on because I'm not allowed to just ride off without her. I tried once and my parents took my bike for a week.

At the end of eighth grade, everybody in school is all jazzed up over summer vacation and starting high school in the fall. Me? I dread it. For me, summer isn't a vacation. No, it's like that twenty-four-hour news station Dad always listens to in the car, the one that plays the same tragedies on an endless loop. Summer was All Ashley, All the Time. *You give Ashley twenty-two minutes, she'll give you a headache.*

But the high school part that comes after summer? Yeah, I'm totally into that for one huge reason.

Ashley won't be there.

For two whole grades, I'll be the only Lawrence in the school.

I have to get through summer first. I'm itchy and desperate and can feel the walls closing in on me. It gets to the point that just hearing Ashley's name makes me coil up into a tight knot.

Until Dad gives me a football. He comes home with it one night after work. Says I have so much energy, he figures I need an outlet for it. Every day, after work, he tosses the ball around with me and Justin. Ashley whines that she wants to play, too. But Dad's firm on this: no girls.

Yes! I pump my fist in the air.

When I finish eighth grade, Justin graduates from high school. He'll be leaving for college soon, where he'll get to live on his own, go where he wants, do what he wants—essentially live the life I want. But when Dad brings home that ball, Justin blows off everything to play.

"Here, let me show you," Dad says one night during our guys-only playtime. "You spread your fingers like this, over the laces and the seam. You see? And you grip it with your fingertips, not your palm."

I do what he says, and he jogs backward to one end of the backyard. I draw back my arm and throw, releasing the ball in an awesome spiral. It propels itself right into Dad's hands and is the most beautiful thing I've ever seen.

I'm instantly hooked.

This is the day Dad saves me from going totally insane.

NOW

LONG ISLAND, NEW YORK

"Derek, you're a guy," Britt says, pulling me out of my trip down memory lane.

"Thanks for noticing."

She smacks my arm. "Do you know how rare it is for guys to get where we're coming from about sexual assault?"

I lift both eyebrows because I'm pretty sure my sister would say I don't get a thing, but before either of us can say anything, Britt's phone buzzes.

She frowns at the text message.

"It's Tara." Her eyes snap to mine, wide with worry. "Derek. They're bringing back football."

I snatch the phone and read Tara's message.

Tara: New coach, new football program, and she ran out of the class. What do I do?

I stare at Britt. I don't need to ask who *she* is. Oh, God. I can't do anything. I'm several states and about six hundred miles away. *Shit.*

"Derek." Brittany grabs my hand. "Sebastian?"

Yeah. I nod. Yeah, Sebastian. I take out my phone and text my former teammate.

Derek: Heard about new coach. Make sure there's no hunt. Please. I'm begging you, protect her.

Sebastian: Already am.

Do more! I want to shout, vibrating with the need to rush home and do something. But I'm not welcome there anymore.

I shove away from the table, spilling my juice. "I gotta go," I mumble, and I bolt, storming through the glass doors like the football player I am. I look feral. Lethal. I always look this way whenever I think about what happened to Ashley.

I wanna tear Victor Patton into tiny little Vic bits, but I can't. The DA warned me—and Dad and Justin—that such a course of action would result in prison terms for us if we tried.

It sure would feel good, though.

I hate Vic, my former friend and teammate. I hate him with that surface-of-the-sun hot kind of hate, and I wish, more than anything, that I could call my sister and tell her I get it now.

I understand *hate.*

And I'm sorry.

3

ASHLEY

I heard about all the times the defendant told people what a nice kid he is. He said it to the police. He said it to everybody at school. He told the press, and he told this court, "I'm a nice kid from a nice family. I don't need to rape anybody." That's because he thinks rapists are scary people in masks who attack in the middle of the night. Victor is much more dangerous than that. The nice kid from the nice family? That's Victor's mask.

—**Ashley E. Lawrence, victim impact statement**

NOW

BELLFORD, OHIO

Locked inside the bathroom stall, I try hard to control myself, to prevent this news from launching me into a full-scale meltdown, but I'm failing spectacularly. My limbs shake, and my heart gallops, and I am so cold, it's like I've never felt warmth. But the worst part is my chest—the pressure, the burn just trying to move air. It hurts so bad, you try to stop breathing, even though you need air or you'll pass out.

Passing out is actually preferable to another anxiety attack. I haven't had one in so long. I used to have them pretty much every day. I *finally* got to a point where I could get through a day and then a week without one. It was progress, Dr. Joyce said. Slow and steady.

And then they bring back football, and now I have to start all over again.

How? How could they do this to me?

I try telling myself it's not personal. It's for the good of the school. The Bengals were on a winning streak two years ago.

Only it *is.*

Personal, I mean.

It's just the latest in a long list of betrayals that started with my brother.

When Andre looked at me earlier in class, I could practically see the comic book thought bubble appear over his head saying, "You lose, bitch!"

Bitch has been his favorite name for me since freshman year.

The names I've been called over the past couple of years don't even register anymore. They're just blips on the radar screen of a wreckage so widespread, I'm kind of surprised I'm still here. There were threats called to our house, to Dad's garage. There was all kinds of harassment. Property destruction. A restraining order against Victor—not my idea, but my dad's. Oh, and let's not forget the righteous condemnation for canceling football from half the stupid team's parents, whose chorus of "My son would never do that, so why must he pay?" was sung loud and often.

What nobody wants to admit, what nobody wants to talk about, is *me*.

I was…raped.

God! I hate that word, hate saying it, hate thinking it, hate how people talk about it and how they *don't*. I hate how it feels on my tongue, and I hate most of all how it just gets worse every time I say it, like a knife in my back. It's been two years!

Rape. Rape. Rape. Stab. Stab. Stab.

The first time I said the word, the world didn't end, but I wish it had.

Most of the time, I avoid the word completely. I know it's really stupid, but I kind of feel like saying it somehow conjures up evil…like saying *Voldemort*.

Talking about it keeps making it real, and I don't want it to be real. Like I said. I lie to myself a lot.

I guess we're not supposed to *ever* get comfortable using a word like that. Maybe that's the point.

But it *did happen*. It is real.

I shut my eyes, squeeze them closed, and try my best not to see my brother's face, but I do. And on it, I see the same expressions I just saw on Andre's face…on Bruce's. That's another problem with the word. Every time I use it, I mourn for what I lost, what was stolen from me. Can you mourn something you didn't even know was there? I don't know that, either.

These are the questions that keep me awake at night.

But I do mourn for my brother. Oh, sure. He's not dead. But he may as well be for all the distance there is between us.

A sob leaks out of my mouth, and I clap both of my shaking hands over it.

This *can't* start again. Football. It's supposed to be just a game. But those guys—guys like Victor and Derek. They think because they win some games, they deserve to get anything they want, that they're heroes and gods who deserve adoration that they can just take even when it's not offered.

Hell to the *no*.

I'm two years older now and a whole lifetime wiser. They want to play ball? They'll have to get by me first. I won't let it happen again. I'm not a little girl anymore.

Victor Patton made sure of that.

......

"How, Mr. McCloskey?" I demand, standing in the principal's office. I'm supposed to be at lunch, but I can't eat. I have trig class after lunch, and I don't really care what the sine of theta is and doubt I will by the time the bell rings.

"Ms. Lawrence," he says, taking off his glasses. "I understand how you feel—"

"Really?" I snap back. "How did you get over *your* rape?"

He jerks in his large chair, the leather squeaking. His face has gone white.

I'm gonna be grounded until I'm thirty.

But instead of picking up the phone to call my parents, he holds up both hands and nods. "Forgive me for that unfortunate choice of words. What I mean is, I understand your disappointment."

Disappointment. That's as bad as Mom's *upset* this morning.

"Mr. McCloskey, *disappointment* is getting a C on some assignment that deserved an A. This is not disappointment. This…this is DEFCON One for me."

"Again, I understand—" He presses his lips together and lowers his dark eyes, trying to find the right thing to say. "We canceled the entire program after your…after what happened to you. We launched a full investigation and have made numerous staff changes since then. But I have a responsibility to the *entire* school body."

Responsibility. Ri-i-ght. "Let me guess. The school needs the money from ticket sales."

Oh my God, who *am* I?

Irritation glints in his eyes, and then he inclines his head. "Ashley. The fact is, these are talented athletes who deserve their shots at scholarships to top schools."

"And what about me, Mr. McCloskey? And the rest of the girls in this school? Don't we deserve something, too?"

"Ashley, the scavenger hunt was an unfortunate incident orchestrated by boys no longer in attendance here. I've already spoken to the coaching staff, the rest of the faculty, and security to make sure activities like that hunt are not repeated. What more do you want?"

I grab my bag and take off. It was a waste of time to come here. Nothing's going to change.

Unless I *force* it to.

......

"So what are you gonna do?" Tara asks me after school. We're sitting on the athletic field, watching Mr. Davidson, the new coach, try out players, waiting for an opportunity to talk to him.

I *have to* talk to him and make him understand in a way Mr. McCloskey never has. But Tara's question makes me anxious.

"I have no idea," I finally admit. "All I know is I don't like the looks I got from damn near everybody in class when that announcement was made. I feel like they just declared open season on me."

Those words trigger something in my stupid brain that sends me sliding back down memory lane to that time when I really had been hunted…and hurt. There's so much I remember about that day, and so much I *can't*. Mom always says *Thank God* to that.

Me?

I'm not so sure it's a good thing.

I remember feeling so happy, I was giddy with it. Vic Patton. A senior! And he wanted to hang with *me*. My belly flipped, like it does at the top of a roller coaster. It kept flipping in all the best possible ways when he took my hand and led me to the field, under the bleachers, and when he kissed me. Even now, two years later, I can still taste the beer on our tongues…feel the tingles. So many tingles. We sat on the ground under the bleachers, but it was disgusting under there. Dirt, cigarette butts, and the smell of sour, moldy bread from the dozens of old beers that had spilled there over time. We drank too much of the six-pack he carried. We kissed, and his stubble scraped my skin. I liked it.

And then I *didn't*. I began to feel sick and dizzy and sleepy. The next time my belly did that flippy thing, all that beer wanted to rush back up. But Vic pushed me down into the dirt. I can feel it, right now, feel the dirt and the bits of plastic and metal and glass—bite into my skin. Nothing tingled, nothing felt good, but he was still kissing me, touching me in places I didn't want him to touch and—

"Ashley. Ashley!"

Tara's hands on my shoulders suddenly bring *her* face into focus. Not Vic's.

Not Vic's.

A shiver of revulsion skates up and down my spine. And I want to just fold up into a tiny ball and roll away.

"Oh, Ashley, it's okay now." She hugs me, and that's when the tears sting the back of my eyes.

"No. No, it's not, Tara." I hold her tight. "And I don't think it ever will be again. I was late this morning because I couldn't get dressed without obsessing whether every outfit I own is *asking for it.*"

"Oh, honey," she says, tightening her hold on me. "I'm so sorry."

I squeeze my eyes shut. "Nobody gets it, Tara. Nobody. They think I should be over it by now. First, they bring back football, and then, in six more months, he gets out of prison. What happens to me then, Tara? How am I supposed to heal? How the hell am I supposed to function when the whole world says this is only *my* problem?" I feel the familiar tightening in my chest and want to sob, but I can't, because if I do, I might never stop.

Damn it, I thought I was past this. I thought this part was over. It's been two years of painfully slow progress trying to forget, trying to put it behind me, and then I find out I'll have to spend the rest of my life living in a world doing its best to make sure I can never forget.

Forget.

I pull away from Tara, swiping my nose, almost amused by that word. God, I used to forget things all the time. I forgot the answers to the chem quiz I studied for. I forgot the steps in the dance routine I'd practiced. I forgot to clean my room and do the dishes. I forgot that Derek told me to take the bus home. No big deal, right? Everybody forgets stuff.

I wish I could forget this. I wish so hard, but the only thing that does is give me a headache.

I try to hold it in, but that sob bursts out of me, loud and raspy. Tara's arms come back around me, and I know my life is never going to be like it was again.

"You're safe now." She repeats it over and over again.

Am I? Am I really?

"You don't have to do this. Let's leave. Let's just go."

Go? Oh, yes! Let's go. Let's hop in a car or on a train and see where it takes us. I can change my name. I can be someone besides the *Bellford High School Rape Victim*.

"This can't happen again, Tara. It just can't."

I have to stop this from starting again. I have no idea how, but I have to try. Nobody should feel the way I feel.

I reach up and squeeze her hand in thanks, then give pacing a shot. The grass crunches softly under my tennis shoes. We watch Mr. Davidson examine his prospects, who seem to be comprised of every single boy in our school. They stand in lines like good little soldiers while he walks up and down the ranks, twirling a whistle around his hand.

I know, somewhere in the logical part of my brain, that football doesn't deserve the blame. It's just a game. But football plays a part. I don't know if it's the flow of testosterone going unchecked that does it or if the players let the entire town's adoration go to their heads. Or maybe it's all that male bonding. I just know that when boys get off that field, they're…different.

Aggressive.

Belligerent.

And feel like they deserve to get anything they want for punishing their bodies out there on that field.

Is it fair of me to blame the game for that? Probably not. I'm basing this on past experience. An experience I seem doomed to keep reliving.

A throat clears behind me and nearly launches me into orbit. "Um, hey, Ashley."

I whip around and find Sebastian Valenti standing there. I force myself to relax.

"I, um, just wanted to see how you're doing. You know." He waves a hand toward the big football meeting happening in front of us. "I figure this has to be pretty upsetting for you."

Upsetting? There's that word again. Try stuff-of-nightmares terrifying.

Sebastian clears his throat again. "Yeah, so. Anyway. I was thinking, if you want to talk to Mr. Davidson, tell him… I don't know. Tell him what happened two years ago. I could go with you. Like, for support."

"Yeah, um, that's a great idea." Tara nudges me. "Right, Ash?"

"Yeah. Sure. Okay."

Sebastian smiles, and it's really sweet. He doesn't smile that much. I don't know why. He's tall and broad—he's built like the football player he used to be. His hair is sandy brown, and it flips in the front in the most perfect way that makes me want to run my fingers through it. It swooshes like the Nike logo. His eyes are green right now. Every time I look at him, all I can think is…sweet.

I turn to Tara. "Will you stay?"

She looks surprised for a second and then nods, her black hair swinging. It's longer now than when I met her two years ago. No longer cut in a chin-length bob, it skims past her shoulders in a shiny black curtain. "Whatever you need, Ashley."

Then Sebastian sits on the grass, kicking out his long legs in front of him, and watches the meeting. After a minute, Tara and I do the same. It's a pretty day. Birds chirp. The sky is bright and blue. A stupid vocabulary word pops into my brain. *Idyllic*. Yeah. That's the word.

As long as you don't peel back the curtain, look too closely.

"What are you gonna tell him?" Tara asks.

My mouth goes dry. I hate talking about the rape, about the hunt, about all of this shit. But I *have to*, if I am to have any prayer of preventing it from happening again. "All of it, Tara. Every minute."

Sebastian and Tara share a glance.

"Even Derek?" she asks.

I squeeze my eyes shut. "Yeah. Him too."

Everything means all the family crap, even Derek's betrayal.

4

DEREK

NOW

LONG ISLAND, NEW YORK

"You okay?"

I jerk when Brittany slides next to me, startling me out of my dark thoughts. "Holy shit, Britt." I scrub both hands over my face to feel something besides numb. It doesn't help. And the thing is, I know she's not making small talk. She's genuinely worried about me.

"Sorry. I didn't mean to scare you."

I shrug. "Don't you have a class now?"

Britt nods and squeezes my hand. "Yeah, but I figured you'd come to the stadium, so…" She trails off and lifts one shoulder in a tiny shrug.

Yeah. *So.*

"Derek, does she hate me?" She shifts to face me head-on,

and her eyes swim with tears. "I mean, she doesn't return my messages." Another shrug. "I don't even know if she's okay with you and me."

Brittany has really amazing eyes. So blue, they're almost purple. I have no damn clue why I never made a move on her back in high school. I sigh and put my arm around her. "Britt, she kind of hates the whole world right now, you know?"

That was a lie. Ashley hates only two people—me and Vic.

"Yeah. But the whole world didn't tell her to relax when she expressed her disgust and outrage over that stupid hunt." She screws up her whole face, and it hits me that the disgust and outrage she's talking about is directed at *herself*. "I told her to let it go. I told her to just roll with it and support the team. I even told her she was wrong that day when she tripped Doug." She jumps up and paces, her flip-flops making that sound I always thought meant *summer*. Now it's just epically out of place.

I stand up and catch her as she paces. "Britt, I did something a lot worse than that."

Brittany's eyes fill with understanding. "You didn't mean it."

God, I wish I could say that. But no. "Yeah. I really did at the time. Trust me. She doesn't hate anybody more than she hates me." Not even Victor, and that makes me want to puke. "Why do you think I'm here at a school so far away from home?"

"Oh, Derek. I'm so sorry."

A tear spills over and slowly rolls down Britt's face, and I'm totally wrecked by it. I pull her in for a hug.

"I live with it. Maybe someday she'll forgive me."

"I hope so. But I think you need to forgive yourself, too."

My eyebrows shoot up at that. Forgiving myself is probably about as likely as winning the lottery or getting struck by lightning. I know what I did. I know I can't ever take it back. And I know there's nothing I can do to make it right.

"Don't give me that look. I'm serious," Britt continues. "I think you should take a closer look at that GAR thing."

"Britt, nothing I ever do is gonna—"

"Not for Ashley. For you." She gives me an extra hard squeeze and pulls away and sits back on the bench. "Derek, I know you. You're a physical person. You need to do something, take action, or you feel useless."

Jeez, we've been at school for less than a month, and she's already whipping out the psych shit. I shake my head and pray for patience.

"And," she continues, obviously ignoring the eye roll I just gave her. "It'll help people here. You're this big strong football player. Your involvement will encourage others to participate. That's how you get a groundswell moving."

"A what?" I ask, even though I don't really care. I sit next to her again. It's the only place I ever feel warm now. Next to Brittany Meyers.

"A groundswell. Think of it like mob mentality, only positive."

"Yeah. Sure."

I love her voice.

I love *her*, but I haven't said the words yet. Probably because I don't know if she feels the same way. Or maybe because I'm chickenshit. She's with me, so I guess that means she likes me. And she kisses me and lets me touch her, which has to mean she *likes me likes me*, right? Yeah. 'Course it does. But I know who I am. And I know *what* I am. So that makes it really hard to accept that there's somebody who could love me who's not my parents, and I'm actually not all that sure about them anymore.

Love. Holy shit.

I feel this pain whenever I think of Britt. It's a good kind of pain, a feeling that says, "Hey! Your heart can race for something besides football, pal!" That's how I feel right now with Brittany sitting next to me.

But I can't tell her if Ashley hates her. I don't know what Ashley thinks about anything anymore.

"I miss her," Britt says after a few minutes.

And that ratchets my pain up to *stab* levels because God, so do I.

"Yeah."

"She's…I don't know. Vacant?" Britt asks.

Vacant.

I try out the word and shake my head. "No, not vacant. It's like she's behind this impenetrable fortress, you know? Something she erected to keep out all the voices throwing shade at her for canceling football." I was one of those voices. *Stab, stab.*

"Oh God, you're right. The girls at school were great, though—most of them, anyway. When she went public, they were ready to pick up pitchforks and storm the principal's office behind her."

I laugh once. "That's cool. You should have. There were too many others who wanted to pick up pitchforks and run her out of town."

"Sebastian was like this real-life hero," Brittany says. "Wish the rest of the guys followed his lead." She doesn't say it, but there's blame implied.

I nod because she's right—we should have followed his lead. I rub my chest where pain is starting to burn a hole. "I hated him for a long time."

"You did? Why? He *saved* Ashley."

I rocked my head, acknowledging the truth in that. "Yeah. He did." *I didn't.* "I just wish…" I trail off, hating to think about what I let happen to him.

"What?" She takes my hands and runs her thumbs over the knuckles in soft, soothing little circles, and the ache spreads out.

"Nothing." But that's a lie, and we both know it. I force myself to be honest with her even though it scares the crap out of me that she'll leave when she finally sees me for the asshole I am. "Okay, that's not true. I was gonna say I wish I'd understood that back then. I thought everything he did was because he was into Ashley, you know? He'd say anything to get her to like him back. But that wasn't it."

"You don't think he likes her?"

I wave a hand. "Oh, he likes her. Even now, I can tell he likes her. But it's more than that. He doesn't do anything unless he thinks it's right. He won't cover for his best friend if that friend did something he thinks is wrong. He won't share his homework.

I used to think he was totally disloyal, you know? I mean, we have this giant mega-crisis coming down on the team after the police arrested Victor. My parents wanted the coach arrested, the principal fired, and the whole school board replaced. They were ready to go on the freakin' *Today Show* to blast the entire school district for that scavenger hunt. So the guys all band together for the greater good, right? Protect the team. But Sebastian won't go along with any of it. God, I *hated* him for that." What Brittany said earlier about mob mentality suddenly hits me like a kick to the nuts. She has no idea how accurate that was. Nobody wanted to be the one voice standing up for what was right. Not even me, and it was my sister who got hurt.

"Protect the team how?" Britt asks, her eyes narrowed.

I swallow hard. "Um. Sticking to a particular story mostly."

And her eyes bug out. "Did you—oh, tell me you didn't lie to the judge."

I shift uncomfortably. "Uh, not exactly."

"Derek, it's pretty much a yes or no thing."

"I know. I know. I mean, it wasn't lying. It was downplaying what happened." *Please, please, don't ask me any more questions.*

I have to change the subject.

Now.

"I don't hate Sebastian anymore," I quickly admit. "He knew what it was gonna cost him, and he did it anyway because Sebastian's the only actual *man* on that team, Britt. The rest of us were all scared boys playing pretend."

I swear I have no damn idea what Brittany's doing with me.

She angles her head, studying me for a minute. "Mmm, maybe. But you eventually agreed with him."

I give her the yeah-right look. "Not until it was way too late." The pain in my heart reaches critical mass, and I close my eyes.

Brittany's hand squeezes mine. "She'll forgive you, Derek. She just needs time."

I laugh once. "Yeah, that's not gonna happen, Britt. It's been over a year since the trial, and she hates me a little more each day. It's my punishment, Britt."

"*Your* punishment?" she asks.

I sigh loudly. "You know what I mean."

Brittany presses her lips into a thin line and watches a jogger hit the track that circles the football field, but she stays silent. I let it go for as long as I can. Her arms come around me, and she holds me tight. I cling to her like she's solid ground after a lifetime afloat in rough seas, but it doesn't help. I still know who I am and still know *what* I am.

And neither deserves her.

I pull away, swipe a hand under my eyes, and grab my stuff. "I have to go. Thanks for—you know—listening and coming after me and—and all of it, but I have to go. I'll…call you or text you later."

I take off before she can say a word.

Like I said. Chickenshit.

TWO YEARS AGO

BELLFORD, OHIO

"Yo, yo, yo! Gather 'round, ladies." Bruce Bishop drops a stack of rubber-banded index cards onto the bench in the locker room. Immediately, hoots go up, and everybody stops what they're doing to dive for the cards. "The hunt is on."

Excitement ripples over me. I've been hearing about this hunt since I was a freshman. Justin never played; he wasn't that into sports. But I can't freakin' wait. The hunt is a tradition at Bellford. Every season, for two weeks before homecoming, all Bengals hunt through town for points as written on the card they choose from the deck. We race around town with our cell phones, snapping images for proof-of-points. Even better if you have a buddy or two to witness you. The items to be hunted are pretty straightforward. Climb to the roof of the elementary school, fifty points. Stand next to a mannequin at a department store in a dumb pose, ten points, but in a—well, crude pose, twenty points. The most points you can get are a hundred, and that's usually for some sort of sexual thing, like getting a blow job on our rival school's grounds. I don't know who thinks these things up, but I'm up for whatever they throw at me. Each card is different. That's because one year, back in the nineties, a bunch of players got into a fight over who found one item on the list first.

Vic grabs the deck of cards and rips off the rubber band. "Seniors first." He takes a careful look around, spots no adults, and fans the cards out. One by one, the senior players take a card. "Okay, juniors next. Hey! No peeking."

Right. We're not allowed to look at our cards until everybody's picked one.

Yes! I wait, not patiently, for my turn. Finally, I pick my card.

"Sebastian?" Vic holds out what's left of the cards to the quiet sophomore, hanging back from the rest of us.

Sebastian holds up a hand and shakes his head. "No, thanks."

"What?" Bruce stares at him in shock. "You're not playing?"

"No. I...well, I don't think it's right, that's all."

"Yeah?" Bruce steps forward, shoving Sebastian back a step. "Well, maybe we don't think it's right that you play football, either."

Vic sighs. "Back off, Bruce. Let's see what we got."

Everybody looks at their cards, and the cursing and laughing begin.

"Aw, shit, guys. Where the hell am I supposed to find a life-size picture of Michael Jackson?"

"Improvise, dude!"

I study my own card. Steal someone's mailbox, play ring-and-run, and kiss a girl in the stairwell while changing classes are each ten points. Flatten somebody's tire, dance on a grave, piss out a car window are thirty points each. Copping a feel is twenty points—ten for each side. And one hundred points for sex with an ex. I grin. I can probably snag two hundred points if I call Dakota *and* Hannah.

Dakota's cool. But Hannah? Not so much. She hasn't even looked at me since the night of the bonfire, when I spilled beer on her. Okay, so maybe not Hannah. But Dakota really liked me. I wasn't all that into her, so I broke it off, but maybe there's still a chance. I take out my phone, snap a picture of my card, and hand it back to Bruce with a wide grin.

Dakota and I have social studies together first period. The next morning I unleash the patented Lawrence grin on her at full strength, and she turns a little pink.

"Hey, Derek."

"Hi. You look really great today."

She rolls her eyes. "Uh-huh."

"So listen. I was thinking." I throw an arm around her shoulders and walk with her to her desk at the back of the room. "What would you say to maybe giving us another shot?"

Her eyes go wide, and when she bounces up on her toes, I know I've got her. "Um, sure. But what about what's-her-name?"

I feign confusion. I didn't get very far with Corinna, the girl I'd dumped Dakota for. "I missed you." I lean in and kiss her cheek.

"Me too," she whispers.

The bell rings, and the teacher walks in, shooting me a glare.

"Wait for me after class, okay?"

She does.

After class, we decide to ditch our second periods and make out in the stairwell.

Woo-hoo! Ten points.

When the bell rings for dismissal that day, I give Dakota a ride home and park in front of her house. She unfastens her seat belt and turns to face me, taking my hand in hers. "Derek, I'm so glad you asked me out again. I really missed you."

"Me too, baby. Me too." I lean over and kiss her.

"I want us to be together, Derek."

"Mm—hmm." I nuzzle her neck.

"I mean, *really* together."

I freeze. Holy shit. Did she mean… I pull back to study her face. She gazes directly into my eyes. "What? You mean you want us to…"

"Yes. I want you to be my first."

Christ on a cracker, this has to be my lucky day. I reach for my door handle. "Anybody home right now?"

She grabs my arm and holds me in place. "Yes. My parents."

I shut the door with a sigh. Was my house empty? Probably. If Ashley had dance practice. "We could go to my house."

Dakota shakes her head. "No, not today. I was thinking after the homecoming game. We could maybe go to the lake, just you and me. I know the whole team likes to do a big party, but…" She trails off, biting her lip, and I don't care if the team plans to meet the president after that game, I'm ditching them.

"Yeah. Absolutely. I'd rather be with you, too," I assure her and kiss her again.

As soon as I get home that evening, I text Bruce, Andre, and a couple of other guys that I will be collecting one hundred points the night of the homecoming game. Meanwhile, I've got to figure out how to clear the rest of my card without getting into trouble.

5

ASHLEY

*Sebastian Valenti saw us and knew something was wrong. He ran
to me, asking if I was okay, asking what happened. He opened his
backpack, gave me a sip of water from his water bottle. He took
off his sweatshirt and covered me. And the defendant said, "Two
hundred points, dude."*

*Sebastian took his phone out, and when the defendant saw that,
he hit him. If this sounds like a "nice kid" to you, we need a new
definition of nice.*

—**Ashley E. Lawrence, victim impact statement**

NOW
BELLFORD, OHIO

The boys take off in clusters. Some head for the school, others
head for the parking lot, and others just walk down the road.
Those who see me sitting here frown, glare, or flip me off.

They *know*.

They know exactly why I'm here.

When Mr. Davidson walks in our direction, I climb to legs that suddenly shake. Beside me, Tara and Sebastian stand, too.

"Mr. Davidson," I say as he reaches us.

"Yes?"

He's a big man. Scary big. Bald head, goatee, deep voice, and giant biceps that strain the sleeves of his Bengals T-shirt. I wish I had a bottle of water because my mouth is Sahara dry. I'm so glad Tara and Sebastian offered to do this with me because being up close with this man is terrifying.

He waits for me to say something. Names. That's a good place to begin. "I'm Ashley Lawrence. This is Sebastian Valenti and Tara Liu."

Recognition ripples across his face.

"You know who I am." It's not a question.

He nods. "Yes. And I'm sorry for what happened. For what was done to you."

"Then you have some idea why I need to talk to you now."

He glances at his watch. Sky-blue eyes meet mine. "Yeah, I guess I do. Is right here good?"

I nod, and he lowers himself to the grass and waits for us to join him. When we do, I can't seem to remember why I thought this was a good idea. He waits, and finally, Sebastian clears his throat again. "So, Mr. Davidson, I was on the football team two years ago."

Bushy eyebrows come together in a frown. "I know. And I would like to know why you didn't come to today's meeting."

Sebastian glances at me and then shakes his head. "I don't play anymore."

Mr. Davidson doesn't like that answer. He turns to me. "Ashley, before I accepted this job, I did a lot of research. I wanted to know what I'd be walking into. I know what happened. I know about the scavenger hunt. And I'll tell you what I just finished telling all those boys this afternoon. This team, this new Bengals team I'm putting together, it's going to be all about the game. There won't be any other traditions. In fact, I'm lobbying against even doing any homecoming events this year."

I exchange a glance with Tara. This is excellent news. Really excellent news. But then I remember the looks I got in class today. And my happiness evaporates. "Mr. Davidson, there are things you should know that weren't in the newspapers."

He leans forward. "Like?"

"Like pretty much all of the boys at your meeting today hate me for canceling football last year."

"I can't force people to like you, Ashley."

I wave that away. "It's not about popularity. It's about *safety*. I don't want them breaking windows at my dad's business. Or surrounding my mom in the parking lot of some store. I don't want them calling my house in the middle of the night and then hanging up. I don't want to come to school and find threats in my locker."

Mr. Davidson stares at me, lips pressed tight. "All of that happened to you."

Again, he states it like he already knows the answer, but I respond anyway with a nod.

"And you're sure it was these boys?"

"I am," Sebastian answers. "I was on the team back then. I heard them planning stuff like that, talking about it afterward. I know exactly who smashed the windows and who circled her mom in that parking lot. They thought it was funny."

"I see."

I almost laugh at that. He sees. And what good does seeing do me?

"Mr. Davidson," Sebastian tries again. "Some of these guys? They don't care about the game. They play because of the power, you know? They like getting to slide out of homework, and they get a rush off the way football is worshiped around here. The second Mr. McCloskey made that announcement today, they started making their plans. I'm telling you. It's all gonna happen again."

Mr. Davidson listens intently while Sebastian talks, and I swear, it's the most I've ever heard him say at one time. Finally, the new coach nods and looks at me.

"No," he says firmly.

No? That's it? I roll my eyes. What a waste of time. I sneer at him. "Thanks for your time," I say with as much sarcasm as possible.

"No. I'm not going to let any of that happen again. Not on my watch." Mr. Davidson shakes his head. "I get what you're saying, Sebastian. But I think *worship* is a bit over the top. Football's a popular pastime around here. I work my players hard so they'll win, and when they do, they deserve respect. But I will not let them slack off homework or exploit their positions on the team. If I see that, they'll ride the bench."

Mr. Davidson seems honest, but what he's saying isn't going to help. Sebastian just told him he knows who terrorized my family back then, but the new coach didn't even ask for their names.

"And the scavenger hunt?" I blurt out the question.

He slices the air with both hands. "Absolutely not. You have my word on this."

Words aren't good enough.

"Mr. Davidson, no offense, but what are you gonna do to make sure?"

The new coach's eyes narrow, and he turns to Sebastian, eyeing him up and down. "That's up to Sebastian. I can teach these boys how to play ball. And I can ensure they keep up their grades. I can even punish them when they mess up. But in my experience, there's only one way to lead a team, and that's from within. That means I have to appoint a team captain with the kind of moral compass I want to see exhibited by my whole team. Other organizations elect their captains, but I don't. I *appoint* them. You should have been at the meeting today, Sebastian. I was waiting for you."

Sebastian shakes his head. "I don't play anymore," he says again.

"Why not?"

Mr. Davidson's voice holds that tone of authority. I can see it working on Sebastian. We're all sprawled on the grass, and yet Sebastian sits up straight, almost at attention.

"Because." He leans forward and stares at the ground, frustration clearly showing on his face. "You don't know what it was like," he says quietly. "It wasn't good." That last part is delivered with a crack in his voice. Sebastian shifts, hunching over his knees.

"I see. So instead of being the example for the team to follow, you quit."

Sebastian's eyes snap to the insulting tone in Mr. Davidson's voice. "I *never* quit. I refused to do the scavenger hunt. I told them! I told them all it was wrong. But nobody listened. Instead, they spent every practice we had until homecoming doing their best to break me. I spent days healing from bruises, and nobody ever did jack shit to them and after—" Abruptly, he clamps his lips together, shaking his head. He shoots me a quick look, and I know what he means.

"Finish it, Sebas," I tell him.

He sighs and shrugs. "After Vic got arrested, when all this stuff went public, I was jumped."

I gasp and stare, horrified, at Sebastian. Beside me, Tara flings both hands up to cover her mouth, and even Mr. Davidson looks enraged.

"I got jumped in the boys' bathroom in the locker room. I was kicked and punched while somebody held my arms, and somebody else had a towel over my head. I was ordered not to say a word. Not to testify. Not to talk to Ashley again."

I knew he'd been unpopular with his team. But I didn't know how bad it was. I should have. I guess I was so wrapped up in my own issues, I never looked at anybody else's. Sebastian is a hero.

After being beaten up by his teammates, he *did* testify. And he *did* talk to me.

Mr. Davidson slowly stands up. "Play ball for me, Sebastian. Be this team's captain. That's the only way I can make sure what happened to your friend and to you doesn't happen again."

"They're not gonna listen to me, Mr. Davidson."

"They will if they want to play."

Sebastian considers that for a minute and then looks at me. "Ash? If you say no, then it's no. I don't want to hurt you more."

Shit. Hurt me more. Is that even possible? Slowly, I shake my head. This is...this isn't my decision. "Do you want to play?"

He shrugs his big shoulders. "Not if it makes it worse on you."

"Forget about me. Do *you* want to play?"

Those pretty hazel eyes latch on to mine—they're green right now—and he nods. "Yeah. I guess."

"Then you should play."

"Good. I'll expect you right here after school tomorrow." Mr. Davidson extends a hand before anybody can say another word. After a few seconds, Sebastian shakes it. Mr. Davidson nods, walks away, but then turns back. "Sebastian? A good captain, a strong leader, throws his support behind a worthy cause," he says with a long look at me. "He expects his teammates to do the same."

We watch Mr. Davidson walk away, twirling the whistle around his hand.

"Well, that went well," Tara says after a minute.

"Actually, it did." Wheels are spinning away in my mind. I

grab Sebastian's hand. "I have an idea, but I need you to make it happen. Are you up for it?"

Sebastian stares at our clasped hands. I quickly let go.

"Yeah. Anything."

I swipe at my phone and open a browser. A few taps and I find what I'm looking for. "That thing Mr. Davidson just said about a worthy cause. Do you think we can make something like this happen at Bellford?"

Sebastian takes the phone and reads the screen with Tara peering over his shoulder. It takes them a few minutes, but when they're done, Sebastian looks up at me, eyebrows raised.

"You seriously want to do this?"

I nod. "I have wanted to do this for a year now. I just couldn't figure out a way to do it by myself."

He and Tara exchange a look, and then he stares right into my eyes. "Ashley, we absolutely can make this happen at Bellford. I promise."

Deeply touched, I nod. "Okay. We should go. There's a lot of work to do."

Tara laughs. "I wish you could see your face right now. You look fierce."

"Uh-uh," Sebastian says, shaking his head. "She looks fearless."

I say nothing because neither is true.

......

We say goodbye to Tara when she turns up the path that leads to the big red door to her house and when it's just Sebastian and me, I figure it's time I register for a driver's ed class. I don't want to walk home from school anymore. Especially now that football's back.

"Hey, Ash."

I look over at Sebastian, and he's biting his lip. "Are you scared right now? Like, with *me*?"

I suck in a deep breath, trying like hell to find the right words to make this sting less. "Truth? Yes."

He looks away, but not before I see the resignation in his eyes.

"Sebastian, it's not something I can control, but I'm trying. I swear. I have to remind my stupid brain that *not all* guys rape. That you, my dad, my brothers are not the ones who hurt me."

Not *that* way at least.

"Is it hard?" he asks.

Nodding, I try to explain. "My body sees something completely harmless and innocent, and for some reason, it associates it with the rape. That forces me into defense mode, and I freak out because a lot of times, I don't know what's causing it. So I have to tell myself I'm *safe*, I'm *fine*, nobody's hurting me." I point directly to him when I say that part so he understands that I'm trying. I really am. "It helps. Eventually."

Frowning, he stops walking, so I do, too. He faces me and holds out a hand. My palms start to sweat. *You're safe.* I swallow hard and repeat the lie. When I look into his eyes, I see the complete absence of things I always saw in Vic's and even in Derek's.

No games.

No challenges.

No lies.

No taunts.

Slowly, I put my hand in his, and wow, my heart is thundering in my chest, and my lungs feel like they might burst, but I'm doing it. I'm touching a guy.

He's good. He's safe. He's good. He's safe. I'm fine. I'm fine. I'm fine.

Even more slowly, Sebastian raises his other hand and puts it over his heart, and I know it's for my benefit, so I won't get scared. "I will *never* give you a reason to be afraid of me."

He walks me all the way home, up the porch steps and to the front door.

"Is anybody home? You'll be okay by yourself?"

I don't mind being alone. It's being alone inside a big house that makes a lot of strange noises that scares me. But I'm afraid to let Sebastian inside. I feel like a traitor. He just made me a solemn vow, but the last time I trusted a boy, I got raped.

"Ashley?"

I jerk back to the present. "Oh. Um. Sorry about that."

"Okay. So, I'll, uh. How about if I just sit right here? You go inside, lock the doors. If you're scared of being alone, you can talk to me through the window. And if you're scared of *me*, you can close the window."

I—I…oh my God. I can't find the words, so I nod and run inside. The house is still. So still, I can hear it settle. I toss my stuff on the sofa and open the window in the front room. Sebastian is exactly where he said he'd be, standing on the porch, right in front of the window.

"Hey." I smile.

"Hey." He smiles back in that way that makes his eyes light up. "Everything's okay in there?"

I shrug. "The house is talking to me."

His eyebrows shoot up. "Your house talks?"

"You know," I say, shaking my head. "All those creaks and whines houses make when you're by yourself?"

He nods. "They scare you."

"Yep." I am so seriously messed up.

I sit down on the sofa, tucking my legs under me so I can face Sebastian outside. "So are you psyched to be playing football again?"

He shrugs. "Not yet. Maybe I will be once we get started. I don't know."

"You're not one of those football-is-life guys, are you?"

He grins and nods. "Hell, yeah, I am. I started playing when I was maybe nine years old. I love the game. But…" He trails off, letting the smile disappear. "It sucked for me, the year you got hurt." And then he winces. "I'm sorry. That came out totally wrong. I mean, obviously it couldn't have sucked as much as it did for you," he amends, and then he gives up, shaking his head.

"What happened?"

He glances at me and then shrugs. "The guys ruined it."

I nod, getting it. "Oh. The hunt."

"That was just *part* of it. The other part started on the first day of practice."

"What part?"

"You know. The tests. Guys push each other, see how far

they can get. Vic was always pushing somebody." He turns, leans against the porch rail, and crosses his arms. "He went after another kid in the locker room, making fun of him, nothing terrible. I let it go until he called the guy a homo."

I lean forward. "What do you mean? You let it go?"

Sebastian waves his hand. "I get that a lot of it's just guys being guys. So I ignore it. I let them have their fun. But the kid's face went, like, gray. I seriously thought he was gonna puke. I figured he really is gay and hasn't come out yet. So I told Vic to back off."

Wow. That's just such a Sebastian thing to do.

"Next thing I know, I'm on Vic's list. Practices were hell. He made sure every guy on that team hit me extra hard."

Jeez. I had no idea. "What you said before, about the guys jumping you in the locker room. What about Derek? Was he one of the guys who hurt you?" I have no idea why I want to know. I guess I need to.

Sebastian shakes his head. "No. I know exactly who they were. Most were seniors, and they're gone now. Graduated. But there are two still left. Don't worry. I know how to handle them now."

I hate this. Those boys, all those boys, punishing me for getting raped, punishing Sebastian for trying to stand up and do the right thing. I hate them. God, I hate them all.

"I'm really sorry he hurt you, Ash."

My whole body jerks. "Yeah. Me too." I pick at the fabric on the sofa.

"You miss him?"

With a start, I realize he's talking about *my brother*. "No." I shake my head, and my voice is firm. "I don't miss Derek *now*. I miss Derek the way he was before high school, back when we were little. You didn't know him then, did you?"

Sebastian shakes his head. "No, I didn't meet him until football."

"You'd have liked him. He was ridiculously cool." I blink because my eyes suddenly burn.

Sebastian angles his head, studying me. "You think you'll ever talk to him again?"

"I talk to him now." I don't mention that the talking Derek and I do now consists mostly of shouting insults back and forth.

"No, I mean, like you did before. When he was ridiculously cool. Could you forgive him?"

Sorry, Ashley.

That phrase, delivered with Derek's trademark charming smile and fake remorse just to appease Mom, suddenly replays in my brain. Derek always got away with everything.

Once he beheaded one of my dolls, and I screamed bloody murder, as one does when her favorite doll is mutilated. Mom came running, expecting us to be bleeding or gasping for our last breaths. When I showed her what Derek did, she ordered him to apologize.

"Sorry, Ashley," he said, and then stuck his tongue out the second Mom turned her back.

"He's not really sorry!"

I kept crying, but it didn't matter. Derek was the golden child in our family. He'd discovered that superpower before he could tie his shoes, and he wielded it like Thor's hammer.

I've already spent most of my life forgiving Derek. I gave him chance after chance, but somewhere along the way, he'd stopped wanting those chances. So damn if I'll ever give him another one.

"Ashley?"

Sebastian's voice startles me.

"Are you okay? You looked really sad."

"Fine." How easily the lies come now. "And to answer your question, no. I don't think I can forgive him. Because when I really needed him, when I needed him the most, he said he could barely look at me."

Sebastian's face turns murderous, and I need an immediate change of subject.

"Sebas," I start, and he laughs. "What?"

"You know you're the only one who calls me that?"

"What? You don't have any nicknames?"

"Sure I do." He takes out his phone, swipes and taps, and joins me at the window. "Got three little sisters. They all call me Baz."

"Baz?" I can't help it. I snort out a laugh and examine the picture he's holding up. The girls are adorable. He's right; they *are* little. One looks like she's still in diapers.

"I should probably call you that, if that's what you like."

His eyes meet mine. "Nah. The way you say it, it sounds like *sea bass*. I like it."

My face heats up. "Okay. Sebas." And now I can't remember what I want to ask him.

Oh. Right.

"That website I showed you and Tara before…do you really think we can make that work? Here at Bellford?"

"Definitely." He stretches, and it hits me how uncomfortable he must be, standing on my porch, talking to me through a window. I could open the door and let him in. But I won't. I might lie about being fine to keep up appearances, but that doesn't mean I actually *am* fine.

"Hang on." I hurry to the closet in the hall, grab a small folding step stool, and bring it to the front door. I quickly open the door, shove the stool outside, and lock it again. "I figured you must be tired of standing."

"Yeah." He smiles. "Thanks."

Sebastian grabs the stool and sets it up right under the window. I laugh because it's just such a Sebastian thing to do. I take out my phone.

"What?"

Shaking my head and still grinning, I record a little bit of video of Sebastian in front of my window. "Nothing. It's just pretty cool you'd do this for me."

"Well, I get that you're scared. I'm your friend. My job is to make you less scared, not more."

I put the phone down. "I don't know if that's how it works, but thanks."

He waves that away and changes the subject. "You know how we always have pep rallies before a big game?" Sebastian asks, and I nod. "I was thinking that this year, we can make the entire thing a sign-up day for the pledge you showed us before."

My eyes widen. "That's a great idea." I take out my phone and start browsing. "I remember hearing about the NFL doing these public service announcements. Maybe we could get some of the AV kids to help with that, too?"

"Yeah, yeah. Good idea." He taps a note into his phone. "We have to come up with a name for this."

I'd already given this a ton of thought. "What do you think of Bengals Against Rape or BAR for short? I was thinking we could do this whole sexual assault awareness program around it called Raise the BAR."

Sebastian looks impressed. "Not bad, Lawrence. How long have you been thinking about this?"

I shrug. "A long time." Almost two years, to be exact.

"So why didn't you ever suggest it?"

I give him a wry look. "Told ya before. I'm the girl who canceled football. Nobody's gonna climb on board with any idea I have."

"I did," he says softly.

"Yeah, well, you're Sebastian Valenti, defender of the weak, fighter of injustice. Did you see the way Andre looked at me during the principal's announcement this morning? That's how almost everybody treats me. Except you."

He doesn't say anything for a minute or two...just scrolls through his phone. "There," he announces. "I sent Mr. Davidson an email telling him I'll play, I'll be his captain, if he'll agree to the pledge."

"'O Captain! My Captain!,'" I say with a grin.

Sebastian flushes pink and looks down with a little huff just as Dad's truck pulls into the driveway.

"Hey, Sebastian!" Dad holds up a hand when he steps out of the vehicle. "What are you doing out here?"

"Joe." Mom extends Dad's name into three syllables so that everybody *except* Dad gets why it's a monumentally stupid question.

"Oh. Right. Well, come in. We're home now."

Sebastian shakes his head. "I gotta get home. Ash, is it okay if I email you later with more ideas?"

"Yeah, absolutely. I'll do the same. We'll compare."

"Cool. See ya."

I watch Sebastian fold up the step stool, place it carefully near the front door, and walk away. When he reaches the curb, he glances back over his shoulder to give me one more wave.

There's this tiny little sigh inside my chest, and I don't know what it means exactly. But I do know this: it doesn't hurt.

6

DEREK

NOW

LONG ISLAND, NEW YORK

I jog through the tunnel that leads out of the stadium. Campus is crowded, full of eager freshmen—unlike me—ready to live the college life. A sea of red Rockets T-shirts fills my vision. Girls in clusters giggle with to-go cups of coffee in their hands. Guys with earbuds bounce to rhythms only they can hear. And everywhere, *everywhere*, are those friggin' rally signs.

"Hi!" an overperky girl greets me with a toothpaste commercial smile. "Will you sign up to volunteer for Rock Stock?"

I'm about to sidestep her because I figure she's going to try selling me on the rally, and I'm sick to death of it already. "Right. Rock Stock."

"Yeah, it's what we call it here because we're the Rockets."

Yeah. I know. "Uh-huh."

"So will you volunteer?"

I shrug. "I don't know. I'm on the football team, so it depends. What kind of help do you need?"

"Everything," she replies with a wave of her hand over the clipboard, indicating various events listed in loopy girly handwriting. "We need guides to show guests and alumni where to park, and we need staff for the barbecue, and oh, do you know anybody in the marching band? Because we really need some more drummers."

"Uh, no. Sorry. It's my first semester."

"You're a freshman? Awesome! Welcome to RHU."

Did this girl drink a gallon of coffee this morning? "Um. Yeah. Thanks."

"You know what would be really great? If you could get the whole team to support GAR." And then she whips out yet another stupid blue-and-white flyer.

Cursed. I am so cursed.

"Not interested." I step around her, but she doesn't shake so easily.

"You should be interested. The rally is really important. A junior was assaulted off campus last week. You didn't hear?"

I freeze where I stand, my eyes pinned on hers. "Are you messing with me?"

Perky Girl shakes her head, sending her long silky hair flying. "It's absolutely true. Here. Take a look." She shows me the back of the flyer, where the whole account is printed. A junior out with her housemates met some guys, shared a few drinks, and did some dancing. One of the housemates drank excessively, so a guy helped the girl and her friends get her home. Once inside the house, he asked if he could sleep on their sofa because he was too messed up to go home. They agreed. Everyone went to sleep. Hours later, the junior awoke to him on top of her.

He raped her while all her housemates slept peacefully in their beds.

"He seemed so nice," the article quoted the victim.

I shut my eyes and shake my head. *He seemed so nice.* Ashley had said almost the exact same thing about Vic.

"Hey, are you okay?" Perky Girl puts a tiny hand on my arm.

"Oh, um. Yeah. Fine."

"So will you sign up?" She holds out her clipboard and clicks her pen. "We're trying to get the guys to come out and show their support."

Yeah, because that'll work. "Support what exactly?"

"Um, you know. Awareness about sexual assault."

"I'm already pretty aware."

She flashes another toothpaste ad grin. "And that's really great. But we need you to help."

How, exactly, am I supposed to help? I mean, don't rape anybody. Duh. I get that part. Seriously, though. I told Ashley to stay home. She didn't listen to me. So what can Guys Against Rape actually do to show this support that's so desperately needed?

"There's so much you can do," the girl answers my unspoken question, and my mouth falls open. "We're having our first meeting tomorrow night." She circles the details on the flyer and hands it to me. "So what's your name?"

"Lawrence. Derek Lawrence."

"Great." She dots the clipboard even though there's nothing to dot in my name. I guess she thinks it's cute.

It's not.

"See ya!" She grins one more time and bounces off to talk to somebody else. I stare at the circle she drew around the meeting details and shove it into my pocket.

I'm not going.

A knot forms in my gut, a thick and oily clot of guilt. I sink on to the first bench I spot, clutching my middle and trying like hell not to puke. Damn it, I wish to hell I'd beaten the snot out of Victor Patton.

Came close to it.

"Hey, man."

I twitch and find some guy sitting beside me. No idea where he came from. He's older than I am, but not by much. Mid-twenties, maybe? Dark hair, dark eyes, some serious muscle.

I nod and shift away, willing my stomach to settle down.

"I'm gonna say something to you," the guy says. "And you can tell me to fuck off, or you can listen. I see you sitting here, green around the gills, gripping one of those rally flyers, and see a look on your face I know well."

I shift back to study him. He meets my gaze without flinching, and there's something in his tone that tells me he's not bullshitting.

"Somebody you love got assaulted," he says, and before I can say anything—before I can even think of something to say—he adds, "Me too."

I stare at him in disbelief. Are we supposed to do some kind of male bonding over rape...some sort of weird bro hug and then share our fucking feelings? That kink in my gut unclenches, and my breakfast comes up and out. I manage to turn away before I ruin this guy's day and spew into the bushes behind the bench. It takes a few minutes. When I'm finally empty and want to crawl into the gutter to die, the guy shoves a bottle of water into my field of vision.

"Take it. Keep it."

Grateful, I crack the seal, chug, and rinse out my mouth. Then I take a nice gulp, sit back on the bench, and wipe my mouth. "Thanks," I offer a few minutes later, when I'm sure I'm not dying.

"Yeah, no big."

There's a long pause. "Girlfriend?" he asks after a minute.

And it takes me another minute to figure out he's asking who I know that got raped. I shake my head. "Sister."

"Oh, man. I'm sorry."

I only nod. What else is there to say? In silence, we watch Perky Girl chase down two guys on Rollerblades.

He snorts out a laugh. "That girl has some serious fun attitude."

I laugh, too. "That's an oxymoron, no?"

Shrugging, he says, "Maybe. Never could keep those lit terms straight."

That makes me wonder about him. "You're not a student?"

"No," he admits. "I graduated a few years ago. Degree in engineering. I work in the city now."

Manhattan, he means. We're on Long Island. It took me a few days to figure out that whenever anybody refers to the city, they mean Manhattan.

"So what are you doing here?"

He sighs and looks back to the quad where Perky Girl's got another pair of guys on the hook for rally duty. "Over there. Under the Rock Stock tent. Black boots."

I scan the area, find the tent, and see a bunch of people under it. But the black boots do it for me. The girl is hot, like off-the-charts hot. Long wild hair, dark sunglasses, jeans, and a black shirt that's held together with a series of metal rings. She looks like the lead singer from some hard rock band.

"Oh, shit. I'm sorry. Was she—"

"Yeah. Back in high school. By my friend. At a party she only went to because she hoped I'd be there."

"Damn." I sigh.

"I came over here to talk to you because you looked like—well, like a guy about to puke."

My face gets hot. I swallow another gulp of water and look away. But I can't deny I'm curious. "How do you…" Deal with it? Avoid killing the guy who did it? I wave my hand, trying to fill in that blank.

He angles his head, studying me. "Get over my guilt?"

Okay. That works, too.

He takes another look at the girl in the black boots and shrugs.

"Still working on it. Being here is part of it. She's doing the keynote speech at the rally. Took me a while, but I finally figured out that therapy's not so bad, either."

My parents wanted us all to go to therapy, but I said no way. Maybe that was a mistake. "Can I ask you something?"

The guy nods.

I swallow more water. "You ever say something you can't take back? Something that made her hate you."

He grins and rolls his eyes. "God, yes. I can't watch a Star Wars movie without wanting to kick my own ass."

"Huh?"

He waves a hand. "Long story. I was a real dick to her, embarrassing her in front of my friends so they wouldn't turn on me. She forgave me. Somewhere along the line, I figured out how to forgive myself so I could be the man she deserves."

Forgive myself. That's exactly what Brittany said. I consider that for a couple of minutes and then shake my head. "I gotta go." I stand up. "Thanks for the water and for—" I wave a hand. "You know."

"Yeah. No problem. Hope we see you at the rally. Trust me, she's something." He jerks a thumb toward the girl in the black boots, and I don't doubt him for a second.

"Yeah. Maybe."

He extends a hand. "Ian."

I shake it. "Derek," I say. "Thanks again."

"Here." He fishes through his pockets and comes out with a business card. "My cell number. I can help. If you want."

I take off, tucking the card into my pocket along with the

blue-and-white flyer. I don't even know why I'm keeping them. It's not like there's any way Ashley's gonna forgive me. I'm not even sure I can forgive myself. I'll never be Leonardo again in her eyes.

TEN YEARS AGO

BELLFORD, OHIO

It's a blistering hot day, and Ashley whines enough to get Mom to take us to the playground so we can run under the sprinkler. Being playground experts like we are, we know you don't wear shorts to the playground or you'll fry on every piece of equipment. So Justin, Ashley, and I wear long pants and pretty much own the tall slide, the one all the big kids use.

Everybody else has red welts on their legs.

Then Justin has this bright idea. Spread our towels on the hot surface and use them to ride down the slides. Works like a charm. Instantly, kids crying over the slide have a second chance at fun.

Teenage Mutant Ninja Turtles towels.

Justin has Raphael. I have Donatello, and Ashley has Leonardo.

What do we care about sharing the towels? We can ride all day with no problems because we have long pants. So we play, make new friends, and have a great time.

The sprinklers are turned on about two hours after we arrive. A squeal goes up, and everybody vacates whatever apparatus they're using to converge on the water fountain in the center of the park. We get soaked, and who cares? It's a hot day, and we have fresh clothes to put on later. Mom calls us over to eat our lunch, and then we go back for more fun in the water. When it's time to change our clothes, the three of us exchange horrified glances. Mom packed shorts for us, not long pants. With heavy hearts, we figure our day of playground fun is over.

And then we remember our Ninja Turtles towels. I grab mine, Justin finds his, but when Ashley asks for hers, the kid who'd just slid down the slide with it pushes her down and says it's *his*. Justin just stands there while Ashley cries, but me?

I lose my mind.

This is *my* sister. She's hurt and crying, and I'm supposed to just *accept* that, to shrug that off?

Hell no.

I tackle the kid, and while he's down, I get back her towel. With apologies to his pissed-off mother, who's trying to blot up all the blood from the fat lip I'd given the little jerk, Mom hustles us all out of the playground and back home.

Everybody is super quiet on the car ride.

"Go to your rooms. Now." Mom points up the stairs the second we get home.

"Sorry, Mom," I say with the smile I patented when I was in diapers. I escaped from tons of trouble with it. It never fails.

Until now.

Oh, man. This is worse than I thought. It means Mom doesn't know what to do with me so Dad will take care of it when he gets home. Ashley and I meet in the bathroom that connects our rooms.

"Thank you for getting my towel back from that mean boy," she says, looking up at me with her brown eyes wide and full of admiration.

I squirm and feel the heat climbing up my face. It feels...I don't know...kind of nice to know I impressed her. "No problem." I shrug.

"If Daddy takes away your video games, you can play mine," she promises me.

I smile. "They're the same games, dopey."

"Oh."

"Well, if Daddy sends you away, I'll sneak into your suitcase and go with you so you won't be all alone."

"He won't send me away." I laugh, but what do I know? I'm eight years old. I've never been in this much trouble before, so I really don't know what the consequence will be.

We whisper back and forth, and then Justin opens the door.

"You guys, we're supposed to be in our rooms." Justin's twelve. Double digits. Way cool. And he knows a ton of stuff. So when he reminds us we're supposed to be in our rooms, Ashley and I both hang our heads.

"It was a really fun day."

Justin's tone makes me take a close look at him. I don't know a lot about tones, but I can tell he's mad. It's like an accusation. *It was a really fun day—until you ruined it.*

At first, I'm kind of embarrassed. Justin's so smart, it's like he's practically an adult. But not this time. Not today. I whip around and push him.

"You're the oldest!" I shout at him. "You just stood there and did nothing."

Ashley's lower lip juts out. "*Derek* saved me. Derek's my Leo."

I roll my eyes even though her words make me stand up tall. "It's Leonardo, dopey."

"I know. He's my favorite."

"Good. 'Cause Leonardo would never let April down."

Ashley smiles up at me like I just handed her a puppy or a kitten, or hell, maybe even an entire unicorn.

Justin blinks a few times, eyes watering behind his glasses. Justin's not into sibling loyalty the way me and Ashley are. He does his own thing, and we do ours. But this is the first time I've ever called him out on it. He turns and leaves us in the bathroom to wait for Dad to come home.

And when Dad does come home, I get grounded for ages, but I don't mind much.

Because from now on, it's me and Ashley—Leo and April—against the world.

NOW

LONG ISLAND, NEW YORK

The next night, I find myself in front of the room where the Guys Against Rape meeting is about to start, with no idea what the hell I'm doing here. I mean, GAR. Really? It feels wrong to make something so serious into a joke. GARRRRR.

The meeting is happening inside the basement of the student

activities building. The SAB—as it's known to students—houses lounges, computer corrals, a market, and Rockets gear shop, plus a number of rooms for lectures and meetings, like the one I'm currently standing in front of.

I hover, ready to turn and take off, when I'm spotted.

"Hey, come on in. This is the GAR meeting." A tall balding man smiles at me. He's wearing cargo shorts and a golf shirt and reminds me of a teacher I had back in Ohio. "What's your name?"

"Derek Lawrence."

"Grab a seat." He hands me a stack of papers and, yep, another rally flyer.

I swallow back the groan, take the papers, find a seat in a comfy-looking leather chair near a window, and eyeball the rest of the room. Besides the bald guy, there are exactly six of us in this room.

Six guys against rape.

Six, in a university where twenty thousand are enrolled.

I pop my neck to the side, listen to it crack, and begin skimming the papers.

"Problem?"

I look up and find the leader looking at me.

"Who, me? No. No problem."

"It's okay, Derek. You can be honest here. You looked pretty disgusted a minute ago. Would you share what you were thinking?"

I scan the room, find all eyes pinned to me, and squirm. "Uh. Well. I was just thinking that there's only six of us here tonight. In a school this big, only six of us give a shit."

"And how does that make you feel?"

I think about that for a second and shrug. He asked, so I'll tell him. "Pissed off, if you want to know the truth."

"Good!" The leader pumps a fist in the air. "You *should* be pissed off by that. Six guys at a university this large? That's pathetic. Thanks for sharing, Derek."

Yeah. No problem.

"I'm Ted Vega." The bald guy smiles for a minute and then gets serious. "Derek touched on something that's actually the cornerstone to GAR's mission, but before we get to that, I'd like to tell you why I'm here. Then I'd like us to go around the room, and if you're comfortable, share why each of you is here, too."

Great. I sink a little lower into my chair.

"When I was twenty-six years old, I was a strong guy. I'd just gotten out of the service…army airborne," he adds with a grin. "I could bench-press my own weight and often lifted more just to say I could." His smile slides off his face. "I was the strongest guy I knew, and even I wasn't able to save my wife. She killed herself about seven months after she was raped."

The breath stops in my lungs.

"I'm here because I spent way too many years blaming myself for what happened to Eileen. I didn't know I needed help or how to find it, so I turned to alcohol instead. I screwed up what was left of my life because I didn't know I needed help to help her." Ted looks down at his hands. They're clenched into tight fists.

A moment later, I notice mine are, too.

"Who else is here because your wife or girlfriend or partner was assaulted?"

Two of the other guys raise their hands.

"You still together?"

They exchange a glance, and each shake their heads. Ted sighs. "I'm sorry about that. What are your names?"

"Gary."

"Jack."

He nods and turns to the guy sitting near the door, a tall guy with glasses and clothes that don't fit. "How about you?"

"Um. My mother...and me." The kid looks away, and Ted doesn't press him for more. "Oh. I'm Zane."

"Same," a guy sitting near the window admits, offering half a smile to Zane. "I'm Steve." He stands up and offers Zane his hand.

"And you?" Ted asks me.

"My, um, sister."

"Same here," the last guy says. He's sitting at the back of the room on a computer stool. "My name's Phil."

Oh, God. Are Phil and I supposed to hug now, bonding over our shared trauma?

"Okay, gentlemen. Show of hands. The attackers in each of our stories...did you or your girlfriends, mother, or sister— personally know them?"

I raise my hand. So does everybody else. Holy shit.

"Take a look at the first sheet in your packets. Studies have shown that rape is more often than not perpetrated by someone known to the victim."

The sound of rustling papers scrapes like sandpaper against my eardrums. The first sheet is a list of statistics. Seven out of ten rapes are acquaintance rapes. And 25 percent are committed by someone the victim is seeing—a spouse, a boyfriend, or a girlfriend.

"And guess where rape is statistically more prevalent?"

I don't have to guess. It's right here on my paper.

On college campuses.

College women are twice as likely to be sexually assaulted than robbed. A chill crawls up my back at the next bullet point: the time when college rapes are highest? August through November.

Football season.

Ted tosses his paper deck aside. "Okay, look. Your handouts have all the stats you could ever need. There's also a list of resources where you can get help, and trust me on this, you want it. But right now, I want to tell you what GAR's mission is." He stands up, powers on a projector, and grabs a remote control. On the wall is a sentence followed by a question.

There is strength in numbers. Are you strong enough to speak out?

"Simply put, our mission is to teach guys that sexualized violence is their problem too. When we get everybody admitting that, owning that, rape crimes will decrease. Part of GAR's philosophy is social justice and putting our strength behind what's right." Ted flexes his biceps. "Let me give you some examples." He clicks the remote, and the image projected on the wall changes to show a fraternity house with a banner hanging from a window that says, *Daughter Drop-Off Point.*

The next image is of a group of guys on a basketball court all staring at a girl walking by. He scrolls through image after image: steel truck nuts, a comedian known for his dirty jokes, ex-politicians and the tweets that cost them their jobs.

"These don't look so bad, right? Maybe you think women are overreacting when they talk about stuff like this. But here's the thing…women keep telling us this crap makes them uncomfortable. And what do we do?" Ted waits a beat. "We ignore them. We tell them to lighten up, accept a compliment, stop making everything about them, and that's wrong. It *is* about them. We should be strong enough to be able to back off when women tell us the things we do scare them."

Ted wanders around the room, stopping occasionally to make another point.

"This is rape culture—this tendency for good men, the kind of men who say they're outraged by rape, to repeatedly ignore and maybe even support the behaviors that excuse rape." Ted puts down his remote and turns to face us again. "How many of you laughed the last time somebody told a dirty joke?"

We all nod kind of sheepishly.

"Or what about this scenario? How many of you have ever been out somewhere…a club or a bar or maybe the beach. You're having a great time, you're meeting people, and everyone's getting along. But then one of your crew gets turned down. Friend-zoned. And you, because you're such a great pal, join in with the rest of your crew telling this girl what a nice guy he is, trying to make her feel bad for exercising her right to say no?"

Holy shit.

I've done that. I've done that a lot.

"I'm not trying to make you all hate yourselves. That's not what GAR is about. We're about change—changing the mind-set, changing the behaviors, thought patterns, responses. Changing the culture."

Ted looks at Zane. "Changing the culture is crucial for all of us, not just women. Did you report your assault?"

Zane shakes his head, and Ted nods.

"How about you, Steve?"

"Hell, no."

"One in ten sexual assault victims is male, yet studies claim that as many as ninety percent of male victims don't report the crimes committed against them because of *exactly* the stigma created by the dirty jokes and song lyrics and attitudes perpetuated by rape culture. Even the legal definition of rape doesn't always address male victims."

I shut my eyes. I remember Carol, the district attorney, repeating that fact. The legal definition of rape is forcible penetration with a penis or implement.

Ted sits back down in his chair facing us. "We need your *strength*. We need guys like you to shut down the dirty jokes and tell your friends to stop harassing girls on the street. It's up to guys like us to show our teammates, our roommates, our friends and family that speaking out against rape and all the stupid little things that trivialize it is cool."

Strength in numbers.

Yeah. Okay. I get it. I take out a pen and sign the pledge form. Then I sit back and listen to everybody share the rest of their stories. Phil's sister, Steve's and Zane's mothers, Jack's and Gary's girlfriends…and finally, me. By this time, my stomach is twisting itself inside out, and I want very much to choke somebody or something, but I tell them what happened to Ashley.

Then Ted powers down the projector and laptop. "Before, when Derek said he was pissed off that only six guys showed up? I have to admit, that pisses me off, too. I've been doing these meetings for a long time now, and they always start out like this…with a handful of guys with direct connections to a victim of sexualized violence. Our job is to go out and find the men of character, the men of honor, who are willing to fight with us, to put their strength behind this cause for no other reason except it's *right*."

I resist the temptation to shout "hoo-ah."

"And speaking of right." Ted grabs a stack of paper and hands a piece to each of us. "These are some upcoming events. Give them a glance and please consider speaking at one or more. Not all of them are here on Long Island, and we could really use a show of strength and support from nice guys."

I glance at the list. There are about forty events from now until the end of the year in a dozen different states. Then I fold it up and stuff it into my backpack. Our first meeting is over.

But I can't shake off my frustration. Six guys. That's pretty damn pathetic.

I spend most of that night reading all the internet sources

listed in my handouts and blow off the next day's classes…and Brittany, who keeps texting me to make sure I'm okay.

I'm really not. I'm annoyed. I feel like I might explode, so I head over to the fitness center inside the sports complex because I'm afraid I'll hurt somebody if I don't work it off.

I cue up my favorite playlist, plug in my earbuds, hit one of the mats, and go through my warm-up routine. I'm restless and itchy, like I might ignite at any second and launch into orbit, taking anybody in a half-mile radius with me.

There are a couple of guys jogging on a pair of treadmills. I recognize them but don't actually know either of them, so I tune them out. With the weight stack on my vertical lift machine set to a punishing level, I start my first set, accepting the burn that spreads across my pecs, maybe even welcoming it. I do another set, grunting with the effort, and stop for a water break.

"And you wouldn't believe the ass on her. I'm putting the moves on her, carrying her tray, about to ask her to hook up. She's totally into it. I can tell."

I suppress an eye roll as the tail end of one guy's statement to his pal hits my ears. I've seen him around. In fact, I think I saw this dining hall drama play out.

"Yeah, right." His pal shoots him a look of disbelief.

"Hand to God, dude," the guy assures him. "She's playing it cool, thanking me for the help and all, and then saying, 'See you around,' but all I want to do is just grab her and shove her up against the nearest wall, you know?"

"Oh, yeah."

"So I say to her, 'Come on, baby. Let's find ourselves a nice quiet spot and make each other very happy.'"

I snort out a laugh and set up the next machine—biceps curl. I *did* see this drama. The girl he's talking about was definitely hot; he's not exaggerating that part. Tall, curvy, and full of confidence. She wears a nose ring and has a floral tattoo on her arm. But he wasn't all smooth and easy. He'd pretty much grabbed the tray from her hands, followed her over to the table where the girl's friends were sitting, and sort of stammered his way through what ended up being, "I want to do you." The girls—shocked, pissed off, and creeped out—gave him the finger and took off, laughing.

The guys glance over their shoulders at me, but they seem to figure it's not them I'm laughing at since I've got headphones on.

"She says, 'Nah,'" he says with a shrug like it's no biggie and then adds, "And I'm like, 'Who do you think you are, bitch?' When I see her again, I'm just gonna do it. Just shove her up against the wall and see how she likes it."

And that's when my fuse blows.

In about three strides, I have *him* up against a wall, his shirt bunched in my hands. "You better not let me ever hear you threaten to assault somebody again."

"What the fuck, man? I didn't threaten to assault anybody!"

"I heard every word you said. It sounded like a rape threat to me, and I'm telling you, straight up, I will not let it happen."

"Dude, relax, bro. It's just talk, you know?" the guy's friend says, tugging on my arm, trying to separate us.

Fuck that. That's bullshit. "I don't know what kind of people

you talk to, but I'm telling you again. Not. Gonna. Happen."
I slowly enunciate every word. "I know the girl you're talking
about. I was there when you tried out your comedy act on her,
and you know what? You're lucky she didn't report your ass." I
relax my grip on him. He gives me a shove that doesn't budge me
even half an inch.

"Asshole."

Yeah, I know that I am. Been called a lot worse.

"Hey, hey, what's going on here?"

"This guy just attacked me for no reason!" the one with the
big mouth informs a campus cop who rushed over to us.

I hold up my hands in a gesture of cooperation. "When
somebody threatens to assault a girl, I don't ignore it."

The guard's eyes narrow when he turns them back on the kid I
had on the wall. "Both of you, come with me. Right now."

"Are you kidding me? I didn't do anything!" he whines.

"Then you won't mind coming with me so I can sort all
this out."

In a small office just inside the main entrance to the complex,
I give a statement. I tell campus police the whole story, starting
with the dining hall drama I'd witnessed the other day and ending
with the guy's boast that had me charging like a bull.

"I never said I'd rape anybody!" the moron protests.

The guard turns to him. "What's your name?"

He blows out a heavy sigh. "Aaron Dreschler. But I never
said rape!"

"Did you say, 'When I see her again, I'm just gonna do it. Just shove her up against the wall and see how she likes it'? Because that's the actual definition of assault, Aaron," the guard counters, reading his notes.

Aaron tries to smile and appeal to the guard's Y chromosome. "Nah, man, come on. You know how it is. It's just talk. I didn't actually *mean* it."

"Then you shouldn't have said it." The cop picks up the phone on the side of a desk and asks for one of the deans. Aaron's face loses all its color.

"You can go, but you may need to make another statement," the officer tells me.

"No problem," I reply.

Outside in the fresh air, I pull in a deep breath. I feel…well, better. That itchy, restless feeling is gone. I feel kind of—I don't know. Proud, maybe? I did something good. *Points for me.*

And then, I freeze. *Points.* I'm still doing shit just for points.

No. No, damn it. I didn't do this to square anything. I didn't shut that asshole up because I thought, *Hey! Here's an opportunity to make up for what I did!* I did it because I couldn't *not* do it. It sounds like it doesn't make sense, but it's the truth. Hearing the way this jerk was talking about that girl almost made my head explode. And the part that sucks the most about this whole incident is that he *doesn't even know her name.* She's just a—a thing. The object of his fantasy world.

I shut my eyes. Ashley had been that for Vic. An object. A *thing.* He didn't think of her as anything besides points. A wave of disgust ripples over me, because I know I'm not any better.

Dakota was never anything besides points for me, either. After it all went down, Mom told me Ashley had been spinning all these fairy tales around Victor…going to his senior prom, hanging out all summer before he left for college.

Ashley might never be the same, and I obsessively worry about that and hate myself a little bit more. Vic killed part of her that day. A huge part. He took what he wanted and left her an angry, frightened, resentful shell. God, I hate him in that volcanic fury way I haven't felt since the day it happened.

The sound of shoes slapping concrete mixed with a few giggles catches my attention. A group of girls is heading my way, and my jaw drops. One of them is the girl who shot down the moron in the dining hall. They see me, and immediately, their laughter fades and caution creeps into their eyes. Their bodies all go tense. I notice one of the girls takes her hands out of her pockets. She's carrying keys.

It hits me—they're *afraid* of me.

I'm the good guy, I want to scream at them. Can't they tell? I want to protest and defend myself and whip out my GAR pledge form so that they'll stop looking at me like I'm…Victor Patton.

But then I remember what Ted Vega said. It's about *them*, not me. It's about how *they* feel.

I clear my throat and hold up my hands, trying to look as unthreatening as I can. Maybe if I'd done more looking out two years ago, I could have prevented the single worst thing that's ever happened to my family.

The girls pass me cautiously. The second I get back to my

SOMEONE I USED TO KNOW

dorm room, I find that list of GAR events Ted handed us last night, and I email the contact name listed for an event that's scheduled at Ohio State University at the end of November. I get a reply almost immediately, thanking me for stepping up and adding my voice.

Could you pick three or four discussion points from this list—whatever you're most comfortable talking about—and let me know?

Comfortable? I almost laugh.

October

7

ASHLEY

When I came to, bleeding and sick, the defendant kept saying, "Two hundred points," over and over again. I was retching in that dirt and garbage, and he, the nice boy, was adding up his points in a team-wide scavenger hunt every single person in that school knew about— knew about and did nothing to prevent.

—**Ashley E. Lawrence, victim impact statement**

NOW

BELLFORD, OHIO

The weather has turned crisp and part of me sighs in relief. It sure makes getting dressed easier. I can wear baggy sweaters, boots, and flannel and not have people look at me like I'm a freak.

But another part of me tightens and braces for impact. October is not my favorite month. October means homecoming.

I shake my head violently. I'm not going there. I've been doing so well, and I'm not about to backslide. I return my attention to the screen in front of me, where the results of my internet research are listed. Sebastian and I got approval to hold a pledge rally in a few weeks. Coach Davidson promised us no homecoming activities at all. No dance, no parade—and absolutely no scavenger hunt. He personally addressed all students over the PA system and assured us that any player on his team who even attempts to resurrect the sexist tradition will be immediately benched.

Bruce turned and skewered me with a spiteful glare at this news. I just shrugged.

We're holding the pledge rally instead of a pep rally the day before the homecoming game. That gives us a few more weeks to figure out our plan. I've been drafting a pledge form, trying to find the right words to convey the message I want to send. I want people to take responsibility for their actions. That means you can't blame the victim for drinking too much if you were drinking, too.

I click a link about dress codes and decide that has to go into the pledge form, too. People need to learn to control their *own* impulses. Someone's bare shoulders or legs are *distractions*? Please.

There are so many other points I can consider making, so many things that were said to me, I can hardly keep them all straight. Things like *Consent is fuzzy.*

It's a yes or no question; I said stop. It doesn't get much clearer! And yeah, I think partners should have the right to change their minds at any time and be able to trust the other person to honor that right. Quickly, I add more notes to the document I've got open.

I skim another link, and my heart twinges inside my body. This one's about hazing and how a phenomenon called group-think can convince decent people to turn their backs on what's right. That scavenger hunt could totally be called hazing. My throat goes tight, and I squeeze my eyes shut, but it does no good.

Sometimes the bad memories are too strong for me to keep contained, and they spill over the dam.

TWO YEARS AGO
BELLFORD, OHIO

"What the hell are you doing, Ashley?" Derek grabs my arm at the exit that leads to the athletic field.

It's now the beginning of October, and after all that intense practicing with Candace and the rest of the girls, I tried out for the dance team's choreographer, a former Rockette named Ms. Pasmore, and made the Fusion team. I was totally shocked. Championship teams have dozens of dancers, but our school's squad isn't very large. There are ten of us. Whatever their reasons for welcoming me to the squad, I'm profoundly grateful.

Practicing with the squad every day after school plus Saturdays and every night on my own is so grueling, I tumble into bed early. I barely even see Derek. During the school day, he hangs out with the rest of the football team. It's his first year playing varsity. Me being on the dance team wasn't a problem for him—until today.

"Let go," I shoot back, pulling my elbow out of his grasp.

"You're actually going through with this?"

Ah, now it makes sense. He'd been betting that I'd quit. "Yeah," I sneer at him while pulling my hair into a ponytail. He still hasn't noticed I cut off about a foot of it. Derek can be downright dumb sometimes, and this is definitely one of those times.

"Okay, listen. You can't be on the dance team or the cheerleading squad."

I look at him sideways. "Uh. Yeah. I *can*."

His frustration is pretty obvious. He grits his teeth and flings out his arms. Yep, Derek is about to blow his top.

"Ash, can't you just go home? I don't want to hang out with you, and you being on the dance team isn't going to change that. What part of that is so hard for you to grasp?"

I hold up my hand. "Don't blame *me*. If you hadn't ditched me on the first day of school, I wouldn't have met these girls."

The look on his face goes from anger to outrage to profound frustration. It really is hilarious, but I manage not to laugh.

"Quit. Right now. Tell them you don't want to dance."

"I *do* want to dance."

"No. You don't. You're a terrible dancer. You say it yourself all the time."

"I'm not terrible anymore. I'm not quitting. Just stop being such a poop head."

Derek's fair skin is flushed, and his blue eyes pop wide. "Oh my God, will you stop with the baby words? It's *shit*head. Just say it. *Shit*head."

I'm totally shocked, so he waves his hands. "Oh, forget it. Just…just stay far away from me. With luck, nobody'll know we're related."

"I will!" I shoot back. "Dance team is for me, not you. Besides, you should be happy. Making my own friends is what you've wanted ever since you started high school."

"Yo! Lawrence!"

We both turn and see Vic approaching. I smile, and Derek curses, ignoring him and stepping right up to my face. "God, Ashley. You are so dumb sometimes."

He strides off, totally oblivious to the way I flinch at that barb he shot at me like a bullet. I stand there, feeling like I'm bleeding, until Brittany and Candace put their arms around me.

"Come on, Ashley. It's *his* problem, not yours."

How could it not be my problem? He's my brother.

"I'll talk to him," Vic promises with a smile, holding his helmet under his arm. He's sweaty and messy, and still, that smile shoots straight to my heart.

"I got a hundred!" I suddenly blurt out.

He cocks his head and frowns. My mouth opens, and the words tumble out.

"On Mr. Wilder's pop quiz. I read ahead. Like you told me." *Oh my God, shut up!*

He laughs. "Good job." And then he winks. "Go do your thing. I'll catch you later."

My thing?

So that's what I do. I take my place and dance. I make the

motions big so they can be seen from the freakin' moon, let alone the top row of bleachers. I smile like nothing hurts, nothing's wrong, but Derek's words still sting.

"Oh, wow," Deanne says much later, with a new and different pitch to her voice. "Chest candy."

We all stop what we're doing to watch the boys strip off their gear, douse their heads with water bottles, and jog by us to hit the showers.

Chest candy. Yeah. I get it now. I lick my lips, my eyes glued to one chest in particular.

"Uh-oh," Candace says, seeing where my gaze is aimed. "Vic the Dick has another admirer. Don't even bother, Ashley. He's a jerk."

I shake my head. Vic's amazing. Besides, it's not like I had half a shot with him anyway. He's a senior. I'm a freshman. I probably have, like, a .0001 chance of a shot.

"Come on. We're having a team meeting. You can stay around longer, right?"

I shake my head. "I have to catch the bus."

"No problem. Brittany can drop us off."

Inside, I tingle. I have a friend who can drop me off. How cool is that? I follow Candace back to the other girls. They sit in a circle on the field around Marlena, who's handing out sheets of orange paper. "Okay, so the homecoming game is in a few more weeks." Groans go up from the older girls. I blink, wondering why this is bad news.

Candace holds up her hands. "We'll use that time to practice the hell out of that new routine because we're dancing the half-time show."

This news is met with squeals of delight. Another tingle shoots through my system. I'd do my *thing* because I totally have a *thing* now.

"Cheer squad, color guard, and dance will share the field, so we'll be putting in long hours practicing."

I can do that. Long hours are fine with me. You know, for my *thing*.

"Now, let's move on to the hunt."

Another groan. Marlena jumps to her feet. "I am *not* putting up with that shit again this year."

"I have no knowledge if they're even planning it. I talked to the assistant coach, and he *claims* he's expressly forbidden it, but you know that doesn't mean much."

"So we're the ones who have to suffer. Great." Marlena shakes her head in disgust.

I try to follow the conversation, but I'm obviously missing something. Seeing my confusion, Marlena explains. "It's become a 'tradition' here," she says with an eye roll and finger quotes. "A scavenger hunt the football players do every year during homecoming season."

"What are they supposed to find?"

"Us," Deanne says with a shrug. "It kind of sucks. The guys get points for how far they get. You know, a kiss is like one point, but getting to second base might get them ten or twenty."

"And going all the way gets like a hundred," Marlena adds.

My eyes bulge. "You're kidding me."

All the ponytails shake.

"That's...that's really low."

"Yeah, so don't accept any dates. They're just for points. But that's not the bad part. The bad part is some of the boys try to get points any way they can. Sometimes, if there's nobody around to see, they'll grab you in the hallway, squeeze a boob, snap your bra, lift up your skirt."

"So," Marlena continues. "That means for the next couple of weeks, everybody needs to wear shorts under your skirts and never walk anywhere alone."

"But...but they can't just reach out and grab you. That's against the law."

I watch the girls sigh and frown and grumble in complete disbelief.

"Wait. That's it? We have to follow the buddy system? Why don't we just tell the principal?"

Candace and Brittany exchange a horrified glance. "Ash, it's football. The team's got a lot of influence."

"So you're saying whatever they say goes?"

"Pretty much." Candace shrugs. "You can go to the principal if you want. But all he'll do is tell you he needs proof. Without proof of any wrongdoing, he won't even consider punishing a single player on that team."

"That completely sucks," Tara says, exchanging glances with me.

"Yeah. It does." Brittany nods. "But there's no changing it. It's been a tradition for years, and the boys know exactly how to get away with it. So do us a favor. Listen to Candace. Don't accept any dates from any of the boys on the team. They won't be real. They'll just be setups to get points."

Oh my God. They're entirely serious. I think about it for a few moments and then decide I'm not going to just sit back and look the other way. If any of those boys try to make their points from me, I won't let them. I'll fight back.

"Oh, hell no." Candace puts both hands on her hips and glares at a few of the players heading our way.

"And so it begins," Marlena adds with a roll of those wild eyes.

"Ladies," the first boy says with a wide grin, and I recognize him. He's one of the players who was in the parking lot the day Derek ditched me.

"Get lost, Brayden. We're busy."

"Yeah? Doing what? Sitting?" the second boy asks. He sits beside Brittany, practically in her lap.

She gives him the same look Mom gives leftovers that have sprouted mold in the refrigerator. "Brayden, take this fungus out of my personal space."

"Give him a kiss first."

"Sure." Candace cracks her knuckles. "I'll give him a kiss." She punches her hand with a fist. The boy just laughs and leans over to kiss Brittany, but she jumps to her feet, still sneering. Undeterred, he gets up and tries to grab her, but she evades, until they're circling us in a sort of duck-duck-goose chase.

The fuse that Derek lit earlier that afternoon still burns, and

I find myself abruptly infuriated by the entire idea of this sexual scavenger hunt. I stick out a foot and trip the boy from my math class, sending him sprawling to the grass.

"Doug! Jesus, you okay, man?" Brayden rushes to his fallen teammate while everyone, including Brittany, stares at me with horrified looks. "What the fuck is wrong with you?" Brayden turns on me. "You could have broken his leg, and we'd be down a player for the game."

"Yeah? Well, maybe your players should think about that before they try to grab people who don't want to be grabbed," I shoot back.

"Oh, please! You're just pissed because we weren't chasing you."

"I don't want you chasing anybody!"

"Ashley, back off." Brittany holds up her hand and goes to Doug's side. "You really could have hurt him, you know."

My mouth falls open. She actually goes to him, prods his ankle, and pats his arm. When, exactly, did I fall through the portal to this alternate reality? I look around our group, and yeah, everyone is mad at *me* for trying to stop this stupid game.

"He fell on grass. It's not like I stabbed him."

"Yes, but he still has to be able to play."

"Yeah. I get it." Football, football, football! I'm already tired of hearing about the football team, and the season has barely started. I mash my lips together, stuff my gear into my bag, and leave. Looks like I'm walking home again.

......

Furious, I stalk out of the athletic field and down the hill to the school's entrance. I cannot believe these people. Poor little Doug almost got a boo-boo. Waaah. Maybe if poor little Doug wasn't trying to molest girls on the field, he wouldn't have gotten tripped. And Brittany defending him was even more messed up than Doug trying to score points from her in the first place.

A horn honks beside me, and I whip around with a snarl. Vic holds up two hands. "Whoa! Don't shoot!"

I try to force my face to look regular or at least less ferocious. "Hi, Vic."

I guess I failed because his "Hi, Ash," has a bite that practically leaves teeth marks. I can't help it. I laugh.

"There she is. So you need a ride or would you rather just stomp on the sidewalk until it cries uncle?"

Shaking my head, I slide into his passenger seat. "Thanks. I really wasn't in the mood to walk all the way home."

"What'd he do this time?"

Another laugh. I kind of love the way Vic just gets me. "Uh, let's see. First, he ordered me off the field and back home, then he said he doesn't want anybody finding out we're related. And because a huge public fight with my brother wasn't already bad enough, I just got yelled at for the way I dealt with Doug and Brayden trying to cop a feel."

He looks at me sharply. "They *touched* you?"

"No. Not me. Brittany. They chased her around the field for points in some stupid scavenger hunt. So I tripped him."

Vic bursts into laughter. "You tripped him? Holy shit, Ash. You are badass."

His words completely dissolve what's left of my anger and turn me to mush. Victor Patton thinks I'm badass. Maybe this day doesn't *totally* suck. He slows down for a red light, and it suddenly occurs to me that he…that I…might be nothing more than points in the same game.

"So are you playing? In the hunt, I mean."

"Yes," he admits without hesitation.

Oh.

I take it back. This day does totally suck.

"It's just a team bonding thing we do. No big deal."

"So is everybody playing?"

"Sure. All the guys pulled their cards, except for that one kid. Sebastian."

"Even Derek?"

Vic laughs again. "Especially Derek. He's well on his way to a hundred points."

A hundred points. "But I thought that was for sex."

"It is," Vic confirms, and my face heats up. "But don't worry. He's got it all under control. He's hooking up with Dakota again."

I stare straight ahead while he turns right at a stop sign, dread weighing me down. I don't know Dakota. I know he went out with her a couple of times, and then he was on to somebody new. Derek may be a jerk sometimes, but he'd never use somebody just for…points. "You're wrong. Derek wouldn't do that."

Vic laughs long and loud. "Oh my God, listen to you defend

SOMEONE I USED TO KNOW

him! He talks trash about you all the time, and you stick up for him?" He shakes his head in wonder. "You are too much."

"Okay, yeah, he treats me like crap, but that's just to me. You know, annoying little sister. But there's no way he'd have sex with a girl just to win some stupid game."

"Trust me, he would." And then Vic waves a hand. "But the hunt isn't all about sex. We have to do other stuff, too."

"Like what?"

"Um. Well, like steal somebody's mailbox or toss a pair of shoes over a utility line and piss on a grave. Oh, and I think at least one card says to do ten shots in less than a minute."

Whoa. I wrinkle my nose. "Couldn't that, like, you know, kill somebody?"

Vic shrugs. "I guess. Luckily, it's not on *my* card."

Just what is on his card? I shift in my seat to look at him directly. "Am I on your card? Is this thing with me just to get your points?"

He doesn't reply, and when I sneak a peek at him, I see he's clenching his jaw just like Derek does when he's pissed off. The dread increases. Victor doesn't say anything else until he pulls in front of my house. He turns off the car, drums his fingers on the wheel for a minute or two, and finally turns to face me.

"There are some items on my card I could ask *you* for, but honestly? I'd rather ask any one of, like, a dozen seniors."

Oh. I look away. I didn't expect such brutal honesty.

"Ashley, the hunt is important to us. It builds confidence and trust, and most girls get that, so they're all totally willing to help us out. But the thing is, I like *you*. And since you're a freshman, you're, you know, a little young for me? I'm used to girls who've already done…things." He finishes with a swirl of his hand, and the dread that's been building inside me finally bottoms out. Tears burn at the back of my eyes, and I fumble with the door handle.

"Yeah. I get it. Thanks for the ride."

"Ashley, wait!" He grabs my arm and tugs me back. "I'm trying to say that you kind of have to help me out here. I don't know where the line is, you know?"

"The line," I repeat.

"Yeah. So I know not to cross it." He smiles for a second and skims the back of his hand down my cheek, and all that dread I was feeling turns to anticipation. His hand climbs to the back of my head and tugs me closer, and I go with it until we're just inches apart. "Like, is it okay to do this?" He moves even closer, and I hold my breath, not daring to move until his eyes close and his lips touch mine.

His lips are so soft and oh my God! Vic is kissing me. Victor Patton, a senior, is kissing *me*, a freshman. Frantically, I try to remember what I'm supposed to do, but I can't, and then I remember I should breathe before I pass out. I gasp in a breath, and when I open my mouth, Vic somehow moves closer. His hands grip my face and angle my head, and he kisses me again. I mean *really* kisses me…*with tongue*. I think I might die of terminal happiness, because this is literally the best thing that's ever happened to me. We break apart, smiling at each other like total morons.

"So…kissing's okay?"

I nod vigorously.

"And…what about touching, like this?" Deliberately, he moves his hand to my right breast, lifting it, squeezing it. My legs bounce, and I'm on total sensory overload, but I nod again, and he laughs.

"Got it." He leans in and kisses me again, his hand still *right there,* and I forget all about Derek and the hunt and points and Doug's stupid leg.

I'm not entirely sure when we stopped and I went inside. In fact, I can't remember anything after that moment until Mom poked her head into my room to call me downstairs for dinner.

The next day, at school, I can't wait to see Vic. Are we, like, together now? Is he…do I have an actual boyfriend? I find Tara at her locker and practically drag her into a stairwell.

"Oh my God, Ashley, what is wrong with you?"

I look carefully around for extra ears to overhear this epic news, but it's all clear. "He kissed me, Tara. Vic."

Her eyes widen, and her lips form a perfect O. "Get out! Are you serious? When? Where?"

I tell her all of it, right up to his hand on my boob. "Tara, tell me the truth. Do you think I'm…I'm just points to him?"

She shakes her head vigorously. "No, like he said, there are tons of older and way more experienced girls he could do that with. He must really like *you*, Ashley."

I float through class that day. Vic drives me home every day for the rest of the week, and every day, our kisses get more and more exciting. On Friday, Tara and I are in the cafeteria during lunch. Vic always eats lunch with his teammates, and I don't get upset about it because he's explained it's for team building.

Doug, the same jerk who'd chased Brittany, walks by Derek's table with his sidekick, Brayden. He leans in and says something that makes Dakota turn on my brother with fire in her eyes. "Oh my God, you *told* the team? Show me your card!" She demands, and Derek shakes his head, smiling at her, trying to calm her down.

"I want to see your card!"

"Uh-oh," Tara says, popping a fry into her mouth. "Looks like your brother is in trouble." She sings the last line. Across from us, Brittany and Candace look over their shoulders to watch the show. Candace looks amused, but Brittany looks really sad. I feel so bad for her. She really likes Derek, though exactly *why* she likes him is beyond my comprehension.

Doug and Brayden, who started the drama, laugh and head to Vic's table. I watch Vic hold up a hand for high fives. Dakota's on her feet now, shouting at Derek, while two of her friends try to soothe her and get her out of the cafeteria.

"No!" she screams. "I want to hear him say it. The only reason we got back together is for your stupid scavenger hunt, isn't it? I thought you were different! But deep down, I knew it all along. That's why I wanted to hold out, but you said you missed me. You said you loved me. I can't believe I trusted you. Ugh! You're paying for my homecoming dress!"

"I'm sorry!" Derek shouts back, but she's not buying it. He

stands up, refusing to look at Dakota, collects his books and his tray, and walks away, while she screams at his retreating back. He stalks straight to the football team's table and hauls Brayden off his seat by his shirt. A rumble grows as anticipation for the fight Derek's about to start ripples across the entire cafeteria. Vic stands up and separates Derek and Brayden and gives Derek a little shove, and all three of them sit down, exchanging some harsh words. Their faces are red, their jaws are clenched, and fingers are pointed in faces.

"Guess Derek's available again," Candace tells Brittany as they turn back around in their seats and resume eating lunch.

Brittany doesn't say a word.

Neither do I. I shove my tray aside, suddenly sick because Vic was right.

I stare at Derek, looking for something familiar, something to prove he's still my brother, still my Leo. But it's not there. He's not there. Derek, my brother, is gone, and in his place is just someone I used to know, someone I thought I knew as well as I know myself.

8

DEREK

NOW

LONG ISLAND, NEW YORK

The GAR meetings are cool.

I can't believe I'm saying that. Ashley would never believe I'm saying that. But they're not what I expected. Okay, I'm actually not sure what I expected, but the truth is, putting my strength behind this cause feels…right, I guess. Reminds me of this old quote I learned in history class once. Something about justice being achieved when those who aren't injured feel as indignant as those who are.

I guess I'm finally indignant.

The statistics alone make me sick, and then when you add in all the additional torment survivors who come forward have to endure, it's a wonder anybody ever gets convicted of this crime. There are stories of police who ask insulting questions and parents and teachers who immediately demand to know if the victims have been drinking. Hell—sometimes, it's even a best friend who doubts an account. Pretty much the only thing that's constant is that survivors will always feel like it's their own fault.

Does Ashley feel that way? I don't think she does. She just blames me.

We started off with just six of us plus Ted Vega. Now we're nine because we managed to convince others to join us. Like Julian Waters, my roommate. I thought I was a big guy until I met him. Six and half feet tall and almost that wide, Julian's a Rocky Hill Rockets offensive tackle, and I'm willing to bet no mere mortal has ever gotten by him. Outgoing and friendly, Julian made friends with half the team on our first day of camp, including me. Like Brittany, he's studying psychology. He's one of the smartest people I've ever met and loves to show off in the middle of conversations and blab about some psych concept he learned and thinks somebody just demonstrated, which is only amusing when it's not *you* he's lecturing.

I told him where I was going, and he stood up and said, "I gotta check this out."

He signed the pledge form that day, and during our next football practice, he began preaching the GAR philosophy in the locker room when one of our teammates told some disgustingly crude joke. I, on the other hand, stood there, dumb and mute.

Yeah. I still have a long way to go.

We're heading back to our dorm room after a meeting, and

Julian asks, "So have you talked to your sister? Told her what you're up to?"

I shake my head. "No. It's better if I don't talk to Ashley. Justin, my brother, says I *trigger* her." The word leaves a bitter taste in my mouth.

Julian nods. Words like *trigger* mean something to him because, you know, psych major, but I can't help feeling resentful. I think that's just an excuse to avoid the real problem. She's pissed off, she hates me, and she needs to punish me.

"I can hear your gears grinding from over here, brother."

I roll my eyes. "Julian, you got any sisters?"

"No, man. I'm the oldest of four boys."

"Wow. Brothers. I wish I had a few more of those."

He laughs. "No, you don't. Trust me on that, 'cause I got the scars to back up what I say."

I think about that for a minute. Justin couldn't ever take me on. I swear I've been bigger than him since birth. But Julian? Yeah, he could totally best me—and has, during our practice sessions.

"Back to my point. You got something on your mind. Gimme."

Sighing, I try to figure out how to explain it. "I've apologized to my sister. Over and over again. But it does no good. She just stares at me with this look on her face..." I trail off and shiver. "It's like she's plotting my death or something."

Julian doesn't say anything.

"I mean, I get it. I was a real little shit to her, but I didn't rape her. And I swear to God, I didn't know what Victor Patton was up to until it was too damn late."

"So what *did* you do?"

I trip over a shoelace that's come untied and curse. "She blames me for the outcome of the trial. Like I had any control over that."

"Why would she think that?" He veers off the path to a bench. I prop my foot on it and retie my tennis shoe.

Julian's pulling the psychoanalysis shit on me, and it's getting on my nerves. "Look, man, I got called to testify about the scavenger hunt. Tell the court what it was, who played, what we had to do. Rape was never part of it. It wasn't on a single player's list."

"So what was on the list?"

"My list had sex with an ex. I didn't know that Victor's list had sex with a virgin until…" I clench my jaw.

Julian looks at me, eyebrows raised, circling his hand in the air for me to go on.

"Until the day he hurt her."

And then it all comes rushing out like vomit.

"I tried to stop him, Julian. I swear to God. I knew he'd been kind of sniffing around her, leading her on, but she was so insanely happy to have his attention, I let it go. When I did find out that was on his list, I went after them, checked every place I knew to look, but I figured he'd just put the moves on her and then hurt her feelings when he dumped her. I never expected him to *force* her." I drop down to the bench, drag both hands through my hair, feeling the nausea bubble in my gut all over again, just like it's done every day since the first. "I swear to you, I never knew, but she doesn't believe me."

"Damn, man. That's rough." He shakes his head. "Just what

the hell was so cool about this scavenger hunt in the first place? I mean, why'd you get so into it? No offense, but sex with an ex? Sex with a virgin? That's messed up."

Yeah. I know it now. "I wish I had a good answer for you, bro. But I don't. I just got sucked into it, like all the other guys." That admission leaves such a sour taste in my mouth, I spit into the grass next to our bench. "Most of the shit on our lists was reckless, you know? Do this, say that, maybe get some people mad at you. But none of it was supposed to actually *hurt* anybody. And you know what totally sucks the most? The way the hunt was set up, the way the items were worded, yeah. People were gonna get hurt. That seems so obvious now, but it didn't then. Am I really that stupid, that clueless?"

Julian doesn't reply. He doesn't have to. The record shows that I am indeed that stupid and clueless.

"Brother, you know what they say about hindsight."

"Yeah, tell me about it."

"So what's this got to do with the outcome of the trial?"

I roll my head from side to side and feel my neck pop. "I was called to testify for Ashley. But Victor's defense attorney tripped me up on his cross-examination. He asked me if anybody made plans about forcing girls, about *taking* points for our items on the hunt lists. I said not to my knowledge because that was true. Nobody did discuss it openly. But the truth is, a few of the guys *did* try to steal points. This one guy? Doug. He cornered my sister in a stairwell, but a teacher broke that up. And I heard some stories about cell phones aimed up girls' skirts. But I didn't say any of that on the stand because he asked me if anybody *planned* to force girls to get their points. How's that for sibling loyalty? My sister's rapist is on trial, and I'm giving testimony that paints the entire team out to be a bunch of choirboys," I say with a sneer. "No wonder she hates my guts."

I'm spiraling down a well of self-pity, so I take a breath and finish answering Julian's question. "He asked me a bunch of other questions, one right after the other. You know, rapid fire? I barely had time to think about my answers. Anyway, the gist of it was I somehow testified, under oath, that Victor Patton wasn't a *real* rapist and shouldn't have to spend a decade of his life in jail for a stupid game." I lean over my knees and hang my head, the shame too heavy to bear. "She wasn't even in the courtroom, but somehow, she knows what I said. Long story short, the jury didn't have *sufficient evidence* to convict on *rape*. They convicted on sexual assault. Big deal right? Well, it is. It means he got two years instead of ten. It means he'll be out soon, man." The thought makes my hands clench into fists.

Julian lets out a vicious curse and jumps to his feet, pacing a few steps away. Sighing loudly, he turns and stares at me. "Man, that is messed up."

"Yeah. Tell me."

Julian walks back toward me and bumps his fist to mine. "You need to let go of whatever it is you're thinking right now."

I'm thinking about how good it would feel to punch this fist into Vic's lying mouth once or twice or twelve times.

"Derek." He waits until I lift my gaze to his. "You know if that asshole breaks a fingernail, you're the top suspect, right?"

"Yes," I reply on a long disgusted sigh. "And don't worry. I've already heard that bedtime story, and it doesn't have a happy ending."

"Sure would feel good, though."

"Yeah, no shit." I stand, and we resume our walk back to our dorm.

"So about the big rally," he begins, and I hold up a hand.

"Yeah, I know. I'll be there. Weirdly, after a few meetings with Ted Vega, I'm kind of looking forward to it. I actually signed up to speak at an event back home." There are probably tons of secondary survivors like me who need advice on how to handle their feelings and how to be the strength their loved ones need so they can heal. I don't know if I can help anybody else. But I have to do something. I didn't do anything two years ago.

Julian shoots me a grin. "Good on you, Lawrence."

Good on me. I resist the urge to swirl my finger in the air. It's not enough, not even close to enough to convince Ashley to forgive me. But maybe, I'll hate me just a little bit less.

9

ASHLEY

Your Honor, it's true I let Victor kiss me and touch me, but that's all I wanted to do. He chose to ignore me when I said stop. He chose. That choice should come with consequences.

—**Ashley E. Lawrence, victim impact statement**

TWO YEARS AGO

BELLFORD, OHIO

On my way down the rear stairs to the exit that leads to the field where we practice, I find Doug waiting, all suited up for football, helmet tucked under his arm.

"Hey, Ashley Lawrence," he says with a grin that sends shivers of panic skating up my spine.

I turn to run back up the stairs, but he blocks my way.

"Get out of my way."

Doug holds up his phone. "Show me your tits. Are they even real?"

Disgust twists inside me. "What? Get lost." I move to one side, but Doug blocks me again.

"You're gonna be late if you don't do it," he says in a singsong voice, aiming the phone at my chest.

"I'm not showing you anything. Now get out of my way." I shove him, but he doesn't move.

"Look, you owe me after tripping me."

"I owe *you*? You are seriously out of touch, dude."

Instead, Doug takes a step closer. Jeez, he's taller than I thought. And with all his gear on, a lot bigger than normal. Panic turns into fear.

"You know, tripping me wasn't cool. We have a big game coming up. It's your job to take care of me—"

Rage replaces fear. "I'm sorry—my job? Are you high?"

The door opens, startling both of us. The assistant coach, Mr. DeMaio, stands there along with two boys. One is Victor Patton, and the other is a boy I remember from the first day of school. Sebastian Valenti. Relief floods through me, and I move toward the open door.

Mr. DeMaio scowls. "Doug, you're late."

"Sorry." But he doesn't move. He just stares at me, grinning like a maniac.

Mr. DeMaio glares at Doug. "Mr. Patton, please make sure Doug gets where he's supposed to be without getting lost."

"Sure thing," Vic says while Doug keeps grinning.

"See you later, Ashley."

With a smack of cleats, they jog outside.

I clear my throat. "Thank you, Mr. DeMaio. Doug tried to touch me."

"Ms. Lawrence, you need to make sure you're where you're supposed to be, when you're supposed to be. Is that clear?"

I blink, not sure I heard him correctly. Maybe he hadn't *me* correctly. "I said, Doug just tried to fondle me. Are you going to do anything about it?"

"There's nothing I can do. I didn't see anything, and it would be your word against his."

"You didn't see anything," I repeat, numb. Oh my God. Candace was right.

......

"Hey, Ashley, you okay?" Candace asks me a few minutes later when I reach the field.

I shake my head. "Doug tried to…" I have a hard time saying it out loud.

"What? Get points off you?"

I nod. "He wouldn't let me pass by him unless I…unless I lifted my shirt."

"That's because he's a little turd who knows he'll never see a girl's boobs voluntarily, so he has to milk the Bengals hunt for anything he can get."

"Candace, I want to tell the principal."

She blows out a loud breath and shrugs. "Well, if you think it'll help, go for it."

"Why? You don't?"

"Ashley," she says with a frown. "I know you're a freshman and don't know everything yet, but trust me. Football's important. McCloskey's not gonna listen to you, especially not if it puts football at risk."

"Maybe that's because he doesn't know about it," I argue, but she just rolls her eyes.

"Oh, he knows about it. They all do and pretend they don't. Ashley, I know it sucks, but it's better to just roll with it."

......

That evening, I stalk into our house and slam the door behind me. Mom and Dad stop talking and stare at me.

"Hey, Ash. Bad day?"

"Ugh!" I respond, sick to my stomach. "You have absolutely no idea. Every boy in that school is just…just…" I'm so mad, I can't even find words.

"Sit down. I'll reheat some dinner for you. Did you mess up your dance routine?" Mom asks, heading into the kitchen.

I flop down into a chair at the table. Dad follows a second later. "No. It's not that. It's…why do people do things they *know* are wrong? I just don't understand."

Dad's eyes sharpen. "What do you mean, wrong?"

"The boys on the football team are playing this stupid game. It's like a scavenger hunt, only the things on it aren't *things* exactly. They're stuff they have to do."

"What kind of stuff?" Mom asks, popping a plate into the microwave.

I lift my arms and let them fall. "Apparently, chase our dancers around the field, demanding we let them kiss us, and…touch us."

Dad and Mom exchange a worried glance.

"Why don't you start at the beginning, Ash?" Dad leans forward.

So I do. I tell them everything. All of it. The hunt, the girls on the team, what happened with Brayden and Doug the other day when I tripped Doug, Derek's big fight with Dakota, and what happened today, with Doug, in the stairwell. I tell them how the teacher *claims* he saw nothing and how Candace and Brittany hate it but won't even try to do anything about it. Suddenly, the full impact of Brittany's betrayal makes me cry. "She took his side, Daddy. I was trying to help her, make sure he didn't touch her, and she took *his* side just because he's *important*. I don't get it. I just don't get it."

"Which was the one who hurt you?"

I bite my lip. "Well, he didn't hurt me exactly. But it was Doug. He cornered me in the stairwell on my way out to dance practice. He wouldn't let me by until I showed him my…"

With every word, Dad turns a little bit redder until he's the color of a roaring fire. Abruptly, he shoves away from the table so fast, his chair topples over.

Mom and I chase him upstairs to Derek's room. Derek's scrolling through phone messages. He looks up when we all barge in. "What did I do this time?" he asks, rolling his eyes.

"Be quiet," Dad orders.

"Dad, I haven't had the best of days—"

"Derek, I said… Be. Quiet." Dad's voice rises.

Derek crosses his arms and waits, jaw clenched, for Dad to just get to the point. But Dad doesn't say a word. He just stands by the door, staring at Derek. The scent of *boy* clings to the air—part sweat and part body spray. One minute goes by, then two, and Derek breaks first.

"Well? Just say it. I have homework to do."

"Your sister was accosted today by one your teammates. He demanded that she show him her chest. Something to do with a scavenger hunt?"

Derek's eyes swing to me, and a little pang of pride fills up my heart. Derek's my Leo. He'll fight for me. He'll tear Doug apart. He'll defend me, protect me.

Instead, he says, "Jesus Christ, you narc'd?"

My heart cracks.

Dad shoots into the room like a bullet, snatches Derek's phone out of his hands, and starts scrolling through it. "Don't you dare put this on her. I want to hear all about this scavenger hunt and your part in it right now." He waves Derek's phone at him. "I get the distinct impression you see nothing wrong with this *tradition* of yours." Dad actually makes air quotes.

Derek laughs once. "Jeez, Dad, it's just a team thing. The guys bond over some spirited competition, and the girls love the attention."

Dad's brown eyes half pop out of his head. "Are you actually listening to yourself right now? Do you hear the words coming out of your mouth?"

Derek sucks in a deep breath, but he's turning as red as Dad. "Yeah, I'm hearing the words. Like I said, it's not that big a deal."

"Derek, I want to know one thing. Did you or did you not get back together with Dakota Harper just to get points in this stupid game?"

Derek doesn't reply but keeps glaring at me.

"Derek?" Mom prompts.

He clenches his teeth so tight, I can hear them grinding from across the room. "It's not as if I don't like her."

"Oh, it's not like you don't like her. That's a really great reason to have sex. 'Hey, Dakota! I don't not like you. Let's sleep together.' I'm sure she just melted at that." Dad laughs, but it's a scary sound, not a happy one. I'm not sure I've ever seen him so mad. "And here it is. Our son's scavenger hunt list." He shows Mom the screen of Derek's phone.

Derek doesn't say a word. But I know what's on it. And now, so do Mom and Dad.

"Sex with an ex." Dad looks up from the phone with eyes that could bore holes through solid wood. "I'll ask again. Is this the only reason why you asked Dakota out again?"

Derek's face goes all the way to red.

"Answer me," Dad snaps.

Derek's eyes shoot to Mom's, but she only angles her head and circles her hands, impatient with his stalling. Derek swallows. "Uh, well…kind of."

"Oh. Kind of. I see. And did you tell her that or pretend you really missed her?"

Derek lowers his eyes. "No."

"Which is it, Derek? What did you tell her exactly?" Dad sits down and crosses his legs, like he's having a pleasant conversation with a neighbor about the weather, except we both know he's furious.

"I...I—" Derek's eyes swing from Dad to me to Mom and back again. "I...um...promised that I'd take her to the homecoming dance."

"Oh, did you? How nice. So you decided that escorting her to the dance was a small price to pay for...let me see...a hundred points?" Dad's voice is reaching new decibel levels.

Derek doesn't say anything.

"And you think—you actually *believe*—this is okay?" Mom demands.

Derek cracks his neck. "Dad, I asked if she wanted to get back together. She could have just said no."

Dad's eyes go narrow as slits at that. "Oh. She could have just said no. Okay, Derek. What about your sister? She did say no. Is it okay with you what your friend did to her today?"

Derek doesn't even glance at me. He just frowns. "I...okay. That's different. They're not together."

"Oh, so that's your line? It's perfectly okay when the girl is dating you?" Dad explodes. "Girls aren't here for you to use, Derek!" He flings up his hands and takes a few steps away and spins back around. "You know what really gets me? You don't even see it! You're still sitting there, trying to find ways to excuse this behavior." He leans in, real close to Derek's face. "I'm gonna make this crystal clear for you. I know football and being on this team are important to you. And I know you've got this problem with your sister. I don't understand it, but I've been trying to give you the benefit of the doubt. But I'm telling you right now, *nobody* treats her the way you treated Dakota Harper. If this is how those players treat girls, I don't want you playing on that team."

Derek's jaw drops. "But, Dad!"

"No, Derek. This"—he waves the phone—"is not right, and you know it. You want to keep playing football?"

"Yeah. Absolutely."

"Then no more hunt. You apologize to Dakota first thing in the morning, or I will drive you straight to her house, and you can apologize to her parents *after* we tell your coach you're finished with football. And you tell every player on that team that Ashley is off-limits to them."

Derek's eyes swing to mine. They were *not* filled with apology.

"Yeah. Okay. Fine."

Dad stands up and tosses Derek's phone to the bed.

"If I hear one more thing about points for sex, one more thing about somebody cornering Ashley in a stairwell, I'm holding *you* responsible. Got it?"

"Yeah."

"What?"

"Yes. I got it. You won't. I promise."

Mom and Dad exchange a long look and head for the door. As

they walk downstairs, I hang back, watching Derek. He just stares at his phone.

"Derek, I'm—"

He leaps up so fast, he blurs. He pushes me out of his room and shuts the door in my face.

......

At school the next day, when I tell Candace what happened, her dark eyes pop, and she shakes her head slowly. "Damn, Ash. Your brother really is an ass."

"I know, right?"

"Do you think he'll go through with it? Tell the guys you're off-limits?"

I nod. "Definitely. He always obeys Dad."

Only, he doesn't obey. Not this time.

I knew this because throughout the day, the guys on the football team grow increasingly obnoxious. One has his phone in his palm throughout math class, aiming up girls' skirts every time the teacher turns away. Doug, the same moron I tripped yesterday, asks Mia, the girl who sits next to him, if he can borrow a pen. She searches through her bag for one, and as soon as she looks up, he plants a kiss on her. The whole class goes wild as Doug high-fives all the guys sitting around him. Mia keeps scrubbing at her lips, looking like she'd just been tricked into kissing a fairy-tale toad.

The worst part? The teacher yells at *her*.

My blood starts to boil.

10

DEREK

TWO YEARS AGO

BELLFORD, OHIO

I walk into the locker room with my temper hitting red-line levels. "I'm out." I drop a printout of my scavenger hunt score to the bench littered with jerseys, shoes, and a couple of cups.

"Dude, are you insane?" Brayden looks horrified as he grabs the score sheet. "You have a hundred and sixty points already!"

My stomach cramps. The last thing I want to do is let down my teammates. But Dad threatened to pull me off the team if I don't, and he doesn't make empty threats.

"What are you, gay or something?" Doug calls out, drawing laughs from everyone who hears it. The only one who doesn't laugh is Sebastian Valenti, a sophomore.

I pull out my phone. "Look. Thanks to you two and your big fucking mouths, my parents heard all about the scavenger hunt.

They know about Dakota's meltdown in the cafeteria. And they know about you cornering my sister in the stairwell. They went practically thermonuclear and plan to talk to your parents. Worse, they said if I don't quit the hunt, I have to quit the team."

"Quit the team? Shit, man," Brayden echoes.

I'm still pissed off at Ashley for tattling, but now that I've thought it over, I can see why Dakota's mad. She's actually amazing, and I'd love to see her again. Maybe take her somewhere nicer than the homecoming dance. But after that big scene in the cafeteria, I don't know if she'll give me a third chance. I guess I have to find a way to deserve one.

"Hey. Let it go, guys. Can't you see Derek's upset about this?" Sebastian steps up.

I will myself to remain calm and try to get Brayden to understand. "Listen to me. I'm telling you, straight up, my dad's pissed. So pissed, he threatened to go to the coach and to Dakota's parents. So I'm out. And if you all have brains under your helmets, you'll stay the hell away from my sister during the hunt. Got it? You put the word out. Ashley is off-limits."

Brayden smirks but nods. "Yeah. Sure. I got it. Ashley's off-limits. Hear that, guys? Ashley Lawrence gets a free pass."

"Yeah. I heard it," Doug says, choking back laughter. I don't like the tone I hear in his voice one bit.

I step up into his face and speak slowly and succinctly. "You seem to think this is a joke. I'm not laughing. If I find out anybody gets points off my sister, I will make you bleed. Got it?"

The smirk slides off Doug's face, and he nods. "Sure."

I back off, eyeballing the other guys, but they each break eye contact first. Damn straight.

Once I'm suited up, I grab my helmet and head out to the field. It's miserable out today. Cloudy and so humid, the air falls on you the second you step outside. Coach Rafferty and his assistant, Mr. DeMaio, are starting drills, so I jog over to take my place. I can see the warning I gave Doug and Brayden ripple across the field as the rest of the guys elbow each other, whisper in ears, and shoot astonished looks my way.

"Yo, Lawrence."

I turn and see Sebastian fall into step next to me.

"Way to take a stand, man." He holds out a hand, and I study him closely, looking for any hint of sarcasm, but his eyes are clear. I shake the hand he offers.

"Thanks, bro."

He jerks his chin toward Brayden, who's busy doing some stretches. "This scavenger hunt is stupid. Half the stuff on those cards creeps out girls, and I'm glad I'm not the only one who sees it."

"Right. You wouldn't play."

"It's not cool, but every time I say that, somebody calls me a pussy or something." He shrugs, but he also clenches his teeth so I know that bugs him.

I think about what he just said. It's pretty much what Mom and Dad said. I just didn't realize any of the guys on the team saw it the same way. I thought the hunt was fun. I'd heard about it since freshman year and was psyched to finally make varsity so I could participate this year.

Mr. DeMaio waves us over. Sebastian and I start stretching out.

"Hey, your sister's a really nice girl, so I think you should know that, well—" He breaks off, shooting another glance over his shoulder as we hit the ground to stretch hamstrings and calf muscles. "Vic's got her in his sights."

The blood in my veins turns to ice. "What?"

"I heard him tell Doug that, um, well, he drove her home—"

"When the hell did Victor Patton drive my sister home?" And why haven't I heard about it?

"Uh, a couple of times, since the first day of school or something? Not sure. Anyway, he said she was all flustered and figures she really likes him, and if he—" He breaks off again, looking miserable. "Uh, if he shows her a little interest, he'll score a hundred points, no problem."

A hundred points. And suddenly, I know exactly what's on Vic's hunt list. My hands curl into fists.

Coach Rafferty blows the whistle, and we run around cones, him shouting out orders, us sweating through our uniforms. And through it all, I keep one eye stuck to Vic.

"Lawrence!" Mr. DeMaio barks. "Any time you plan on getting your head in this practice would be helpful."

"Yes, sir," I say, but don't take my eyes off Vic.

Vic catches me staring at him and steps up. "Problem, Lawrence?"

"Maybe. Depends."

"On what?"

"On whether or not you stay away from my sister."

Mr. DeMaio blows his whistle. "Tackle drills. Form up."

I take my position, crouching low and face off against Vic.

"Your sister has great tits," he mutters so only I could hear him, grinning behind his mouth guard. "They feel so good."

I explode before the whistle even blows, sending him sailing. I wrestle off his helmet and land a solid punch, but then we get separated.

"Lawrence! What's wrong with you?" Coach Rafferty shouts.

"Ask him," I answer, not taking my eyes from Victor, but he just smiles and holds up his hands when the coach turns to him.

"Okay, Lawrence, you're done for the day. Hit the showers." Coach Rafferty jerks a thumb over his shoulder.

I tell Vic straight up, "Stay away from my sister."

Again, he throws up his hands, but he never loses that stupid smile.

"I said, hit the showers!" Coach roars.

I stare down with Vic for another minute and then take off, unfastening my helmet in disgust.

"Hey, Derek. Hey! Derek!"

The soft voice finally penetrates my rage as I walk into the building. I look around and find Brittany Meyers near the stairs, just inside the door on the ground-floor corridor.

"Hey, Brittany," I give her a halfhearted wave and put one foot on the staircase that leads up to the locker room.

"Derek, wait. Listen. Ashley's really upset. She's going to the principal's office to complain."

"Aw, hell." I take off in that direction. If I don't get to her before she gets to the principal, I'll be *watching* football instead of *playing* it.

FIVE YEARS AGO

BELLFORD, OHIO

"Derek, I can't do this." Ashley shoves aside her fourth-grade math homework, her lower lip sticking out about a mile.

I close my textbook and take a peek at her worksheet. Reducing fractions…everybody's favorite lesson. "Fractions, huh?"

"Fractions. Ick."

I laugh. Pretty sure I said the same thing in fourth grade. "Okay. I can help. Be right back." I head upstairs to my room and come back with a bag of Lego blocks.

"Hey, hey, what's this? Playtime after homework time. Dad's picking Justin up, and as soon as they get home, it's time for dinner, so get moving." Mom waves a finger from the kitchen where something cooking is making me seriously hungry.

"This *is* homework, Mom. Ashley's got fraction distraction."

Mom laughs, and Ashley frowns. "I do?"

"Yeah, you do. Come on. Look." I dump the blocks out on the table. "See this one? How many pegs does it have?"

She counts the pegs and grins. "Eight!"

I write an eight on a piece of loose leaf from my binder and put the brick above it.

"Great. That means we need eight of these tiny red ones to totally cover that brick." While she carefully counts out eight single-peg blocks, I write a dash with an eight under it. "Each one of these blocks has only one peg, right?"

"Uh-huh."

I write a one over the dash. "So this block is one-eighth the size of that one."

She shrugs, and I can tell she's not getting it. I keep going, first with four-peg blocks, then with two-peg blocks, writing the corresponding fractions above them. "Remember, this brick has eight pegs, and this brick has four." I snap them together and ask, "How much is covered?"

"Um, half."

"Yeah. Half. Here's how you know it's half." I write four over eight and then show her how to divide to get one over two.

"Oh!" She takes another brick with four pegs and covers half of it with a two-peg block. "This one is two over four."

"Yeah. And it's also one-half. Do you understand now? If we had a Lego block with a hundred pegs on it and another block with fifty, it would still be—"

"Half!"

"Right." I grin at her.

I show her a few more combinations of blocks, impressing her when she realizes any number over any same number always equals one and totally blowing her mind when she discovers that two pizza pies of the same size are always the same size no matter how many slices they're cut into. When she was little, she used to think eating four small slices was better than eating one larger one.

"Mommy, Derek told me how to do fractions, and now they're so easy," she informs Mom. And then she gasps. "You could be a teacher when you grow up."

Uh, yeah. So not gonna happen.

"Good job, Derek. You guys done now? Set the table."

"I'll put the Legos away," Ashley announces.

"What do you say to Derek, Ashley?" Mom prods.

"Thank you, Leo!"

"No problem, April." I grab all my books and stuff them into my backpack.

When Dad and Justin get home, Ashley shows them her math worksheet and announces she's over her fraction distraction. Justin rolls his eyes, and Dad laughs, messes up my hair, and says how lucky Ashley is to have a brother like me.

TWO YEARS AGO
BELLFORD, OHIO

I jog down the corridor to the principal's office still wearing my gear, cleats making a racket on the floor. Ashley walks smack into me as she comes out the door.

I grab her shoulders, and she recoils, wrinkling her nose. Yeah, yeah, I need a shower. But this can't wait. "What the hell are you doing, Ash Tray?" I use the nickname she despises so much *because* she despises it. I want her to hear me this time. "Bad enough you narc'd to Mom and Dad. You go to the principal, and they'll punish everybody on the team."

"Stop calling me that," she snaps, wrestling out of my grip. "Yes, I reported Doug. What he did was wrong."

She's right, but that's not the point.

"Look. You have to see the bigger picture here. Just quit the dance team and you'll be fine. You'll be on the first bus out of here every afternoon, and the football team can't bug you."

Her dark eyes pop wide. "But Daddy said—"

And my temper erupts with maximum velocity. "Oh, will you just grow up? Daddy said, Mommy said," I mimic in a high-pitched voice. "This is high school, not kindergarten. And for what it's worth, I did what *Daddy* said. I told the guys you're off-limits, and you know what they said? Nothing. In fact, half of them laughed."

"Then say it again," she snaps back with a crack in her voice, and I know I hurt her feelings. "Say it like you really *mean* it. I know you don't care what happens to me, but what about all the other girls in this school? It's okay for them to get cornered in a stairwell?"

"I *do* care what happens to you. That's why I want you to go home." I care. I really do. Okay, I've been a real dick to her, but it doesn't mean I don't care. "And all the other girls can take care of themselves. You, on the other hand, can't, and I'm getting sick of you always needing my help."

"Wow, Derek. Just wow. You are seriously delusional. I haven't needed your help since fractions in fourth grade! You said you didn't want me around, and I listened. I found my own friends. I like dancing. But that's not good enough for you. You don't even want me in the same zip code as you. Why? Huh, Derek? Why do you hate me so much?" she demands.

"I don't hate you. I'm just, you know. Kind of sick of you," I fire back and then shut up. Jeez, that was mean, even for me. But it's also true. I just want some drama-free time with guys like me. I cross my arms, sighing loudly. "Ash, just forget about you and me and think of the Bengals. The hunt is a tradition that goes back years. It's nothing that ever hurt anybody. Except for you tripping Doug."

She rolls her eyes. "I still don't understand why *that's* such a flippin' federal case, but when he corners me on the stairs, you just shrug."

"First, you're not hurt, okay? I told the guys everything Dad said last night and threatened to bloody up anybody who puts a hand on you. And second, you could have *ended* his football career forever. How do you not get that? You ever seen what a tib-fib fracture does to an athlete?"

Ashley shoots out a hip and folds her arms. "Derek, I'm telling you it's not cool for guys to demand we show them body parts. It's even illegal. And it's really not cool for you to get back with an ex-girlfriend just because you need sex with an ex to get some stupid points. You have absolutely no idea what it's like to be a girl. None." She sneers at me, a twist of her lips and narrowing of her eyes that shrivels me up to something on the level of pond scum.

I pace away and fling up my arms. "Are you even serious right now? It's a game, a dumb game I already said I'm not playing anymore. What else do you want from me?"

"I want you to be my brother!" she shouts. "My Leo."

Her Leo. "For God's sake, Ashley! Will you just open your eyes and realize I'm not that goofy little boy who thought it was cool to push some other kid around for hurting your feelings? I'm seventeen years old, and I'm over it, and I'm done playing with you. This team has a real good shot at state this year. Stop trying to ruin that just because you're pissed off at me."

A tear slips down her cheek, but I refuse to cave in.

"We're kind of scared, Derek. The girls in this school really hate this hunt," she says, wiping the tear away.

I look up and down the corridor. It's deserted except for us. "Then why are you the only one here?"

She only shakes her head. "You really are a lost cause." She turns and runs to the main exit while I sag against a locker and rake both hands through my sweaty hair. I know I should probably feel guilty. But all I feel is relief.

11

ASHLEY

I couldn't wait to start high school. My brother and I are only two grades apart, so I was excited to hang out with him and his friends again, like equals instead of siblings who, for whatever reason, can't stand to be around each other. Now my brother can't even look at me.

—**Ashley E. Lawrence, victim impact statement**

NOW

BELLFORD, OHIO

"Ashley, these are all good. I mean, *really* good." Tara shuffles through the printouts I handed her when I sit down to lunch.

I crack the seal on a bottle of water and take a sip. "You don't think it's too much?"

She shakes her head, making the sun bounce off her shiny

hair. "Nope. I think you covered all the basics without making this seem like a test, you know?"

A test. Hmmm. That's not a bad idea. Maybe I could do a quiz or something that we can post to the web page that Sebastian wants to create.

Speaking of…

"Hey." Sebastian stops at our table and runs a hand through his Nike swoosh hair.

"Hi, Sebastian," Tara says, scooting her chair over to make room for him, and I kind of love that. There's no question—will he or won't he? We just assume he will.

He does.

"These your ideas?" He jerks his chin toward the pages Tara left on the table. When I nod, he picks them up and skims them. When he's done, he stacks the pages carefully, tapping their edges on the table, and hands them back to me without a word. By the time he opens his cellophane-wrapped sandwich, I'm burning with curiosity.

"Well, what do you think?"

"I love the idea of making a speech. I can help you with it, if you want."

"Yeah. I'm gonna need lots of practice."

Sebastian shakes his head. "Don't rehearse. It's better if you're you. Real, you know? Just get up there and tell the school what happened." And then he squirms.

What is wrong with him? "Okay, what else?"

Shrugging, he bites into his sandwich and talks with his mouth full. "Think the pledge signing is awesome. Everyone will think it's a pep rally, so they'll be psyched to get out of class."

"Okay. Cool. What else?" Oh my God, just tell me already!

He lifts his eyes, and they're kind of yellow today. "Um. The pledge form."

Uh-oh.

"I think it's good…"

"But?" I prod because I totally sense a *but* coming on.

"But I think you should maybe change one thing."

I glare at him because really, who's the expert here?

"It's not a big deal, Ashley. But this one part, about how it could be your sister, your girlfriend, your mom? I think it's wrong to say that."

He taps the page on the table between us, and I straighten my back.

"Wrong," I echo. "Wrong, as in not correct, or wrong, as in morally reprehensible?"

Sebastian's lips twitch, and he rocks his head from side to side. "Maybe somewhere in the middle of that scale."

Tara's brown eyes bounce from him to me and back again, and Sebastian holds up both hands.

"Ash, I just think it's wrong to tell guys they need to do this because of the girls in *their* lives. They should do this for all women, not just the ones they know, because it's right."

Oh, wow.

This guy isn't real. Did I dream him?

Tara's eyes meet mine, and she's thinking the same thing.

"And we have to remember, it's not just women who get raped," he adds.

That's a really good point. I lower my head, ashamed I'd forgotten. Sometimes…well, most of the time, it feels like you're completely alone in this. "Yeah. Yeah, you're right. Um. Thanks for, you know…looking out."

He smiles in acknowledgment, but it's a serious smile.

I sigh as he heads to the trash bin and tosses his sandwich wrapper. There was a time when I wished all boys were just like Derek.

Now I wish all boys were just like Sebastian.

NOW

BELLFORD, OHIO

By Thursday, the signs of panic are circling me like vultures. Homecoming is Saturday. I don't think I can do this. I don't think I can stand up in front of the entire student body tomorrow and tell them my story. It was all my idea, and I can't do it.

I can't.

But I can't let this happen again.

I obsess all day and finally come up with a plan B. I grab my laptop and start recording a video.

"Hey." I offer a lame wave and tight grin to the webcam. "I'm, well, I *used to be* Ashley Lawrence. Before I was raped two years ago. Seven hundred and twenty-three days ago. It's not like I want to count the days. I can't help it."

I frown and move around my room, feeling like the biggest, most awkward thing alive.

"I have flashbacks, anxiety attacks, and a ton of totally irrational reactions to normal, everyday things. It used to happen a few times a day. Now, it's a few times a week. So, yeah. I count the days because I figure there will be one day when I'm *me* again. Ashley. And I want to know how long it takes me to reach that day so I can celebrate my accomplishment."

Oh my God, this sucks worse than anything. I pause the recording to regroup and start again.

"So here's the thing. Getting raped pretty much sucks. It's, like, almost the worst thing that can happen to you. Because it makes you *want to* die. And every time you remember that the person who did this to you was someone you knew, someone you maybe even liked, part of you *does* die."

I pause the recording, rolling my eyes. Not exactly upbeat and encouraging.

"It sucks to have something you value get taken away by somebody else. It sucks that you didn't do anything wrong but got the blame for it anyway, even from people you thought knew you. And it sucks that the court looks at the person who did this thing to you, did the worst thing that anyone's ever done to you, and says two years in prison is justice, and everybody, even your therapist, tells you that you should feel proud that you won. It sucks when you *finally* figure out that there's no such thing as justice."

I pause the recording again and just stare into the camera, wondering if anybody will get where I'm going with this.

"I never hear anybody saying Victor Patton did a terrible thing and deserves to be punished for it to the full extent of the law. I never hear anybody say Ashley Lawrence's life was ruined and you feel really bad about that. I don't hear you saying we shouldn't blame Ashley Lawrence for canceling football because she didn't ask Vic to rape her."

I stop recording and think about my next point. When I'm sure I've got it, I start a new file.

"Say you have this car. It's a really nice car. Expensive. Super cool. Took you years to save up for it, and now it's all yours. You love this car. You're driving one day, and you stop at a red light. Maybe it's a red light on a road you drive all the time. But this day, this one day, bam! Somebody crashes right into your really nice car. Totals it. How would you feel?"

I really hope they understand the point I'm trying to make with this.

"You'd be upset, right? You'd be furious. You know you would. You call the police and report the accident. And the police ask *you* questions like: Were you drinking? Do you drink a lot? What were you wearing? You wonder what any of this has to do with some moron crashing into your car. You keep telling the police *he* hit *you*. Your car wasn't even moving at the time! But they keep asking *you* questions. How fast were you going? Do you always drive down this street, at this time, alone? Do you always drive such nice cars? And then, the police say something that hurts more than your car getting wrecked. They say maybe you shouldn't drive such a nice car if you don't want it wrecked.

They say by driving down that road alone you were just *asking for* somebody to crash into you. They say that poor other driver is never going to be the same. He'll probably lose his driver's license because of you."

The power flows through me, and I sit up straighter and stare, unblinking, directly into the webcam.

"Maybe they arrest the other driver, and then you go to court where the lawyers ask you more questions. You thought the cops' questions were insulting, but the lawyers ask you all about a car you drove the year before, or two years before, and ask if *those* cars got wrecked. The whole time, every single time they ask you a question, you wonder how *any* of this is your fault. But they're not done. They save the worst for last. That's when they ask your brother, your own brother, what he thinks, and *he* tells the court the other driver shouldn't have to spend his whole life getting punished. You wonder when anyone's gonna notice that you are the one getting punished for it—every day, for the rest of your life."

I'm mad now. I'm so fucking furious that this isn't obvious to people. That it has to be explained in third-grade terms.

"This is how I feel! Victor Patton took something from me. He wrecked *me*, not some car. But *I'm* the one who gets all the hate and the blame."

I end the video and start a new one because I didn't realize I had so much to say. I tell them how I was late the first day of school because it sometimes takes me hours just to get dressed. I tell them about the nightmares I keep having. And then I tell them about the brother who can't look at me.

Suddenly, I notice I've got half a dozen video files saved, and I still have more to say.

"Guys, let's play a game. It's a trivia game this time, not a scavenger hunt. Take out a pen. Ready? Here's the first question. It's for the boys. What do you do if you don't want to participate in the scavenger hunt?" I pause and hum a game show tune. "Okay, first, why don't we ask what the girls did during the last scavenger hunt? I'll tell you. We wore shorts in case guys decided to look up our skirts. We never walked alone. We had our parents pick us up after late practices. Okay, boys, show us your list now. Oh, wait! You didn't write anything down? Too bad. Guess you lose."

I drop my notebook and lean into the camera.

"Are you seeing the problem yet? No? Okay. I'll connect the dots for you. Every time girls try to tell boys what we're afraid of, you hold up your hand and say stuff like, 'Whoa! I'm not that kind of guy. I'm *nice*.' A whole team of boys thought it would be fun to harass girls to collect points. Did any of you boys congratulating yourselves on not being that kind of guy say, 'Wait! What if they don't want their skirts flipped up or their bras snapped? What if they don't want their boobs squeezed?' Nope. You went along with it. This is the problem. Every time you laugh at a sexist joke, every time you defend an athlete just because you like his sport, every time you assume a girl who accuses somebody of rape is lying, you're shouting to the world that she does not matter! Believe me when I tell you it's not okay. *I'm* not okay!"

I am shouting now. My voice is crackly and hoarse, but I keep going. "Every time there's a terrorist attack, everybody starts screaming for border closings and tighter security at airports. Does anybody ever shrug it off and say, 'Oh, it's just extremists being extremists?' So why do you say, 'Oh, it's just boys being boys,' when you terrorize girls? Because that is what you're doing. Terrorizing us."

Slowly and quietly, I lift tear-filled eyes to the camera. "I just don't get why *all* guys aren't mad at the ones who make it so unsafe for girls to exist in this world. Guys, you want us to think you're brave and strong, but when you don't stand up to your friends who do this kind of stuff? It shows us you're anything but."

I hover over the Pause button, debating about this next part. Finally, I decide I may as well go all in. Full disclosure.

"You're all probably sitting here wondering why we're doing this, why we're asking you to sign this pledge. It's to ask you an important question. Are you ready to *raise the bar*?"

I end the video and sit back. I said the dreaded *R* word over and over again and didn't burst into flames. Guess my therapist is right about that, at least. But my hands are shaking. It may be *easier*, but it's still not even in the same zip code as *easy*.

I drum my fingers on the laptop for a couple of seconds. Am I done?

I already know the answer to that question. I have more to say—a lot more, about the ways Derek tore my heart out, about how the harassment from the entire community that occurred after Vic's arrest and all during his trial chipped away at the once rock-solid foundation of my family, leaving it about to collapse in a strong gust of wind, and about the way the court's ridiculously

SOMEONE I USED TO KNOW

light sentence told the entire country that a good football player's future is worth more than a good dancer's. But I don't think there's enough hard drive space in the world for all those videos.

I save what I have and then text Sebastian, wondering if this will change somebody's mind.

After all, I *never* was able to change Derek's.

12

DEREK

NOW

LONG ISLAND, NEW YORK

I snag a table, and while Brittany drowns a stack of pancakes in maple syrup, I eyeball another sexual assault rally sign. Then I study her. She's really beautiful. Ashley used to say all the time I have no idea what it's like to be a girl. Brittany never talks that way, but now I wonder. Does she ever get scared that way?

"Britt, I have a question," I begin, flipping the rally sign around in my hands. "This." I hold up the sign. "Anything like it ever happen to you?"

"I've never been raped, if that's what you're asking."

I let out a happy sigh. Thank God.

"But…"

And the breath stalls in my chest.

"But I've been harassed. A lot," she adds with an eye roll.

My spine snaps straight. "A lot? Define a lot."

She stabs another bite of pancakes with her fork and swallows it. "Um, well, why are you asking?"

I shake my head and shrug. "I...well, I signed up to speak at a GAR event back home, and I'm not entirely sure what to say."

She raises an eyebrow.

"It's just something I need to do, okay?" I snap.

Both eyebrows go up this time. "Did I say anything?"

"You didn't have to. The Eyebrows of Disappointment spoke for you."

She laughs. "Now you're projecting. And for the record, I am anything but disappointed right now."

Good to know. I crack the seal on my orange juice bottle and chug half. My phone buzzes, and I sigh when I read the message.

"What?"

"My mom. School, like, *just* started, and she's planning Thanksgiving already." The thought of going home fills me with horror. Ashley might kill me in my sleep. And no jury would convict her, either.

"Ooh, Thanksgiving. I can't wait to go out east and visit the pumpkin farms."

I grin and toss a napkin at her. "You are such a girl."

"Lucky for you."

My phone buzzes with a text message. I sigh after reading it. "I've been summoned to the dean's office to retell my account of the gym incident."

Brittany looks up at me with a smile. "You know I think

you're really awesome for doing that, right?" she offers after a minute.

The way she's looking at me makes my knees weak and my cheeks burn. "No. I'm really not. I'm pissed."

"Good. You should be pissed. I wish more guys got pissed. Maybe then we wouldn't have so many assholes running around."

I drop my fork and angle my head. She never did answer my question. "You said you get harassed a lot. Why don't you ever talk to me about it?"

She gives me the *seriously?* look. "Uh, because that's probably all we'd talk about."

I give her the same look right back. "Exaggerate much?"

"I'm not exaggerating at all. It's true. Every day, there's a hassle of some kind—like the other day, this guy just cut in front of me at Starbucks, so I said, 'Excuse me, there's a line.' And he said, "I'll let you go ahead of me if you smile. I bet you've got a great smile." I was too mad to smile because—*hello*, he still cut in front of me. But it's not like any of the other people protested. So, I had to let it go, even though it just *killed* me."

"But not enough to tell your boyfriend about it." I shoot her a look, and she snorts out a laugh.

"Oh, Derek," she says with a little shake of her head. "It would literally be all we talked about. You have no idea! You don't stop to think about where you've parked your car and whether it will be dark when you get back to it. You don't worry about the guys who step onto an elevator after you. And you probably never had to deal with dates who actually expect services in exchange for the money they just spent on you. It literally happens *all the time.*"

I'm stunned into silence. I really thought she was exaggerating, but now? Jesus.

We eat in silence for a minute and then head to class. Britt presses her lips to mine and leaves me with the taste of maple syrup. "If you want more info, just search these hashtags." She shows me the Twitter feed on her phone, and I see two—#MeToo and #YesAllWomen.

We go our separate ways. I'm halfway through my statistics class when my mind starts replaying some of the things Britt said. *It would literally be all we talk about,* she said.

I've known Britt since high school, and okay, sure, we didn't start dating until a month ago, but I think I know her. She's not the kind of girl who flips out over every little thing like—

My back snaps into a straight line when I realize where my thoughts are leading me.

Like Ashley. That's what I was thinking. Ashley doesn't just exaggerate; she makes giant Kilimanjaro peaks out of the smallest little molehills.

But she didn't exaggerate the scavenger hunt. She was totally right. I just couldn't see that back then. Someone should have looked out for her…like maybe her brother.

"Okay." The professor startles me out of my thoughts with a clap of his hands. "Let's move to page thirty-two."

I flip the pages in my text and see the list of practice problems he wants us to tackle. I rifle through my backpack for a pencil because—math. Instead, I find another one of those rally flyers. Tucked inside a fold is a business card.

Ian Russell, Mechanical Engineer

This is the guy whose girlfriend is delivering a speech at the rally. I tuck the card into my pocket and suddenly realize Ashley *did* have someone looking out for her. It damn well wasn't me.

It was Sebastian.

After class, I figure it's time I acknowledged Sebastian's efforts, so I sink down onto a bench in the quad, pull out my phone, and shoot Sebastian a text.

Derek: Hey. Thanks for looking out for Ash.
Sebastian: No problem.
Derek: I mean it. I never thanked you for what you did that day.

He doesn't reply. But a few seconds later, my phone rings. It's him.

"Hey, man."

"Hey, Derek. I figured this would be easier."

"Uh, yeah. So anyhow. Thanks."

"Didn't do it for you."

"Yeah, I get that. And I'm sorry."

"Yeah, well, I'm not the one you should be saying that to."

I get that, too. "Yeah. I should. The guys treated you like shit, and I should have done something. Stopped them. Stood up for you. I'm sorry I didn't."

I hear his loud sigh hiss through the phone. "It's okay, I guess. I'm captain this year."

Wait, what? "Wow. That's…that's really great, Sebastian. You'll be a great captain."

"Yeah. I will." He says it all solemn, like a promise.

"You'll make sure there's no hunt this year."

"Definitely not. We've got a pledge happening all week, with a big rally on Friday instead of the usual homecoming crap."

I lean back and kick out my legs. "A pledge for what?"

"A pledge to raise the bar. That's what Ashley's calling it. Raise the Bar. You know, B-A-R. *Bengals Against Rape*."

Holy shit. Ashley thought of it? "That's really cool."

"I know, right? She's been working on it since the first day of school. I'm helping where I can, but it's her story."

Yeah. Her story.

"I was the first Bengal to sign the pledge. Then Coach Davidson did. Ashley doesn't know this yet, but I got your dad and your brother to sign it on video. It's cool because she decided to record video, too."

What about me?

I don't ask him, though. I already know the answer.

"Our goal is to get the entire football team signed up by the game Saturday, but other teams are pledging, too. Even the girls. It's like a competition now. Which team gets a hundred percent participation."

I can't seem to stop being impressed that *Ashley* thought of this. A memory replays of Ashley, lying small and way too still in a hospital bed, and I shake my head to erase it. I like thinking of her as a fighter way better.

"That's cool, Sebastian. Really cool."

"Yeah. It is. You can go online and check it out. Mr. Davidson got it posted to the school's website."

"Yeah, I'll do that."

"So how's college, man?"

"Good, good. There's a big rally here too for sexual assault awareness. And I joined GAR."

"GAR?"

"Yeah. Guys Against Rape."

"I like BAR better."

I laugh. "Yeah. Me too."

"That's great, Derek. That you joined GAR, I mean. Ash would like that."

I doubt that. It would probably just upset her. But suddenly, I want nothing more than to do something she'd like. That she'd be proud of.

"Yeah. Maybe. Hey, Sebastian?"

"Yeah?"

Don't do it. Don't ask. "Do you think I could maybe...you know, sign a form on your video?"

He doesn't answer for so long, I think maybe the call dropped.

"Derek, it's—"

"Yeah, never mind. It would piss her off. I get it." I let him off the hook and change the subject. I knew I shouldn't have asked. "So how's she doing?"

SOMEONE I USED TO KNOW

There's a long pause, and I hear him sigh again. "She's okay, Derek. She's...strong, you know? A real fighter."

Ashley, a fighter... Hadn't I just been thinking the same thing? That completely confounds me because when we were kids, she was so damn *needy*.

"But she had a flashback or anxiety attack or something, and it messed her up."

"Oh, shit. She's still having those?" My stomach pitches and rolls, and I fold over, rocking. These attacks or episodes or whatever they are started right after it happened, and I...I thought she was faking it to get back at me. *I'm sorry, April.* I'm so sorry.

TWO YEARS AGO
BELLFORD, OHIO

Dad knocks on my door.

"You talked to your sister?" He sits on my bed, looking like he hasn't slept in a week.

I shake my head. "No. Her door's shut. I don't want to bother her." I'm afraid to talk to her. I'm a big chickenshit coward. Justin's not. He's in there practically all the time.

She hasn't come out of her room since they let her out of the hospital.

"You need to talk to her. Reassure her. Tell her you're sorry and still love her."

I blink. "Why?"

"Because she thinks you hate her, Derek. She's thought that for a long time."

Oh. Right. That. I never wanted her to think that. I just wanted... Forget it. It's all just stupid now. All that guy stuff I thought I wanted. I'd give it all just to have Ashley back the way she used to be. April, looking at me like I'm a superhero.

"Yeah. Okay."

Dad smiles at me—one of those tight-lipped, no-teeth smiles. He stands up, and it takes me a second to get that he means right now. We walk through the shared bathroom to Ashley's door.

"Hey, April," I say, calling her by the Ninja Turtles nickname she always loved, bracing for more stupid when she calls me Leo.

She's in bed with blankets pulled up to her chin even though it's like seventy degrees. She's curled up in a ball, Mom next to her, rubbing her back. A hundred balls of tissues litter the bed.

At the sound of my voice, she jerks. "Hey."

No Leo.

No tone in her voice.

No sparkle in her eyes.

No puppy/kitten/unicorn smile.

There's...nothing.

Dad nudges me. I clear my throat. "Um. Yeah. So, I was thinking of playing video games. Want in on that?"

Her brown eyes stare at me, unblinking. "What?"

"Video games. Wanna play?"

She shifts, sending half the tissue balls sailing to the floor. "You want to play video games. With me. Yeah, right."

I shove my hands in my pocket. "I do. Really."

She stares straight through me with those flat eyes and finally shrugs. "Whatever."

I take that as a yes and go to fetch the game console. Mom's beaming, and Dad looks satisfied. I connect the game, hand Ashley a controller, and sit with her on the bed.

And she completely and totally freaks out.

She claps both hands to her face and covers her mouth and nose. Her eyes are wide and unfocused, and she keeps making this sound, this sound that's tearing my guts apart, like she's being tortured.

Mom's on the verge of losing it. "Ashley! What's wrong? Tell me what's wrong!"

Dad takes Ashley's shoulders and gives her a little shake. "You're safe, Ashley. Open your eyes!" But they are open; they just aren't seeing what's really happening.

She cowers and screams. "Stop! Stop, please!"

Mom cries and tries to stroke Ashley. "Ashley, it's Mommy, honey. You're safe."

But Ashley just kept doing that deep breathing thing. "The smell. Oh, God, the smell."

What a drama queen. "Come on, Ash. Knock it off. You're making Mom nuts."

That's when Dad looks at me with disgust. He grabs me by the collar and hauls me away from Ashley's bed. I land in a heap across the room by her dresser. "He's gone, baby. He's not here. I promise you, he can't hurt you again."

"Oh, God!" She keeps shrieking.

Mom and Dad both have tears flowing down their faces. Dad rushes over to where I'm sprawled and—and *sniffs* me. "Derek. You showered at school?"

I nod.

"Shower again. Right now. Use Ashley's stuff. Wash that smell off you *now*."

And he shoves me out the door, slamming it after me. I go back to my room, grab fresh clothes, and hit the shower, scrubbing myself raw. When I'm done, it's quiet.

Too quiet.

I open the bathroom door on my side of the room. Mom and Dad are sitting on my bed, waiting.

"She's sleeping. I…I had to give her one of the sedatives they gave us." Mom stares at her hands. Dad looks about a hundred years old. Suddenly, he stands up.

"I'll go to CVS and buy you some new stuff. Deodorant, body wash. You pack it in your bag, you hear? Don't use the locker room stuff ever again."

"I'll…I'll go with you."

We drive all the way to the CVS without exchanging a single word. Inside the store, Dad opens up every bottle of body wash. "Too musky. No. No. No."

He's gone through four or five bottles before he finds one he likes. "This one."

I give it a sniff. It smells like chocolate, that cheap, really bad kind of chocolate they sell at Easter time. "Ick."

He shoots me a look. "It's that or flowers. Pick one." His eyes gleam with a rage I've never seen before so I just stick the bottle in the basket I picked up when we walked in.

Next up, deodorant. We grab a baby powder–scented one.

Finally, shampoo. I just used the body wash on my hair, but he goes through the same procedure, opening up bottles, sniffing all of them, finally settling on plain Head & Shoulders. Lastly, we go to another aisle and grab a zippered case to hold them all.

Outside in the car, I can't take it anymore. "I'm sorry, Dad. I'm sorry."

He finally looks up, bewildered, like he has no idea how he landed in the middle of a CVS parking lot. He scrubs both hands over his face and makes a sound kind of like the sound you make when you first get up in the morning, only it's not fatigue. It's frustration.

"They warned us about this," he says. "The crisis counselor at the hospital said to expect flashbacks. We're just lucky she kept saying she could *smell* him. I could figure out right away she meant you. You both use the same stuff in the locker room."

"I'm sorry," I repeat because I really have no fucking clue what else to say.

Dad nods, and his face changes right before my eyes, drooping and trembling, and it hits me that this is where that old saying about *falling to pieces* comes from. A sob escapes his mouth before he clamps his jaw tightly shut, and then he grabs me in a hug so tight, I'm sure I hear a bone crack.

God. *Shit.*

This is my dad, the guy who carried me and Ashley at the same time that day at the amusement park when our legs were too tired to walk. This is my dad, the guy who taught me to throw the football that changed my life. This is my dad, the guy who chased away the monsters that lived under my bed, taught me to ride a bike, taught me to drive. This is my dad, crying like a baby in my arms, holding on *to me* like I'm suddenly big enough, strong enough, smart enough to battle *this* monster without him, but I'm not. God, I'm not, but I hold him, hold on, until he can catch his breath, and the whole time, the whole fucking time, I don't say it. I don't tell him that he was right, that the only reason I asked Dakota out again was because of what was on the list.

I don't say any of it because I don't like what it means about me.

13

ASHLEY

Memories used to be these cool things that made me feel happy. But now, all of my memories—every one of them—have the defendant in them. If I remember a fun time, a happy time from when I was little, it always ends with today. Right now. When nothing is fun or happy and can't ever be that way as long as he is free.

—Ashley E. Lawrence, victim impact statement

NOW

BELLFORD, OHIO

I flip through the pages of the photo album and find a shot of Justin taken in his freshman year at college. I wasn't even in high school yet, and Derek had just started. We're sitting on the sofa in the family room. There's a Christmas tree in the corner and a thick blanket over all three of us. Justin is in the middle, and

Derek and I surround him like bookends. We spent an entire day watching all the silly holiday movies we could find. *Elf, Home Alone, National Lampoon's Christmas Vacation, The Santa Clause.* We did that every year.

Until the last one.

My cell phone vibrates, and when I see the caller ID, I just shake my head.

"Justin. You are some kind of psychic."

"Uh, sure. Okay, we'll go with that. So, um, what are you up to?"

"Nothing. Just looking through old photo albums and was thinking of you. Then you called."

"Oh. Cool. So I, um, called to ask, uh, you know—"

"I'm fine," I cut him off.

"Uh-huh. Okay. So when's the last time you talked to Derek?"

My stomach knots as soon as he mentions Derek. "I don't talk to him if I can help it."

Justin sighs loudly. Through the phone, the sound is like a gust of wind. "Ashley. Look. I talked to Mom and Dad and to Derek. Everybody's hurting."

I roll my eyes. Like anybody could possibly hurt the way I am.

"And I get that none of us can possibly understand how you feel, but you need to give us a break."

Well, at least he tried to soften the sting of that statement.

"I'm worried, Ashley. I think Mom and Dad are separating."

My heart slams into my throat. "What?"

"I don't know for sure. It's just…I don't know. A feeling. You live there. Don't you see it?"

See what? "They go to work, they come home, and we eat dinner and watch TV. There's nothing to see."

"Really? Nothing to see? When was the last time you saw Mom kiss Dad on his nose the way she always does? Or see Dad tickle Mom?"

I put a hand to my heart, and then I remember it's cracked in so many pieces, it's probably not even where it used to be.

"Look, my point is," he says quietly, "deliberately making anybody suffer isn't your style."

It is now. "That was before, Justin. Before the rape, before Derek stuck a knife in my back."

"Jesus, Ashley, will you get a grip? He testified. He was under oath and obligated to tell the truth as he perceived it."

"Well, his perception was pretty conveniently flawed, wasn't it?"

"No. Actually I think yours is."

"Whatever. The trial isn't even the worst thing he's done."

"Yeah? So what's the worst? What was so bad you're willing to break up the entire family over it?"

I don't want to talk about it. I don't want to even *think* about it. A wave of exhaustion flows through me, and I suddenly don't want to talk to *this* brother anymore, either.

"Did you call for any particular reason or just to fight Derek's battles?"

"Yeah. I did. I wanted to let you know that I'm coming home. I'll finish school there."

Really. "Why?"

"Reasons."

He ends the call without saying goodbye, and I toss my phone to my desk where I left the photo album. With a sigh, I sit up, grab the book, and flip through the photos.

In this picture, Justin wears his university sweatshirt. I wear Christmas reindeer pajamas. Derek wears his football jersey. We all sport identical toothy fake grins, the kind you flash when someone shouts, "Cheese!" Our arms are wrapped around Justin, who'd finished one semester away from home and was back for just three weeks.

I flip the pages and find the next iteration of that photo. This one was taken last Christmas. In it, the three of us are scattered around the room, each under our own blanket. I'm not even looking at the television. I'm just staring off into space, seeing nothing. My hair is way shorter.

I'd hacked it off after the rape in the first of several overpowering fits of rage.

Justin is sitting in his usual spot—center of the sofa. His arms are crossed, and his jaw is tight. He's not watching the movie, either.

He's staring at me.

Funny how Justin's always the one in the middle, even though he's the oldest.

Guess some things never change.

And then there's Derek. He's off to the right of Justin, laughing at the screen. But it's one of those same toothy fake grins we used to flash for Mom so she'd take the picture and leave us alone.

It's not real.

What *is* real are our eyes. Behind his glasses, Justin's eyes are cold and dark, full of hate. Oh, not hate for me. I know that much, at least. No, hate for Vic. It was pretty damn scary, actually. Justin has always been, well—sort of a nerd. He loves stuff like Dungeons & Dragons, chess club, and really odd music. He belongs to online groups and spends hours discussing games and books and movies. He actually played on a Quidditch team at his school in northern Ohio. It was a bunch of college kids with brooms between their legs chasing a volleyball around a field, while some other player who was not on either team ran around with a tiny golden snitch strapped to his ass.

Justin was rarely very serious.

Now he's *always* serious.

In this picture, he has a bruise on his jaw and a cut on his nose. He never did tell us what happened. Derek thought Justin's battle wounds were cool. I hadn't given them a thought until now, and that was only to wonder whose business he stuck that nose into.

There's a strange feeling inside my chest. It's not pain exactly. More like an open wound that's been numbed, the space where something used to be. Only whatever used to live there has been gone for so long, I'm not even sure what it is I miss.

With a snap, I slam the album shut and shove it to the end of my desk.

One more video.

Yeah. I think I have to shoot one more video for the pledge rally.

I sit in front of my laptop, take a deep breath, and press Record.

ONE YEAR AGO

BELLFORD, OHIO

I've been looking forward to Victor's trial for months. Imagining the righteous sense of justice I'll feel when the judge declares him guilty. I've been preparing for it, planning life around it. I'm waiting, anticipating, *salivating* for the judge's gavel to come down after declaring Victor guilty, but first, I have to endure the whole stupid trial. It's almost a year to the day since I was raped, and I think it's kind of poetic that the trial will take place at homecoming time.

Time.

It's funny how time plays tricks on you.

It goes by so fast when you don't want it to, but when you're looking forward to something? Oh, then it drags by, glacially slow, infusing you with all these superpowers of epic proportion. I can hear the ticks of a clock on a wall clear across the courtroom, smell the body odor on somebody sitting a few yards away and the lemony-scented wax used to polish all the wood. I can count the beads of sweat pooling at an attorney's hairline. Random thoughts fill my brain at warp speed, like: *Each unhappy family is unhappy in its own way.* I can't remember where I saw or heard that quote, but it keeps replaying in my mind. Tolstoy? Maybe.

I'm suddenly an expert at reading body language. Sneaking glances at my family's faces, I note Mom's expression, like she's frozen in a silent sob. By the direction her gaze darts, I can tell she's thinking about Victor's mom, sitting on the other side of the courtroom, wondering how her son could have done this thing, this horrible thing to me, and if he did it because she was a bad mother. But Victor's mom doesn't look like a bad mother. She looks just like my mother. And that expression on my mom's face? I can tell her heart's breaking.

Across the courtroom, Victor's mother sits like she has no bones and might spill over the sides of her chair. She missed a button on her blouse. She sits just behind Victor and his lawyers, her hands coming up in a jittery motion whenever he moves, like she wants to catch him in case he falls. Next to her is Victor's father, wearing a crisp suit and sitting with his foot propped on his knee, like sitting in a courtroom is no bigger deal than sitting on his backyard patio. Every few minutes, he shakes his head and shrugs, glancing my way, which makes the rest of my family react in ways that make my stomach hurt.

Dad's jaw is clenched so hard, the cleft in his chin vibrates. Next to him, Justin and Derek wear identical expressions of tension. They keep their eyes fixed straight ahead, refusing to look across the room like Mom. They hate Victor, hate his family, hate what happened to me so much, it takes all of their self-control to keep that tension from fraying at the edges. All it'll take is one more sneer, one more glance from Vic's father in my direction, and I'm afraid all three will attack, descending like animals on prey.

I swallow hard, wincing at the pain. There's this sour lump stuck in my throat, but it's not because of that tension.

It's the *distance*.

Maybe that's why that quote is on my mind. I'm not sure where I read it. It's just this odd piece of trivia that got stuck in my brain some time over the past year, when my family realized we weren't happy anymore. Maybe we never were. It's not like I paid attention to what made us happy.

Until *now*.

Somewhere, somebody's tapping a foot to a beat only they can hear. It's in sync with the ticking of the clock across the room and gives me a soundtrack for all the tension and random thoughts circling my mind. I'm suddenly painfully aware that my heart is keeping time, too, and try not to believe it's some kind of omen.

A hand grips mine and gives it a squeeze. Mom. Our eyes meet, and she manages a fairly convincing smile. Dad sits up a little straighter. Justin adjusts his glasses, and Derek rolls his wide shoulders, joints cracking like gunshots. The tapping stops, and for a second, I'm afraid I might fade away without that beat to hold on to. I shut my eyes and drift, not sure if five seconds or five minutes pass.

"It'll be okay, Ashley. We have a strong case," Carol Bryce, the assistant DA, assures me. She's told us that repeatedly. "We have eyewitnesses, and the rape kit evidence was positive for Victor's DNA, which proves penetration, plus it shows the various bruises and scrapes you suffered during his assault."

Carol told us the legal definition of rape requires *proof of penetration,* and God, I hate that word. *Penetration* from the Latin root *penetrare.* The dictionary says it means *to enter by overcoming resistance.* The thesaurus says words like *invade, enter, insert, pierce, perforate,* and *force* are synonyms, so I hate those words, too, because none of them tell you the object of the stupid verb was me.

Victor penetrated, invaded, entered, forced *me*.

"We got this, Ashley. Just breathe," Carol says, squeezing my hand.

But breathing, it turns out, is hard to do under the circumstances, so I grip the smooth waxed wood of the railing—the *bar*—in front of me, hold my breath, and don't let it go because if I do, I'll have to feel that greasy knot of grief lodged just under my heart. Or maybe it *is* my heart now.

Carol makes her way to the jury box and talks about that legal definition of rape.

I tune her out, and somewhere, in all the random firing going on in my nervous system, it suddenly hits me that no matter what happens in this courtroom, I still lose.

I lose.

Because real justice would be for what happened to *not* have happened, and that isn't possible. Real justice would be for me to have my brother back, my family back the way we were. Real justice would make it possible for me to sleep through the night, to dance again, or even look at that stupid warm-up outfit without wanting to vomit. Real justice would *reset* my life.

Suddenly, my name is called. I'm supposed to stand up and walk across the courtroom, but my legs have disappeared. But I do it. I put my hand up, swear an oath, lean toward a microphone, and answer all of Carol's questions.

Then I answer the defense attorney's questions. I hate him.

His name is Barry Young. He's a little man, bald with a large nose, and reminds me of a cartoon character. He asks the same questions in different ways, and a few times he ask questions that make me see red, but Carol immediately objects.

"You let Victor kiss you, correct?"

"Yes."

"You let Victor touch your breast, correct?"

"Yes."

"Why did you let him have sex with you?"

"Objection, leading."

"Did you say no to sex?"

I don't know how to answer this question. "I couldn't."

"You couldn't say no or you didn't want to?"

"I couldn't say no. He—"

"So you didn't say no."

As soon Victor's lawyer says he has no more questions and sits down, Carol is on her feet. "Redirect, your honor." She approaches me. "Ashley, you just told Mr. Young you couldn't say no. Why not?"

"Because Victor put his hand over my mouth."

"For how long? For how long did Victor keep his hand on your mouth?"

"Until Sebastian found me."

Question after question after question. I could feel the eyes boring into me. I could smell the disapproval from everybody watching. *It's her fault*, they were thinking.

"Ashley, you need to step out now."

Oh. Right.

I stand up on shaky legs and leave the courtroom. I'm not allowed to be present while witnesses testify because I'm the *complaining witness.* Carol says it could somehow taint testimony, so I have to leave. Outside in the corridor, I wonder where I'm supposed to wait. Before I can figure that out, the door opens again, and as Dad steps out, I hear a voice say, "Victor Patton to the stand."

My heart stops as the door shuts with a soft click.

"Hey, princess." Dad slings an arm around me and leads me to a bench. I sink down beside him and try not to think about it. It turns out testimony takes a while, so Dad takes me home. I remain home for days. But I'm back in court to read my victim impact statement.

I'm there when Carol, a worried look on her face, explains Victor's claiming it was consensual.

I'm there for the closing arguments, when Victor's attorney tells the court he doesn't believe Victor should be treated like a criminal for *a few minutes of fooling around.*

I'm there when the jury returns a conviction on Victor for sexual assault, not rape. What's the difference? About ten years of prison time.

I'm there when the judge decides two years in prison is plenty for *the boy with such a promising athletic future.*

I'm there when Carol tries to explain that even with the eyewitnesses, DNA evidence, and the cuts and bruises, the court believed Victor, not me. Victor, who said *we just got a little too carried away.*

After the trial, we go home, take off our fancy clothes, and just sort of stare at each other. It's been a year, and now, it's over. We've done all we can. And now we move on.

Yeah, right.

Justin disappears. Derek changes into sweatpants and grabs the TV remote. Mom and Dad sit in the kitchen with cups of coffee, repeating the same stupid sentiment. "At least we got some justice."

By the way, I hate the word *justice* most of all.

Life goes back to what's supposed to be normal, except it's anything but. Justin doesn't want to, but Dad makes him go back to school. Derek avoids me. Mom and Dad tiptoe around me. School is sheer torture because the cancellation of football also means everybody hates me. Funny how nobody hates Victor.

Mom or Dad, sometimes both of them, pick me up immediately after school, to protect me. But one day, at the final dismissal bell, I head for the parking lot and start walking toward my father's truck. Suddenly, a woman appears out of nowhere, sticks a microphone in my face, and asks me what I think about my brother's testimony. Mom and Dad both run from the truck, shouting at her to leave me alone.

"What testimony?" I ask when we get home.

Neither answers me.

"Mom. What did Derek say?"

"Ashley, there was a reason you were not permitted in the courtroom during testimony," Dad reminds me.

"The trial's over, Dad!" I shout. "What did Derek say? Whatever it was, that reporter thinks it's her next big story."

They refuse to tell me.

As soon as we get home, I hole up in my room, start web surfing, and find the truth.

Brother of Bellford High School Rape Victim Says, "Don't Jail for a Game"

I click the link and read the story, which claims that during questioning, the brother of the Bellford High School rape victim, which would be me, couldn't be sure the crime in question was real rape.

Oh my God.

The words blow a hole straight through me. My breath hitches, and my head swims, but I read every damn word.

Bellford, Ohio—For the seventeen-year-old Bellford Bengals football player accused of raping a fourteen-year-old freshman, testimony from teammates, including that of the victim's sixteen-year-old brother, could exonerate him of all charges.

Appearing as a witness for the prosecution, the victim's sixteen-year-old sibling testified during direct examination that the crime the seventeen-year-old defendant stands accused of was the result of a scavenger hunt gone bad. However, during cross-examination, the witness testified that the high school senior wasn't a real rapist and shouldn't have to go to prison for a dumb game.

I close my laptop and slowly move away from the computer, folding my arms over my churning stomach. Oh, God, Derek. I slap a hand over my mouth and run to the bathroom in time to lose my last meal. I retch for ages, and when I'm finally empty, I slide to the floor next to the toilet, arms wrapped around my middle to stop that gaping hole inside me from swallowing me alive.

When I'm able to stand again, I return to my computer and set up a blog. The first thing I post is Victor Patton's mug shot. The second thing I post is my victim impact statement. And the third thing I post is a question.

Why is my promising future worth less than Victor's?

I get lots of answers. And then I disable commenting.

14

DEREK

LONG ISLAND, NEW YORK

"Derek? You okay?"

I stare at the phone in my hand and remember where I am. "Oh. Yeah. Sorry, Sebastian. I was just thinking of something."

"Yeah. No problem."

"Well, good luck with your BAR thing. It sounds great." It does. I'm not blowing sunshine about that.

I end the call and am just sitting there on the bench, staring off into the distance, when my eye gets stuck on a swatch of blue. Another rally sign. My bag sits on the ground near my feet where I dropped it. I search for the flyer that guy gave me and find it at the bottom of the bag. I read every word this time about secondary survivors needing to find meaningful ways of handling their own emotions.

And then I call the number on the business card.

"Hello?"

"Yeah. Hi. Is this Ian? Ian Russell?"

"Yeah. Who's this?"

"Um. Derek. Derek Lawrence. We met on campus at Rocky Hill. You gave me your card."

"Yeah, I remember you. You were sitting on a bench trying not to puke."

I wince. "Yeah. That would be me."

I hear him mumble something that sounds like *Be right back,* and then he asks, "You okay?"

I laugh once. Am I okay? I'm not sure if I remember what okay even feels like. "Sure. Fine. I just…"

"Talk to me, Derek." His tone changes. "How can I help?"

Suddenly, I forget how to talk, how to string words into sentences. I'm silent for so long, Ian asks again, "Derek? It's okay. You can tell me anything. That's why I gave you my number."

So I do. I tell him about Ashley. And Vic. And me. I tell him how I feel like I broke my whole family. That I'm afraid to go home because I know my parents and Ashley—they blame me.

"I need to *do* something, man. Anything. I made my sister feel like she doesn't matter, and she does." More than anything. "I don't know what I can do." My words feel thick and salty from the tears I'm swallowing back.

There's a long heavy sigh on his end of the phone. "Derek, you need to understand something fundamental."

"Okay."

"This isn't about *you* and your feelings. It's about your sister's. There's a real possibility nothing you *ever* do will be enough in her eyes."

I nod. "Yeah, I know. She'll probably never talk to me again. But I still need to do something. I joined GAR," I blurt out.

"Yeah? That's great. Guys Against Rape is a great organization. I'm a member, too. That's where I learned about secondary survivors."

I just read that in the flyer he gave me. "I don't feel like a victim."

"I didn't, either." Ian's tone was definite. "But you *are* a victim. We both are. When someone we love is hurt, like it or not, we're affected by it, too."

I do. Believe him, I mean. And that surprises me. I don't know this guy, but there's something about him that's…I don't know… *real*, I guess.

"Here's what I mean," he continues. "Rape is a power thing. Everybody has this power inside them…what to wear, what to say, what to do. You never think about it. It's just there. And when it's *taken*, you do a lot of shit to try to convince yourself that you still have that power. This is why some rape survivors go on self-destructive binges—changing their appearance or getting wasted a lot, maybe even having a lot of sex with different people."

"Yeah. Ashley, my sister, she did that. Changed her appearance, I mean. She locked herself in her room, wouldn't open the door. Dad finally got it open, and we rushed in, found her hacking at her own hair with a pair of pink Hello Kitty scissors. I…um. I don't really know if she's, uh, doing the binge thing." Or the other thing he mentioned. God.

"Derek, this is pretty normal. And it's okay."

"Okay?" On what planet is any of this okay?

"Yeah. It's important that survivors find ways they can take back control—ideally, healthy ways instead of ones that can lead to more trouble. Your job is to do whatever she needs to help her heal. If she seems to deliberately lash out at you, shut you out, whatever, you need to *not* take that personally because—"

"Because she needs to feel like she's back in control."

"Yeah. Pretty much," he says on a sigh. "You have to sort of prepare yourself for that. You have to understand it may be part of her process, and that your own process is gonna be a lot different."

Process? "Jeez," I say on half a laugh. "You sound just like the shrink my parents dragged us to after it happened." Not to mention Brittany and Julian, shrinks in training.

"You should *still* be seeing one," he shoots back, all serious. "Your whole family should be. I wish I'd started seeing mine a lot sooner because she would have saved me and my girl a lot of pain."

Pain? "What do you mean? What pain?"

He's silent for a minute. "Well," he says, and his tone is different. Softer maybe. "Secondary survivors feel a similar loss of power. We feel like it's our job to protect, to take care of our sisters and girlfriends, and we failed. They were hurt. So the guilt we feel over our loss of power sometimes shows up in inappropriate ways. Like Grace and me? I got so busy bulking up, trying to become this big bad bodyguard so she'd feel safe, I didn't notice that the things I was doing to protect her were stripping away more of her control instead of giving it back. And by the time I *did* finally figure that out, she was close to not wanting me around."

His voice cracked, and he cleared his throat.

"Groups like GAR? They can teach us—boyfriends, husbands, fathers, and brothers—to be what the people we love need, not what *we* need."

For a second, my heart stops. Then it takes off galloping, beating against my ribs with a vengeance. Against my will, I start imagining life without Ashley in it all. No April and Leonardo, no playground escapades, no joining forces against Justin. No fighting over who has to sit in the middle in the car's back seat. No one to build blanket forts with in the living room. No one to back me up when I tell Mom I didn't break something. I may be a year older, but I can't remember life before Ashley.

Without Ashley.

I squeeze my eyes shut and lean over my knees in case I puke. Again.

"Derek, trust me on this—it doesn't matter how much weight you can bench, it doesn't matter if you have a black belt, nobody's strong enough to deal with this alone. You have to know what to expect so you're prepared to handle it, to *help her* handle it. And that means you have to find ways to deal with your own rage and pain, which, if you're like me, you have in truckloads."

I snort out a laugh at that because it's the biggest understatement I've ever heard. "Yeah. I guess. So what if your girlfriend needed you gone for good?"

I hear him swallow hard. "Then I'd go. I love her, maybe more than I love me. So yeah. I would go if she wanted me to."

Jesus. Go. Could I do that for Ashley? Could I leave our home so she never needs to look at me like the reminder I am?

You already did, a tiny voice whispers in the back of my brain.

Sighing loudly, I admit the truth. "I left, too. Fled so fast, I think I left skid marks. I accepted a scholarship to Rocky Hill. But it's still not enough." I tell him all about how I thought I was helping when I reported Aaron, but I'm not sure that will actually prevent him from hurting somebody.

"Come to the rally. Start there."

"I will." I mean it. I suddenly feel like I can't miss it.

"I'll see you there. We can talk after if you want."

We end the call, and I shake my head.

Talk. Listen. Listen. Talk.

I don't get how this helps anybody.

15

ASHLEY

I know football was canceled because of this. But it wasn't canceled because of me. I never asked for that. Some of our neighbors, some of our friends won't let their kids near me, pretend they don't see us. Some even insult us to our faces. They blame me. They think the court should let the defendant play football because that matters more than some stupid little freshman girl who got what she asked for. I wanted a kiss, a boyfriend, just like every freshman girl. I never asked for this.

—Ashley E. Lawrence, victim impact statement

NOW

BELLFORD, OHIO

On the day before the homecoming game, the school gym is nothing but noise. Shoes squeak on the waxed floor, students shout and laugh, and the band plays the school song. Tara and I are sitting on the bleachers—first row—and I'm huddled into my hoodie, waiting for people to point and stare and whisper behind their hands the way they did when the word got out that Victor Patton had raped me under the football field's bleachers two years ago.

Today, they mostly ignore me, pretend I'm not there so they don't have to acknowledge me and they don't have to face what happened. I try to convince myself I'm cool with that, but I'm not. I wish one person, just one person, would look at me and say, "Hey, it really sucks what happened to you."

My heart keeps skipping beats, and inside my stomach, there must be an entire colony of butterflies. I felt so brave when I recorded all those videos. But now? This is a huge mistake that won't have a prayer of changing anybody's minds.

A hand touches my elbow and just about launches me into orbit. "Sebastian. Hey."

He goes still and shoots both hands up in surrender. "Hey," he replies, waiting. When I say nothing else, he asks, "Are you sure you want to go through with this?"

"Not one bit. But we're gonna do it anyway."

"Ashley—"

"No." I put up a hand. "Let's just do it. It's stupid to pretend they're not all talking, that everything's fine. This way, they'll get what actually happened."

I walked into the girls' bathroom one day last term and heard a few girls a grade behind me talking about *my side* of the story. As if there were teams they could cheer for. That seriously pissed me off. It was a *crime*. I was the *victim*. There are no teams, no sides to take.

So now, I never say "my story." The videos I shot last night for Sebastian are my version of *events* because you can't argue with events.

Sebastian smiles with tight lips, nods once, and disappears into the crowd.

At one end of the gym, beneath the scoreboard, there's a portable projection screen erected on a large tripod stand. The noise level in the gym drops by decibels while Sebastian and another guy spend several minutes connecting a laptop and cables. The lights fade, and then my voice echoes around the huge room.

I'm, well, I used to be Ashley Lawrence. Before I was raped two years ago. Seven hundred and twenty-three days ago. It's not like I want to count the days. I can't help it.

On the screen, the video blinks into life, only it's not me talking into my webcam. It's me walking down the school's main corridor, eyes darting left, right, left again, looking at everybody with undisguised distrust, shoulders hunched up, steps uncertain. Fearful.

Oh my God. Where did this video come from? Is this what I look like every day? Sebastian's voice plays. "Hey, Ashley."

My fingers inch along my collar to the short ends of my hair. Two years ago, my hair had been long and pretty. After I begged, Mom let me cut it to the middle of my back for dance. And then I'd hacked off the rest of it after a really bad flashback when I remembered Vic pulling it.

I redirect my fingers to my bare lips. That's another thing that's different. I used to have a collection of lip glosses in dozens of colors and flavors. Vic said my lips tasted sweet, so I never wear gloss anymore.

I'm different. Do they not see that? Do they see that thing all over my face that I can't ever stop wearing?

It's *fear*.

Video Me stops at her locker, looking over her shoulder every few seconds and jumping like she was shot when someone slams another locker nearby.

My voice talks about why I count the days since the rape.

The video changes to the one I recorded of me talking to Sebastian through the screen on my front window, because I was too scared to let him into the house.

So here's the thing. Getting raped pretty much sucks. It's, like, almost the worst thing that can happen to you. Because it makes you want to die. And every time you remember that the person who did this to you was someone you knew, someone you maybe even liked, part of you does die.

Heads swivel, and dozens of pairs of eyes stare at me. Oh God, oh shit, oh crap. I feel my skin start to crawl. This was a bad idea. A really bad idea.

In the video, Sebastian bleeped out a curse word I'd used, and nervous laughter rings out across the gym. A few of the gazes pinned to me look away because Sebastian added a bunch of news article headlines to the video that scream how many sexual assaults there were last year and how old the victims were.

And how few of the perpetrators got punished.

Suddenly, it's me on the huge screen, staring across the gym. There are tears in my eyes, which is funny, because I don't remember crying while recording the videos. I'm mad and disgusted, and it shows. With a sneer on my face, I tell them exactly what I think.

It sucks to have something you value, something you maybe worked really hard on, get taken away by somebody else. It sucks that you didn't do anything wrong but got the blame for it anyway, even from people you thought knew you. And it sucks that the court looks at the person who did this thing to you, did the worst thing that anyone's ever done to you, and says two years in prison is justice, and everybody, even your therapist, tells you that you should feel proud that you won. It sucks when you finally figure out that there's no such thing as justice.

Sebastian's video splits into two screens. I'm on one side, and on the other, there's a really awesome car that rolls to a stop at an intersection, while I tell the car analogy.

In slow motion, another vehicle approaches the intersection and loses control, T-boning the gorgeous car just sitting there. Pieces of it break off and fly into the air in an explosion of energy. The car is totally, painfully, and obviously ruined. The driver steps slowly out of the wreckage, dazed and heartbroken when he sees what's left of his car. While I continue the car analogy on the video, I notice some people lean forward and frown, and a few others nod.

A chill skates down my spine because it's working. The video is working.

All those eyeballs are pinned to the screen now. Not me.

Not me!

On the screen, the guy whose car got wrecked sits with his head in his hands, a look of such heartbreak on his face, I almost laugh. I mean, it's just a car, right?

And then I remember it's not.

It's *me*.

The video goes back to a single screen. This time, it's video of four feet walking. And then I hear Sebastian ask me if I'm afraid of him right now. *It takes work to remember that not all guys rape.* My voice echoes across the gym. That was the day we talked to the new coach. I didn't know he was recording. I want to be mad, but I'm not because, like I said, it's working.

The scene changes, and now, it's the video I took of Sebastian from my window, with voice-over from one I recorded last night.

Where is your outrage? Every time there's a terrorist attack, everybody starts screaming for border closings and tighter security at airports. Does anybody ever shrug it off and say, 'Oh, it's just extremists being extremists?' So why do you say, 'Oh, it's just boys being boys,' when you terrorize girls? Because that is what you're doing. Terrorizing us.

Sebastian's video cuts to a clip of a girl walking down a street while men harass her.

My brother told me to stay home if I was so scared. He thought it was my problem. He's wrong. And if you agree with him, you're wrong, too. It's everybody's problem. And only everybody can end it. So I'm here to ask you an important question. Are you ready to raise the bar?

The last few words echo, and the video freezes with my furious face staring directly into the crowd.

Then my jaw drops when my dad's face appears on the screen. "Raise the bar," he orders, a car up on a lift behind him.

Justin's face is next. "I'm raising the bar," he says proudly, holding up a document and pointing to his signature.

Justin fades away, and the principal appears. "Help us raise the bar."

I wonder if Derek was too busy to be bothered to sign a pledge as the video fades to black, and across the dark screen, white words appear.

Raise the BAR! Bengals Against Rape. Sign the pledge today.

The screen freezes right there. There's an eerie calm hovering over the entire gym. No shouts, no squeaking shoes. I look around, and everybody seems to be shell-shocked.

Motion from across the room catches my attention.

It's Sebastian, wearing his football jersey with the large *C* patch. He holds up a piece of paper. "Raise. The. Bar. Raise. The. Bar," he chants, keeping the rhythm with the hand holding that document.

Next to me, Tara claps in time. It spreads from Tara to the people next to her, and soon, the entire gym is chanting and clapping, and I have never felt anything so powerful. I look around and see tears in people's eyes, which makes me want to cry.

Sebastian powers off the projector and takes out a stack of forms he puts on a table in the center of the basketball court. Seconds later, Coach Davidson strides to the table, sticks two fingers in his mouth, and lets out a whistle so shrill, it stops everybody.

Without a word, he makes a big show of taking a pen out of his pocket, picking up a form, and signing his name to it. He shakes Sebastian's hand. "Good job, Captain." He hands the paper to Sebastian and steps to the side, folding his arms over his chest.

That starts a stampede. At once, the athletes wearing jerseys stand up. One by one, they approach the table and line up, waiting for their turn to sign a Raise the BAR pledge form. Tara grabs my hand and gives it a squeeze, but I all I can do is nod. Emotions I hardly recognize flood me. I think they're relief and pride and gratitude, but who cares? It's working. My video is working.

I watch the line to sign the pledge get longer, and suddenly, I'm standing. I walk across the gym to Sebastian. He's behind the table, answering questions, pointing to the website link on a brochure that he set up with the principal's blessing to explain the Raise the BAR idea. He stops in the middle of a sentence when he sees me and swallows hard.

I walk around the table, his eyes following me the entire time until I stop directly in front of him. Then I put my arms around him and hug him hard. So hard. For a minute, he does nothing but stand there, stiff and still. Then he hugs me back, but his hands shake just a little bit.

"Um," he says, clearing his throat. "Wow. This…this is okay? Me hugging back?"

"Yeah. It's okay." Sebastian smells really nice. Laundry soap. Maybe shampoo. I don't know, and I don't care. All that matters is he doesn't smell like *him*.

"So does this mean you liked it?"

"Yeah. I did. I really, really did."

"Uh." Another throat clear. "That's good. Right?"

"Yeah." I laugh.

Oh my God, I'm laughing. It actually hurts my cheeks a little because it's been so long since I did this. We pull away from each other. There's no panic. No anxiety. No flashbacks. No pain. There's just us.

Us.

Holy crap on a cracker, this is it. A moment. *The* moment. A normal teenager kind of moment. I want to trap it, cage it, keep it forever so I can take it out and use to recharge the next time the darkness closes in and makes me feel like a freak.

"Ashley?" he says. He's still sort of hugging me.

"Hmm?"

"Would you, maybe, like to, you know, go out sometime? Um. With me, I mean?"

My heart floats, and it's not an anxiety attack this time. I look right into those pretty tea-colored eyes half hidden by his Nike swoosh hair and say, "Yeah. I would. Totally."

He grins and hugs me again, and for the first time in two years, I think I'm happy.

I should have known it wouldn't last long.

The next day is game day.

And I'm in bed, shaking and shivering. Mom checks on me a bunch of times, wondering if I have a fever or flu, but I don't.

I have memories. Bad ones.

Today was the day. Two years ago on this day.
But it's not Vic that I can't get out of my stupid head.
Derek. My Leo. I miss him. God, I really miss him.

16

DEREK

NOW

LONG ISLAND, NEW YORK

I wait for Brittany outside her dorm building, frowning at my phone. There are no fewer than a dozen messages from Mom.

Mom:	I know Thanksgiving isn't for weeks yet, but I miss my baby boy.
Mom:	If you can be home the day before, I think it'll help me convince Dad to close the garage early.
Mom:	How did your game go? I'm sorry we couldn't make it there. Dad didn't want to leave Ashley home alone.
Mom:	I love you. Please remember that.
Mom:	I can't wait to have all three of my babies in the same house again! I'm making all your favorite dishes.

"Hey," Brittany says, pressing a kiss to my lips when she joins me. She lets me go, but I hold on for a few more seconds because I need to. "Oh. This is nice," she whispers.

Yeah, it is. Her hair smells like sunshine so I kiss her head, too.

"You look so pretty." The words sound seriously lame to my ears, but not to hers.

"Thank you." She lowers her eyes and grins.

God, I love when she does that. She always gets embarrassed by a compliment.

"Derek." She rises up on her tiptoes to whisper in my ear. "We don't have to go to the rally. We could go back to my dorm. My roommates are out."

The blood leaves my head, and my stomach does a long, slow roll. I tighten my arms around her and kiss her deep. I want to take her up on that offer like I want to breathe. It's *all* I want to do. I kiss her again, and with a couple million regrets, let her go. "I can't believe I'm saying this but yeah. Yeah, we do. I'm meeting somebody there."

I take her hand, and we start walking. She gives me a look that I can't decipher. "Okay. So who are you meeting? Julian?"

I shake my head. "No, it's this guy. Ian. His girlfriend is one of the speakers tonight. We talked a couple of times. He wants to help me."

She gives me a look, and I squirm.

"What? What's wrong?"

Her hand tightens on mine. "Nothing. I just think you're really awesome for doing this."

My face burns. It's cool that she thinks so, but I'm the furthest thing from *awesome* there is. I change the subject. "Britt, I've been thinking about Thanksgiving. Do you wanna maybe take off somewhere? Maybe camping?"

"In November? Are you nuts? We'd get shot by hunters."

Can't say I'd mind. I lift a shoulder. "Whatever. It doesn't have to be camping. I just...you know. I can't go home. I knew when I left in August that it would be better if I never went back. I think my mom kind of knows that. She's texting me like crazy."

Britt runs a hand along my cheek. "You should do it. Go home, I mean. Not camping."

The thought of stepping foot into that house and facing Ashley's cold, flat eyes and my parents' tension makes me shiver. But that's not why I won't go home.

It's because they need a break. All of them. If not seeing me means Ashley has a peaceful holiday, than I should do whatever I can to make that happen for her. Not having to referee us should lighten Mom and Dad's load, too.

"No. I can't help anybody there. Here... I don't know. Maybe I can." I shrug, thinking of Aaron Dreschler. I like knowing maybe something I did stopped somebody from getting hurt. "Ashley's never gonna forgive me, and it is what it is, you know? But I'm doing this for me now. Maybe figure out how I can *not* be one of those assholes hassling girls like you."

Her eyes lift to mine, and inside them, I see this sort of glow. She smiles softly. "I wish Ashley could see you like I do. If she did, she'd know what I know."

I slowly shake my head, not sure I want to ask this question, but I do. "What do you know?"

"That you're a good person."

I snort and pull back, but she grabs my face and turns it toward hers.

"You *are*, Derek," she insists. "Look, you're not perfect. You don't know all the answers. You don't have life all figured out, so you improve. You fix. And yeah, you mess up a lot, but the point is, you *change*. Do you have any clue how freakin' rare that is? If my dad were like you, maybe my parents would still be married."

Frowning, I try to talk with her hands mushing my cheeks together. "So what. Messing up means I'm good?"

Britt rolls her eyes skyward. "No, you jerk. It's *knowing* when you mess up. You don't hide it. You don't downplay it. You *own* it. That's what makes you good."

Pretty words. And yeah, really pretty girl.

A cheer rises in the distance. "Come on," I say "We should get going."

In front of the campus student activities building, the crowd is already big. Members of the marching band, out of uniform, bang drums, and everywhere I look, I see T-shirts bearing the Take Back the Night moon emblem. In front of the building, there's a booth where two guys are handing out those T-shirts. Opposite the booth, four girls are unfolding an enormous banner. Grinning, Brittany tugs on my hand to walk faster. We sign in and get our T-shirts, a couple of candles stuck into cardboard drip guards, and a program.

Past the booth, there's what looks like a clothesline strung up between a couple of trees. Clipped to the line are clothes and posters that say things like *This is what I was wearing the night I was raped.*

It's a pair of flannel pants.

I swallow hard, and I keep reading.

He said I was so sexy, he couldn't control himself. We'd been dating for four months.

This is a dress. It cannot give consent.

He told me, "You make me so hard."

Stop telling girls how to dress and start telling boys NOT to rape.

He asked me, "How was it?" I cried and fought the whole time, and he wanted me to give his performance a score.

"Derek. Derek!"

I look down, find Brittany staring anxiously up at me.

"Derek, breathe. Just breathe."

I shake my head, my whole body coiled when I spy people around us staring at me like I'm a bomb about to blow. I guess I am.

"Here. Have some water." She presses her bottle into my hands.

I pop the cap and realize I'm tight as a spring. "I'm okay, Britt."

"You're flushed and look like hot molten lava is about to pour out of your ears. I know those signs are hard to see. Believe me."

I shake my head again. I don't even know what I'm feeling anymore.

"Come on," she says, tugging my hand.

I let Brittany lead me to an area near the fountain where

the crowd is thickest. There's a mic standing on top of a small temporary stage and a sense of anticipation in the air I recognize from my football games. But I don't feel anticipation. Jeez, those posters messed me up. I don't know what Vic said to Ashley.

I should. But I never asked because I wanted her to forget. To heal. To move on.

Which isn't true.

I never asked because I didn't want to know.

My phone buzzes. I pull it out and glance at it. It's from Ian.

Ian: Hey, man. You nearby? I'm at the sign-in booth.
Derek: Yeah, I'm by the stage.

Less than a minute later, I spot him, holding hands with a girl dressed head to toe in black. This is his girl. Grace. She's supposed to speak tonight. Her boots have metal studs on them. Her shirt is more metal than material. Her hair is long and straight and a sort of light brown, but it's her eyes that make my throat close. They're bright gray—almost silver—and they don't stop darting around, taking in everything and everybody.

Ashley does this, too. After…after Vic. She hangs back and studies the environment. If Justin's there, she edges closer to him. If he's not, she moves to Dad.

Not me. Not anymore.

Ian flashes a smile when he spots me. I stand up and raise a hand in greeting.

"Hey, Derek."

"Hey."

Ian's eyes dart to Brittany.

"Oh, um, this is my girlfriend, Brittany."

"This is—um—Grace. The girlfriend."

She shoots him a silver glare, and he laughs at our questioning expressions. "Grace has a thing. Hates when I call her *my* anything."

Sure. Okay.

"Hi, Grace. I love your boots," Brittany gushes.

While the girls make small talk, Ian studies me. "You okay, man? You look like you want to start flattening people."

I spread my hands out. "I don't know. I'm just…feeling like a complete ass, you know? Did you read those posters?"

Understanding crosses his face, and he nods. "The posters. Yeah. I read them. Did you see the one that said something about being so sexy, I can't control myself?"

When I nod, Ian looks down and clears his throat, and says, "I used that exact line on the girl I lost my virginity with—and then, didn't talk to her for over a year."

My mouth falls open. I stare at him like he just sprouted horns.

He smiles halfway. "I hated her, you know. Grace, I mean. When it first happened. I was sure she was making up the whole story. Zac, the guy who did it? He was my friend."

I wonder if he *hated* her in the universally accepted definition of the word or if it was true hate, but I don't ask.

"Then Grace and I had to serve some stupid weeklong

punishment together for mouthing off to teachers and got to know each other. When she told me what happened, it was a way different story than the one Zac told."

I consider that for a minute. "So why did you believe her and not him?"

He shrugs and then shakes his head. "I didn't at first. But the entire school called Grace a whore and a liar, and she never quit and never tried to hide. I figured nobody would do that to themselves if it wasn't true."

The posters hanging on the clothesline snap in a sudden gusty breeze. "You know, I told Grace that they should put up the stuff everybody says to a rape survivor after they go public instead of the things the rapists said." He turns to watch Grace, smiling kind of shyly at something Britt is telling her. They're standing near the stage. "It's ridiculous, the things people say, people who are supposed to help."

My eyes go wide. "Yeah, but some girls really do lie."

He looks at me sharply. "Some do. About the same as people lie about any other crime. Do you think your sister lied?"

I think about that for a minute. "I really hoped she did."

"I get that. It's hard to accept that someone you know, someone you consider a good friend, could do something like that. Harder still to look back on moments when you could have said something, done something, only you didn't because you didn't want to be the buzz killer."

Sebastian's refusal to play in the scavenger hunt picks that moment to haunt me. God, we really ganged up on him over that.

"And because enough guys like you and me don't step up when we have the chance, this kind of stuff keeps happening." He waves his hand at the posters on the clothesline. "To somebody we love."

If I'd refused then, if I'd stood next to Sebastian when the scavenger hunt lists were distributed and said, "This is wrong," could I have prevented Ashley from getting hurt?

The thought breaks my damn heart.

......

Somebody with a mic standing on the stage tries to quiet the crowd.

"Welcome! Welcome everyone! We're here to Take Back the Night!"

The crowd erupts into cheers and we're again quieted down to listen to the order of events. We'll light our candles and walk around the fountain at the north side of the campus to right back here, where the stage is. Then, there will be an open mic, when anybody can share their story. But first, we'll listen to Grace Collier deliver the keynote speech.

Grace moves closer to Ian and he holds out his hand. She clutches it in both of hers, lips twitching into something that tries to be a smile but fails. She breathes heavily and I hear him murmur, "You're okay. You're safe. Do the counting."

The counting. My stomach twists.

Ashley does that. She holds her breath for three seconds and slowly lets it go. Ian counts softly, just under his breath, the same way Mom does for Ashley, only he counts backward. Grace holds her breath, then exhales slowly as he counts, tapping one finger against her hand. I remember hearing about the Laurel Point High School Rape case. It was so many years ago.

And Grace still suffers.

Viciously, I kick a water bottle lying on the ground, send it careening toward the stage. I hate this, I fucking hate it. Is this what it'll be like for Ashley? Grace jerks like I just fired a gun in the air. Ian shoots me a dark glare, and Brittany looks at me like I'm insane. I think I am.

"Sorry," I mutter and step away from them so they can have whatever time they need.

Grace lets go of Ian's hand and walks up three steps to the platform. Ian's eyes are glued to her and he looks like he's ready to pounce if she so much as trips on a crack in the sidewalk.

"Hi," she says into the mic and laughs once at the reverb. "I'm Grace. You might know me as the Laurel Point rape victim. I was pretty famous about six years ago."

The crowd cheers at her joke. Six years. I would have been in seventh grade then.

"So we're here to *Take Back the Night*!"

Another cheer goes up.

"But we can only do that if we talk about something nobody wants to talk about. And that's rape culture. See, a lot of guys believe women like me hate men. That we're a bunch of man-hating feminists who worship Satan."

The audience laughs.

"These are men who think it's okay to harass women they see on the street, demand that we smile for them or give them our numbers, and then call us bitches if we don't. These are the men who protect and support the athletes, the celebrities, the coaches and teachers, the priests and next-door neighbors and politicians accused of rape instead of *listening* to the accusers."

The cheer that goes up at that makes my ears ring.

"For the record, I don't hate men. But I do hate feeling scared of men. That's why we're here tonight. Tonight is about us. As women and men. It's about our society. It's about taking a long, hard look at why the crime of rape is so significantly underreported. It's about asking why we're still teaching girls not to get raped instead of teaching boys not to rape."

Cheers ring out across the quad, and I glance at Ian, and he's in some kind of trance, watching his girl work this crowd. His lips are parted, and his eyes gleam. It's pretty obvious that he'd do anything for her.

I...I wouldn't do that for Ashley. I'd proven that, hadn't I? My sister hadn't asked for much. Just for her brother to act like her brother and not some stuck-up dick who'd rather hang out with his friends instead of her.

Grace doesn't talk about her rape. Instead, she talks about *after*. She talks about nobody believing her.

About losing her friends.

About her dad's inability to deal.

About the police refusing to make an arrest.

She talks about the school protecting their star athlete, about his teammates harassing her, calling her a liar. She talks about the bone-deep feelings of guilt and loneliness that almost compelled her to take her own life.

The crowd continues to listen and cheer in the right places. But then, Grace says something profound.

"I didn't get it until much, much later, that I *wasn't* alone. What happened to me, what was done to me, impacted more than just me. It impacted my family. It impacted my entire community. Because when I pointed my finger at one of our own, I showed everybody that the monster doesn't put on a scary mask and hide in the bushes, waiting for his opportunity. No, he doesn't *hide* at all. He lives in plain sight, takes off his mask of total normalcy, and attacks only after you trust him. When you believe a nice kid like him, a guy from a great family, is a monster, it means you have to redefine what a monster really is…and own your share of the blame in creating those monsters. For way too many people, that's as bad as admitting you're a monster, too."

Oh God.

Lights flash in my visual field…little twinkling lights interrupted by flashes of Vic tracking Ashley while she danced on the field, of Dakota's hurt expression when she discovered I'd wanted to get back together just to score points. *Those fucking points.* Of Ashley's bruises when…Sebastian found her. Of me yelling at Ashley to leave me alone, to quit the dance team. The lights beat brighter, faster, until I swear I'm back there again, back running across the field so fast my lungs are on fire, back under those bleachers where Victor is with Ashley…only this time, it's *not* Ashley and Vic.

It's me.

It's me with Dakota. *A hundred points!*

Gasping, I drop to the ground and wrap my arms around my middle. I feel like I'm gonna hurl…or maybe die. And I don't care.

"Derek! Derek, what's wrong?" Britt falls to her knees next to me.

Ian tears his gaze from Grace and studies me.

Our eyes meet, and he nods once. He doesn't say anything. He doesn't have to. He tried to tell me, but I think I already knew.

I'm the monster.

Dad pulling me off Ashley's bed, insisting I go shower off Vic's smell. Because I'm just like Vic.

A *monster*.

I sit on the ground for a minute or two and try to hold my shit together. Ian's studying me like I'm a slide under a microscope, and Brittany looks like she's about to call an ambulance and have me committed. Grace doesn't look at us. She focuses on what's directly in front of her.

After a minute, it smacks me with all the force of a tackle that I'm probably making Grace nervous. I scramble to my feet, dust off my ass.

"Sorry, man. Sorry."

Ian shakes his head. "Don't worry about her. She's done this a few dozen times now, Derek. You won't rattle her." And then he flashes a fierce grin. "You can't."

Brittany grabs my hand, which is shaking. I want to run, head back to my dorm room, plug in headphones, and get lost in some headbanging music until this rally is over, but I can't. The entire football team is supposed to be here. I pull the hood of my sweat-shirt over my head and shove my hands into my pockets.

Grace finishes her speech to thunderous applause, and the rally organizer takes the mic, instructing everybody to light their candles and start the march. It takes about fifteen more minutes to get the crowd organized. Brittany's got her candle lit and holds it out to me.

She says she loves me. How does she not see the monster in me? I don't belong here. I'm exactly the reason why these people are out here tonight.

"Derek?" She waves her candle at me.

Mechanically, I pull the stupid candle out of my pocket, and she lights it. We start the march. Everybody chants, "We are women. We are men. Together we fight to take back the night!"

Brittany nudges me with an elbow. "You're scaring me. Are you okay?"

No. I shrug and shake my head. "Working on it."

"This is pretty great, right?"

"It's not at all what I expected."

She smiles, teeth flashing in the low light. "There's hope for you yet."

Hope.

The word kind of hangs there in midair, taunting me, forcing me to face it, but I don't want to.

The chant is growing, getting louder, and has suddenly split by gender with the women shouting out, "We are women," and the men answering in a deeper pitch, "We are men."

It's working its way inside me, a challenge. A dare to be better than what I am. All this time, I thought I was a man, but I wasn't. I was a pretender, a wannabe. Now these protestors are daring me to be a real man, a man who's not afraid to tell other dudes when their jokes aren't funny, when their behavior is scaring someone, when they're coming on way too strong…and a man who's not afraid to hear it when he's the one being a jerk.

I take a good look around and decide there must be about a thousand of us marching. The light of all those candles reflecting off the gold trim of so many Rocky Hill University sweatshirts holds back the darkness. I see my coaches, guys from the team, my fellow GAR members.

"Yo, Lawrence!"

I whip my head around to find my roommate, Julian, grinning at me.

"This is sick," he says, grabbing me in a one-armed hug that practically lifts me off my feet.

I wrestle free, anxious to keep our candles from setting our faces on fire.

"Yeah, it's…powerful." I have this completely ridiculous urge to grab a microphone and apologize to the entire female population, but I know it won't do a damn thing to fix stuff with Ashley.

"Hey, Julian," Britt says. "This is Ian and Grace."

Julian's face changes, a look of awe spreading across it. "Damn, girl. That speech was amazing."

Grace smiles, shrugs, and leans a tiny bit closer to Ian. "Thank you."

"Uh-uh. Thank *you*." Julian falls into step beside us, marching to the rhythm of the chant. "Hey. Did Derek tell you about what happened in the fitness center?"

Ian frowns. "What happened?"

Julian tells them the entire story about Aaron Dreschler in the gym talking about how he wants to grab somebody. "And my man, Derek, goes caveman on his ass."

Grace's face snaps toward mine. "You beat him up?"

I shake my head. "No. I just threatened to. I let campus security deal with him."

Brittany's hand squeezes mine. I look down at her, and she's got this bright smile for me that makes me feel all warm inside.

"And what did they do about it?" Grace asks.

I look away. "I actually don't know if they did anything."

"Maybe you should check."

Bristling, I shake my head. "I don't run the university."

"That's not what I mean," Grace says, waving a hand in the air. "You could have gone to all your football teammates and told everybody what this guy said. Make sure they know why it's wrong."

A hundred protests form, and I open my mouth to argue with her. But the exasperated look on Ian's face stops me. "Oh." I suddenly get it. "I did exactly what you just said in your speech. I didn't see it as my problem." My jaw tightens, and I stare straight ahead. Once again, I'm the bad guy. Once again, I'm getting blamed for shit I tried to prevent.

I cannot do this anymore.

"It was nice meeting you," I tell Ian and Grace. Then I tug on Brittany's hand. "Come on. Let's get out of here."

"What? Derek, I—"

I don't listen. I just pull her out of the parade of marchers. We cut across the quad, elbowing through the crowd until finally, I find a spot where it's quiet, relatively speaking.

"Derek, what's going on?"

"I don't fucking know!" I explode, flinging both arms up.

Britt jerks like I hit her.

"You're angry."

"Yeah."

"Why?"

I cross my arms and glare at her. Didn't we just cover that I don't know? Not much has changed in the one-point-two seconds that elapsed to suddenly fill me with knowledge.

She puts up both hands, palms out. "Come on, Derek. Psych major, remember? What's fueling your anger?"

Sighing loudly, I fling myself to the ground, my back against a tree. "Failure, Britt. A total systemic complete failure of me to do my job!"

"Your job?"

"Yeah. As a brother. As a man. As a fucking human being!" Jesus, how does she not see this about me? "Did you listen to Grace? Did you hear those words?"

She waits for me to connect the dots.

"I'm one of the monsters Grace was talking about."

She looks at me, blue eyes big and round. "No. No way. You're no monster. You're not a rapist."

"Might as well be!" I shout and scramble back to my feet, needing to move. "I didn't do anything to prevent it. Or anything to fix it. Hell, it was Sebastian who insisted we find them, not me! And I sure didn't do anything to help after. No, the only thing I did was take off, after I told an entire courtroom he's not a real rapist." I finish with a sneer of self-directed disgust. "And you just heard Grace say I didn't do enough about Aaron."

Brittany puts herself right in front of me, hands on my chest. "Derek. Listen to me. Nobody's attacking you or blaming you for anything. Tonight is about seeing a different perspective, you know?"

"*I* blame me," I snap back, thumping my chest with a palm. "I—God! I *am* seeing things from a different perspective—my sister's. *She* blames me. My parents, they can barely look at me. My brother? He's suddenly the referee, telling me to do this because Mom's upset or not to do that, because Dad is. Didn't you see the way Grace controlled her anxiety? It's been *years* since Grace's assault and she's still doing all the things Ashley has to do, like deep breaths and counting. You know what that says to me, Britt? What happened to them isn't a twisted ankle or a pulled muscle that heals after some ice, some meds, and some therapy. It's—" My voice cracks on a sob. I rake both hands through my hair and rock back and forth, barely able to keep my shit together.

"It's…it's an amputation, Brittany. It's always gonna be here."

"Okay, Derek," she says after a long moment. "You're right. If you're so sure it will always be there, why do you keep trying to deny it? Find a way to live with it. That's what you need to focus on." She gives my hand a squeeze. "Come on. We should get back."

I let Brittany lead me back to the rally, her words ringing in my ears. How do you find a way to live with something you hate about yourself with every cell in your body? I'm a big guy. Strong. I can take a lot of pain.

But this? I don't know if anybody's strong enough for this.

We catch up to the crowd back at the stage. The rally organizer is at the podium and leans into the mic. She's a tall woman with short hair and a big voice.

"I have a question for you!" she shouts to the still-cheering assembly. "Rape culture—is it real? How do we end it? The mic is open!"

She steps back and waves her hand to the crowd, encouraging people to step up, to share.

My stomach drops and rolls, and I don't know how much more I can take.

A small girl who looks like a high school freshman approaches the mic. She adjusts it and then says in a loud, clear voice, "I was raped by my stepfather more than once. My mother didn't believe me. We have to listen to victims when they come forward instead of assuming they're lying! That's how we'll change things."

As the crowd cheers, Tiny Girl looks straight at me, like she knows I didn't believe my sister.

Another girl walks up to the podium. "We can change it by making the punishments a lot harsher. When I was harassed by my softball coach and told him I would report him, he just shrugged and said, 'What are they gonna do? Fire me?' They didn't even do that, and that creep is still coaching."

I squeeze my eyes shut. Victor Patton is gonna be released from prison because I told the judge not to punish him too harshly.

The next person approaches the mic and lowers her—wait, *his* hood. Holy shit, it's a guy. "We can change it by accepting that rape is *everybody's* problem. It can happen to guys, too. It happened to me when I was fourteen years old and in Little League. My own parents asked me if I was sure I wasn't just imagining things." He turns his head and looks at me.

Jesus. What the hell is this? *Imagining things.* I'd used those exact words.

Another guy walks up the three steps leading to the stage. A chill runs down my spine. "I don't know if we can change anything. But I do know that when it happens to somebody you love, you always have to remember your job is to support them. You *be* there for them. You keep loving them. You don't turn your back. My mom was raped by our landlord. My dad couldn't look at her. They're divorced now." He turns his head, his eyes boring through mine, and a lump the size of a baseball lodges in my throat. How can he know my parents are on the verge of splitting up? How can he possibly know this?

On and on, they come. Dozens of them, all talking *straight to me.*

I take off running in the dark, where the monsters are supposed to be, and don't stop until I reach the woods that border the campus. I can hear traffic on the main road that runs north from the Long Island Expressway to Rocky Hill, but thank God I can't hear any more of the open mic stories. I lean over my knees, breathing deep against the burn. Jesus. All those stories. All those survivors.

All that pain.

The burn inside my chest climbs to my throat, and I'm on my feet again, running a few steps before I trip over a branch and face-plant into the weeds. I climb back to my feet and brush off the leaves and dirt. I grab the branch I tripped over, hold it like a club, and beat the tree it probably fell from, curses flying, until I'm too weak to move.

I drop the branch, slide to the ground, and sit there, panting, trying to figure out how the hell I'm gonna address a crowd like this next month when I'm no better than the guys who cause all that pain.

17

ASHLEY

I don't remember getting to the hospital. I was so dizzy and sick and in pain. But I remember the nurse who took care of me. After she finished combing my hair for dirt and garbage and traces of the defendant, after she finished taking pictures of the blood and the bruises, after she finished packing my clothes into a paper bag that said 'Evidence,' she took me into a shower and said I could wash. I remember wishing she could take my whole body like she took my clothes. Just unzip, peel it off, and stuff into a bag where I would never have to look at it again. It's his now. He took it. It smells like him sometimes...even today.

—**Ashley E. Lawrence, victim impact statement**

TWO YEARS AGO

BELLFORD, OHIO

They make me strip while standing on a large white sheet.

Paper.

No, plastic. Maybe.

It's frustrating how some details are so blurry while others are etched onto my retinas like sun flares.

My clothes get put in bags, and I get put in a gown. I don't know why they bother giving me anything to wear because the nurse examiner keeps opening it to take pictures of every part of my body. She combs my hair *down there.* She swabs every soft part of my body, pulling dirt, bits of trash, and even glass from my skin and hair. It takes a long time. Crying and trembling through most of it, I'm comforted by how kind and patient she is with me. She gives me medication and painkillers and stays with me after the detectives show up, asking the same questions over and over again. I'm okay—mostly—until she tells me my family's outside and anxious to see me.

My heart beats so fast, it makes my chest hum. There's an ice-cold ball spinning in the center of my body, growing bigger and bigger, spreading that icy cold pain to every cell in my body until I'm not me anymore. I'm ice. Every breath hurts, and soon, I can't get breath past the pain into my lungs. I gasp, my hands clawing for air, and then my vision goes gray and blurry.

The nurse examiner takes my hands, tells me to hold my breath and count to three, but it doesn't help. It doesn't work, and then I can't see. My vision fades and then goes completely black. I'm dying. I am going to die, and just when I think I can't take another second of this agony, I let everything go and welcome death with relief.

Escape.

Only it's not death.

I wake up who knows how much later, lying on a stretcher with a sheet pulled all the way up to my chin. I'm woozy and weak, like I've just recuperated from some illness. I'm not in the same room where I'd been examined. I'm in a regular room now. Mom, Dad, Derek, and even Justin are there. They all jump up and surround me when they see my eyes open. Mom and Dad cry. Justin looks dazed. Derek?

He looks pissed off.

They all talk at once, asking me questions, but I can't seem to make sense of their words. But their emotions? Those register. Shock, pain. Disapproval so huge, it's like another life-form. I float, disconnected. The nurse who examined me tells me she has to leave me. I try to hold her hand, keep her there, keep her with me, but I have no strength. She takes my family into the hall with her, and I wish I could say thank you, but I'm too tired even for that.

So I sleep.

Every time I move, I jerk awake, remember where I am…and why I'm here. The ice-cold pain in my chest starts right up exactly where it left off, and it's too much. I muster up enough strength to rip some sensor from my finger, the sheet off my body, but I can't stand up. I crash to the floor, more pain squeezing its way past the agony I already feel until I'm sure every nerve ending in my body is lit up.

I have no memory of getting up from the floor. I wake up again, much later, back in the bed, again with the sheet up to my chin. My room's dark, except for a slice of light from the open door. A shot of fear goes through me when I see a figure silhouetted in that light, but then I recognize it.

Derek.

He stands there for a long while, saying nothing. The light bothers me, but I'm too weak, too fuzzy to protest. Finally, the door shuts, and I relax, but then he speaks.

"God, Ashley," his voice whispers, thick and harsh in the dark. "Why couldn't you just stay home like I told you to?"

What? But I can't move. It takes all of my strength just to keep my eyes open. I want to apologize and tell him I didn't mean to do it, but Vic wouldn't stop. I want to tell him he was right. I should have stayed home. I shouldn't have made such a big deal out of the scavenger hunt. If I'd listened to him, would this have happened?

"The police arrested Vic. Sebastian is a witness."

No. No, he can't be.

There's a noise, loud. Deep. Almost animal.

It takes me a few seconds to figure it out.

It's…it's a sob.

A sob from my big strong football player brother, the one who never apologizes and means it, never cries and means it.

Am I actually dying? Why else would *Derek* be crying? I wish I can get out of this bed, hug him, tell him I'll be fine, but I still can't lift my limbs.

"Damn it, Ashley! Why? If you'd listened to me, this wouldn't have happened! We're never gonna be the same after this. Mom can't stop crying, and Dad says he's buying a gun. Justin wants to quit school. The whole family is hurt. We can't even look at you. You should have just stayed home. God. Goddamn it." He kicks something in my room. Hard.

The slice of light appears again, and he's gone, the sound of whatever he kicked still echoing between my ears.

The next day, I don't feel so floaty, so tired, but I still wonder if maybe I dreamed the whole thing.

"It wasn't your fault," everybody tells me, but I see through their well-rehearsed lines taken straight from the rape survivor's handbook they give my parents before they let them take me home.

The only one who never says it is Derek.

If you ask me what I think, I'm gonna tell you. Ask somebody else if you want compliments.

That's what he always used to say.

So I don't ask. If I don't ask, he can't tell me what he really thinks, what he told me while he thought I was sleeping.

18

DEREK

TWO YEARS AGO

BELLFORD, OHIO

"Derek."

I look up and find Sebastian Valenti, pale and anxious, running toward me. The homecoming game is later today, and I just got to school for a team meeting our coach called.

"What's up, man?"

"Your sister. Any idea where she is right now?"

I look away. Ashley's pissed off at me for what I said by the principal's office. I haven't seen her this morning. When I stumbled out of bed this morning, Mom said she went to school early for Fusion practice. "Uh, the girls' room, getting ready for dance?"

"She's not," he says, shaking his head emphatically. "I already checked."

An instant uneasiness prickles just under my skin, and I squirm. "Well, maybe she's already out on the field."

"I checked there, too, Derek."

I step forward. "What the hell's going on, Sebastian?"

"Something bad, bro. I think Vic is with her."

Panic ignites inside me, and my entire body snaps to attention. "What the fuck do you mean, *with her*?"

"With her, Derek. It's on his card."

The bottom falls out of my world. "What's on his card?"

"I don't know for sure. It's just a feeling. I heard some of the guys in the locker room talking about Vic's scavenger hunt list. Sex with a virgin. Two hundred points. They *doubled* the points."

I grab Sebastian while all the blood drains from my brain.

"Did you hear me, Derek?"

I blink and shake my head. "No, I told them Ashley's off-limits. You were there. You heard me."

Impatient, he slashes a hand through the air. "I know, and I'm telling you, they're not listening. They decided she's worth double if Vic…if Vic…you know."

No. My vision turns red around the edges, and my mouth goes dry. "Who? Tell me who!" I scream at him.

"They didn't know I was there. Brayden. Andre. Vic. But Vic left. I don't know where he's heading."

I pull out my phone and call Ashley, but it goes to voicemail. I tap out a fast text warning her not to go near Vic.

"His car?" I ask, and Sebastian takes off running. I'm right on his heels. We race to the parking lot where students typically park, up one aisle and down another, but Vic's black Chevy is nowhere—

"There!" Sebastian spots it at the end of the next row. We run to either side.

It's empty. I slam my palms to the hood. Where else could they be?

"Classroom?"

"No, I checked. The security gates to the main corridor are down. Only the locker rooms are open."

"The field?"

We take off running again, through the parking lot, around the building, across the main visitors' lot, and through the gate to field. The Fusion dancers, cheerleaders, and color guard are clumped up under the goalpost.

"Anybody seen Ashley?" I shout.

Brittany, a girl in my grade, smiles up at me. "Hey, Derek."

I snag her by her arms. "Have you seen my sister? I gotta find her. Now."

Brittany pulls away. "Um, she and Victor Patton took off together, like, twenty minutes ago." And then she frowns. "Why? What's wrong?"

"Vic's got his eye on her. For points."

Brittany shuts her eyes and groans. "I'll help you look."

Ten more minutes go by. I've got cheerleaders checking the girls' bathroom, Sebastian checking the woods that border the school, and I'm about to lose my damn mind when shouts go up at the other side of the field. I whip around, find Sebastian and Vic in some kind of shoving match. It takes me a few seconds to notice, to connect the dots. The cheerleaders, the dancers…they aren't shouting at the two fighting guys. No, they're all running under the bleachers.

I take one step, two…and then I'm running at full speed.

SEVEN YEARS AGO

BELLFORD, OHIO

"Ashley, stop that before you hurt yourself!" Mom shouts at Ashley from the other room. She's been running around the living room with thick fluffy socks on her feet, trying to skate on the bare floor.

"Your move," Justin prods, somehow ignoring Ashley's antics.

Chess is ridiculously dull. I move another pawn that he immediately murders in cold blood.

"Come on, you guys! Skate with me." Ashley slides into the table where we've got our board set up, scattering pieces.

"Ash, will you stop? Look what you did." Justin chases a queen that rolled under the table while I retrieve my pawns.

They're probably trying to escape before they're all slaughtered or die of boredom.

"Chess is dumb!" she shouts as she runs back to the entry to gather momentum for her next slide.

Justin frowns and replaces the pieces on the board.

"How do you remember where they all were?"

He shrugs. "That's part of the game. You keep track of where every piece is and what they can do." His voice cracks, and I laugh once. It happens, like, all the time. He shoves me. "Knock it off and play."

"She's right. This is boring."

Ashley does a kind of cool sideways drift from the center of the room to the sofa.

Justin looks at me, adjusts his glasses, and shrugs. "So go skate if you don't think you can beat me."

Beat him? Oh, it's on now. "I can beat you. Let's start again."

We reset the board and start again. Two pawns are already off the board when Ashley blurs past us. This time, her trajectory has her sliding directly toward the tall bookcase in the corner of the room. I'm on my feet before she crashes, but I'm not fast enough. Time sort of freezes and then starts in slow motion. The bookcase bounces off the wall and falls forward, spilling books and pictures on top of her. My feet feel like they're frozen in concrete.

"Ashley!" Mom runs in from the other room.

There's this second, the longest second of my life, of complete silence. There's nothing—not even the hum the house makes. Then all three of us are hefting the bookcase up and out of the way, moving books and all the other crap aside.

Ashley's on the floor, blood dripping from a gash on her forehead, and suddenly, my own forehead hurts, too.

"Justin, first aid kit!" Mom shouts, and he takes off running.

I fall to my knees next to her. Ashley's not moving, but her eyes are open, and they latch on to mine, her terror a living, breathing thing.

"Hey, April," I say. "You're supposed to say 'Cowabunga' when you wipe out."

She tries to laugh and move and then cries. "Mommy! It hurts!"

"I know. Don't worry. We'll fix you all up." Mom tickles her feet, and when Ashley wriggles both, Mom squeezes her eyes shut.

We spend hours in the hospital emergency room, Dad rushing in soon after we get there. There are X-rays and stitches and some loud scolding that gets Ashley all sniffly, but soon, we're on our way back home with takeout bags and a new movie to watch. Ashley's cuddled up on the sofa between me and Justin, a bandage over her stitches.

She falls asleep before the movie's credits finish. Carefully, I put my arm around her and adjust her so she's leaning on me.

I look into the corner where Dad fastened the bookcase to the wall with two thin cables. Lemon cleaner tickles my nose. There's no more blood on the floor, but I swear I still see it. My forehead throbs again, and I rub away the pain. Dad's kicked back in his favorite chair. Mom's curled up on her side, and Justin's reading a book. Carefully, so carefully, I lean over and kiss the bandage on Ashley's head and then settle back to watch the movie.

I don't know if any of that kiss-the-boo-boo stuff really works, but if there's a shot, why not take it?

TWO YEARS AGO

BELLFORD, OHIO

They won't let me near her. Jesus, this is *my sister*, my fourteen-year-old sister. They say they have to preserve evidence.

My sister. *Evidence.*

I want to tear Victor Patton's head off his body with my bare hands. But he's safe in the back of a cop car, hands cuffed behind his back.

Forty or fifty people are now standing around, aiming their cell phones at her, and I lose my shit. "Turn them off!" I shout over the roar inside my head, this screaming white noise that drowns out everything but my own thoughts. "Turn them off now!" They stare at me like I'm about to detonate, and I am. Why doesn't anybody get that?

Cursing, I stalk to the ambulance. "That's my sister. What did he do to her? Tell me!"

"Calm down." A paramedic says. "We're taking her to the hospital. She needs to be processed—"

That word send an icy chill down my back. "Processed? What the hell does that mean?"

"It's standard procedure in sexual assault ca—"

"Sexual assault," I repeat, the words cutting deep trenches into my soul, yet my brain can't seem to interpret them. *Sexual assault. Sexual assault.* I repeat the words until they play by themselves in my head, and suddenly, I whip around with one goal. One mission.

And that's to end Victor Patton's miserable little life.

"Whoa, whoa, stop." Strong hands hold me back, but I'm too blinded by rage to get that.

"Let go of me. He raped my sister! I'll kill him!"

"Friendly advice, son. Never threaten to kill somebody in front of a cop." The hands tighten to the point of pain. "Calm yourself down, or I'll put you in cuffs, too."

"That's my sister!"

"I know. You want to help her, get your temper under control. You can't help her if *you're* under arrest."

I close my eyes and suck in oxygen, but it does little to kill the urge to rip Victor's face to shreds.

"Good. If I lift my hands up, can I trust you not to move? Because if you move, I will have to assume you're dangerous and arrest you."

I nod and open my eyes.

"What's your name, son?" the cop asks, hands still clamped on me.

I exhale slowly. "Derek Lawrence. That's my sister." I stab a finger toward the ambulance.

He slowly lift his hands. "I need you to tell me what happened. And then, you're gonna want to call your parents."

My parents. I rake both hands through my hair. Holy shit. How am I supposed to tell them Ashley was… Oh, God.

I can't remember getting to the hospital. Suddenly, I'm just there. The cop who'd held me back earlier is gone and in his place is a pair of detectives. They make me sit in a waiting room, Sebastian at one end, me at the other. When had he gotten here? How had he gotten here?

They ask us question after question after question, and I still haven't seen Ashley. The detective wears this wrinkled suit and smells like an entire pack of cigarettes.

"I want to know more about this scavenger hunt. Did you boys both play?"

Sebastian shakes his head while I lower mine. He refused to

play from the very beginning. Didn't care how much shit we gave him over it, just wouldn't play.

"Are you and Victor Patton friends?"

"We play on the same team. But we're not friends." I've had enough. "Just tell me how she is," I demand. "Nobody will tell me. Was she…" I break off, unable to say the word. "How bad did he hurt her?"

Before he can answer, the door bursts open, and my parents rush in.

"Derek!" Dad's at my side in two strides.

"Where is she? What happened? Is she okay?" Mom's sobbing out the words, mascara running down her cheeks.

I stand up, hug her so tight.

"Mr. and Mrs. Lawrence? I'm Detective Lansing."

"Our daughter. Where is she?" Mom turns back to head out the door, but the detective bars her way.

"They're still treating her, Mrs. Lawrence."

"I need to see her!"

"You will when they're ready. Right now, your daughter must be examined and evidence collected."

Dad's spine snaps so straight, I could hear it crack. "Evidence of what, exactly?" His voice is suddenly shaky.

Detective Lansing turns to Dad and answers bluntly. "Of rape, Mr. Lawrence."

Dad makes a sound like he's been gut-punched, like air gushing out of a popped tire. A second later, he picks up the chair closest to him and heaves it at the wall, where a bunch of magazines and leaflets hang on a wooden rack. Dad's big; I get my height from him. But he isn't violent. Even when he's mad at us, he's never scary.

But right now, he's terrifying.

The second cop leaves Sebastian in his corner and hurries over, muscling Dad down into another chair. "Mr. Lawrence, I understand your anger. But right now, we have to let the medical team do their jobs."

Dad finally remembers me sitting there. "Derek! Is this more of that scavenger hunt bullshit? Is it?" When I don't answer, he leaps to his feet, eyes wild, and has my shirt bunched in his hands before either detective can twitch. "Answer me! Do you know who did this?"

Oh, I know. And I am going to gut him the first chance I get.

It takes a few minutes, but Lansing's partner gets Dad back into a chair and slightly calmer.

"The scavenger hunt. What can you tell me about that?" Detective Lansing asks, flipping pages in his notebook.

Mom cries in a chair next to Dad.

I swallow hard, tugging my shirt back into place. "It's a team thing," I try to explain. "I told the team. I told everybody Ashley was off-limits."

"Derek, I swear to God—" Dad says through clenched teeth.

"He did, Mr. Lawrence," Sebastian adds. "I was there."

Lansing turns his balding head in his direction. "There for what?"

Sebastian explains the whole ugly story. He tells the detective about the scavenger hunt, about the points and how we collected them, about how my parents flipped out over Ashley being targeted, and how I lost it and tackled Victor for what he said about Ashley. "If he hadn't have done it, *I* would have. Vic is a real ass—uh, jerk."

Lansing exchanges a look with his partner, a younger guy with a better suit and much better hygiene. "Stay with Mr. and Mrs. Lawrence. I'll take the kid through it again."

He does.

I lose track of how much time we spend with the detectives. The roar in my head grows louder but not loud enough to muffle the sound of my own conscience.

Why couldn't you just be nice to her? it keeps asking.

November

19

ASHLEY

Every day, I wonder, Will this be the day I turn some corner and walk right into him? Will this be the day I have an anxiety attack so bad, I pass out in the middle of the street? Half the people in this town think I'm lying, but nobody is that good an actor. Why would anyone want to be? I want it to stop. I just want all of this to end.

—**Ashley E. Lawrence, victim impact statement**

NOW

BELLFORD, OHIO

I survived October.

I'm not entirely sure how I did, but I did. Even though I missed the homecoming game, Sebastian totally understood. He told me nobody got assaulted in the stairwells or under the bleachers, nobody had to wear shorts under their skirts, and absolutely nobody got hurt—except for Bruce Bishop, and that's only because he got sacked in the third quarter.

And then he told me it was all because of me.

So, um, I now have an actual *boyfriend*.

On Monday morning, I jump out of bed, like *literally* spring out of it. October is over, and I have a boyfriend, and tonight, we're going to the movies.

I haven't been to a movie theater in two years. I don't like the dark. But I feel like I can do it now. Like maybe I can do anything now.

I feel strong.

That's because the Raise the BAR campaign has not only seen lots of pledges at *my* school, it's now made it into other schools across the district. In fact, the school board president emailed my principal, and we had a meeting about changing the name from *Bengals Against Rape* to *Bellford Against Rape* so the entire district can adopt the program.

I've been asked to speak at other schools. I'm thinking about it, even though I wasn't technically able to speak at my school. Every time I do though, I start to breathe harder. Maybe they'll let Sebastian come with me.

"Ashley! Come on. You'll be late!"

I glance at the alarm clock next to my bed. I grab my bag, head downstairs for one of the bakery muffins Dad brought home Sunday morning, and skid to a stop. Both of my parents are still home.

"What's up, guys? Closing the garage today?"

Dad shakes his head. "No, sweetheart. Sit down. We have.... news."

Uh-oh. By the looks they exchange, I can tell I'm not going to like this news. My heart skips a beat, and I hold my breath. Slowly, I pull out a chair, bracing for impact.

Dad clears his throat. "We..." His voice breaks, and Mom lays a hand over his. "We heard from Carol."

"Carol, the assistant DA?"

Dad nods. "He's out, Ash," he says, shoving out the words like they're trying to choke him. "Victor. He's free."

I try to process the words I just heard. Free. Victor Patton, free? I knew this was coming. I'd prepared myself for it. And now that's it here and real—no. Just...*no*.

"But...what about me?" My voice sounds small and...*weak*.

"I know, baby. I know." Dad cups a big rough hand around my cheek and catches a tear before it can roll all the way off my face. "He can't come near you. We have a restraining order. He won't want to go back to prison, so we're confident he won't violate the order."

"What if he—"

"He won't get near you, I promise." Dad's lips thin into a straight line. "I want you straight home from school, no hanging out. I want your phone on you at all times. And I need to talk to Sebastian. Is he picking you up?"

Dizzy, I nod and absently wave a hand toward the street. Mom gets up, heads to the front door, and lets Sebastian in. I hear them talking.

A minute later, he's there, kneeling next to me, his beautiful eyes dark and stormy.

"Sebastian, I'm counting on you to help keep her safe," Dad says.

He nods gravely.

"Home right after school."

Wait, no. "We're going to the movies," I protest.

Dad shakes his head. "Watch a movie here."

Sebastian nods. "It's okay, Ashley. We can go out another time."

Something deep inside me coils up. I can feel it...the outrage, the fury, this absolute sense of injustice. "No," I say. And then more loudly. "No. I am *not* the criminal here!" I stand up, shaking from rage. "It's not fair. Damn it, it's not fair."

"But, Ashley, we're only—"

I hold up a hand. "I know. And I'm telling you I am done living like a prisoner. *He's* the one who should stay home, not me. Come on, Sebas. We're gonna be late."

Sebastian nods, and we leave the house.

He has his mom's car. We're silent all the way to school, but inside, I'm still seething. He parks the car and cuts the engine. Outside, I see Tara walking up the school's road, shuffling through a pile of leaves, and I smile. I want that. I want to be able to walk wherever I want, without looking over my shoulder.

"Ash." He says my name quietly.

Turning to him, I'm kind of shocked to see him wearing his game face, all tough and *don't mess with me*. Sebastian is always so careful around me, making sure I know he'd never hurt me, so this is....confusing.

"Your dad's right. You need to be extra careful."

I wave that away, making a sound of frustration. "I get that he wants to protect me. But do you not see how friggin' unfair this is? This is why we have a justice system! So the victims, the people who already suffered, don't have to keep suffering every day for the rest of their lives! I'm not doing it, Sebastian. I finally reached a point where I don't freak out over the scent of somebody's deodorant, and they let him out? Fuck that!" I slam a fist on his dashboard. It feels so good, I do it again. "Fuck the whole stupid system."

"Okay, I get that it sucks, but, Ashley, you have to figure out how you're gonna manage this. He lives here! You could see him on Blaine Boulevard, walking into the diner. You could see him at the supermarket. What if you're by yourself and have an anxiety attack? Who's gonna stop him from hurting you again while you're just trying to breathe?"

Tears sting the back of my eyes, and I swallow hard. I will not cry. I am done crying. I am done being scared. And I am way past done wasting my life worrying. It comes to me in a flash. "I have an idea about that."

"What?" he asks, looking at me sideways.

"Tell you later. I have to think about it some more."

And think about it, I do. All morning. I think it about it so much, I get in trouble in math class for daydreaming.

By lunchtime, I'm standing on a cliff about to fall. Tara and Sebastian catch up to me at the cashier and exchange a glance.

"Me or Tara?" he asks, and I swear, I fall a little in love with him for just asking, for somehow knowing that I'm not ready yet to lean on him this much, and for being cool with it.

"Tara."

He nods and says, "I'm eating with the team, but you call me, text me, whatever, when you're ready, okay?"

I nod. Fine by me. "Sebas."

He turns back, eyebrows raised in question.

"How do you feel about cutting class?"

His eyes dart around like I'd just suggested we go on a serial killing spree. "Jeez, Ash. Like right now?"

Sebastian's honorable. My mom says he's straitlaced, but he's not weird about it or anything. He tries hard to do what's right.

"No, not now. But maybe later?"

He steps closer and holds out his hand. I really love when he does that. He never just touches me. He offers first, and if I want to touch, I will. I grab his hand and squeeze it. "Is this about Vic?" he asks.

Nodding, I tell him the truth. "This is really pissing me off."

"But not scaring you."

It's not a question, and I nod because until Sebastian said it, I hadn't realized I'm more pissed off than I am scared.

"Yeah. I just can't believe he gets to go free so soon."

A muscle in Sebastian's jaw ticks and jerks his chin toward Tara. "Go eat. Reach out when you're ready, and I'm there."

"Just like that?"

"Yeah. Just like that."

I watch him walk away, trying to figure out how a boy like

SOMEONE I USED TO KNOW

him would want a messed-up, pissed-off, whacked-out girl like me.

"Ashley, what's up with you? You've been zoned out all morning." Tara grabs a bottle of water.

I slide my tray to the cashier station and hand over my student card. "I need to talk to you."

She gasps. "You and Sebastian didn't break—"

"No, no. We're okay." I say nothing more until we slide into an empty table. "It's Vic."

Her eyes go wide.

"He's out."

Tara's face scrunches up. "Oh, Ashley. I'm so sorry."

"You and me and everybody else." I crumple up the wrapper around my sandwich and crunch it into a ball.

"But he was guilty. I don't understand."

"He was guilty of *sexual assault*, not rape." I grit my teeth and try not to wish a long and painfully torturous death on my brother. *It's just a game,* he kept saying. Sighing loudly, I pull myself out of that thought spiral. It's over. It's done.

I have to live with it.

"There are two things I need to do, and I need your help."

"Anything." Tara nods, and for a minute, I can't talk because of the lump in my throat that formed the second she said that without even knowing what I need.

"Off Main Street, there's a place called Street Warriors. I want to sign up."

"Kickboxing?"

I nod. "That and any other form of fighting they're willing to teach me."

"Done. What's the second thing?"

Instead of answering her, I pull out my notebook and show her the doodle I was working on when I got in trouble for daydreaming this morning. "I want to plaster these all over town. The courts may think he's paid his debt to society, but society should know this face and this name."

Tara pulls out her phone, swipes, and taps. "Okay. I'm looking up slander and libel."

"It's neither," I informed her. "As long as it's true. The court already convicted him, so I'm safe."

Tara looks down and says nothing. I can tell she's not on board with this. "What's the problem?"

"This feels like revenge, Ash."

I shake my head. "No. It's justice, which is what I should have gotten in court, but I didn't because nobody could prove it was *real* rape. I mean, seriously, is there such a thing as fake rape?"

A few heads swivel my way, and I realize I'm talking too loud. I lean over my sandwich and tell Tara straight up, "It's not fair, Tara. None of this is fair. He says the sex was consensual, and just like that, the charges go from rape down to sexual assault, and he spends what? A stupid year in prison and gets to come out, go back to his nice life, like nothing happened? And what do *I* get? A brother who can't stand me, parents on the verge of divorce, and oh, yeah, let's not forget about the list of psychological problems I now have."

Tara gives my hand a squeeze. "They're not psychological problems, Ashley. They're scars from a trauma. Every day, you get stronger. Give yourself a break."

"Not strong enough. And not fast enough." I shut my eyes and drop my chin into my cupped hand. "I need to *do* something, Tara. I need to make people get how unfair this is."

Tara cracks the seal on her bottled water and swallows a sip. "Ash, the Raise the BAR rally was a huge success. You're gonna talk to other schools, right?"

"Yeah, and that's something, I guess. It's just not enough. I need to do more."

"Okay, but is hanging a bunch of posters around town really gonna make an impression?"

My eyes pop at Tara's words. *Make an impression.* "No," I say slowly. "They're not." And I bounce out of my seat. "You're right. Thanks, Tara." I grab my backpack and tray.

"Wait, where are you going? You didn't even eat!"

"No time. I need to take care of something. See you later."

Ten minutes later, I'm in the library, scouring through the search results displayed on a workstation monitor. I read about Emma Sulkowicz, the Columbia student who carried her mattress around campus after her university permitted her rapist to continue attending class. I read about Grace Brown's Project Unbreakable and studied the haunting images on her website. I visited Ithaca College student Yana Mazurkevich's website and viewed the graphic photo series called *It Happens*.

Thank God I hadn't eaten my lunch.

"Ashley, are you all right?" Mrs. Hudson, the librarian, puts a hand on my shoulder.

I nod and swipe my eyes with my fingertips. "Yeah. I'm okay."

Mrs. Hudson studies me and glances at what's on the screen. She pulls out the chair next to me and sits down, uninvited. "How can I help you?" She waves at the search results.

All I can do is shrug hopelessly. "I don't think anybody can."

"Why not?" she asks, removing her glasses.

"Because people can't stop judging. And because they can't understand, I mean, not completely...unless it's happened to them. They let him out, Mrs. Hudson, and I—" I bit back the sob building up in my throat. "I can't deal with this, can't accept Victor Patton will be walking the same streets, shopping in the same stores, breathing the same air as me. It's just not fair. Everybody says I should be happy because I got a conviction, that justice was served, but it's not true! I don't know if there's any such thing as justice." I slouch down in my hard wooden chair and cross my arms over my chest. The primal need to do something ripples just under my skin, driving me mad with my inability to scratch it.

"I understand," she says. "*Completely,*" she adds a second later.

My eyes snap to hers, and she meets my gaze, unflinching.

The tears spill, and I can't stop them now because I get it. "Oh, no. I'm so sorry."

She nods and covers my hand with hers. "I wasn't much older than you are now. It happened when I was in college. And no one believed me. They let him remain in school. I had to see him every day or transfer out, which is what I ended up doing. I gave up a scholarship, much to my father's ire."

"You still talk to him? Your father?"

She laughs at that. "I didn't for many years, but we finally came to a mutual understanding."

Whoa. My mind instantly thinks of Derek. Will we ever reach that point?

"Ashley, I want to say something to you," she begins.

I sit up straight and angle to face her.

"The work you did on your video…on Raise the BAR. It—" She shakes her head. "It is absolutely astounding to me. I wish I'd known you back when I was…I wish I'd had someone like you."

I blink. "Like me?"

Smiling, she rubs absently at the open collar of her blouse. "You are so courageous. My parents wouldn't let me talk about it, wouldn't let me *think* about it, but you? You won't let anyone forget it, and I envy you."

Envy me? What alternative reality did I fall into?

She rubs her blouse again, and I see it. Just under her collarbone, there's a scar. She catches me staring and squirms.

"Sorry, I didn't mean to stare."

She waves away the apology, opens the collar a bit more, and shows me the scar. "I was raped at knifepoint. And still, my father blamed me. Said I shouldn't have been walking alone, shouldn't have gone to that school. You know the drill." Mrs. Hudson's pretty dark eyes dim.

I do. Too well.

"Anyway. I saw you here, and you looked upset. I just wanted you to know you can talk to me anytime. Talking helps, more than you probably know right now. Talking saved me, Ashley. I wish I could have taught my dad that."

Her words reach right into my heart and squeeze. Teaching a lot of people would be awesome. I'd start with all of the football players from two years ago.

And I'd end with Derek.

......

My last class of the day is art, an elective I chose because I thought we wouldn't have a ton of work to do. Turns out, I was wrong, so now I sort of hate art.

Sometimes it's fun, like when we learned to create blackout poetry to reveal new meanings in the ways words are arranged on the page. But most of the time, art annoys me. I can't draw or paint or sculpt or even take decent photographs, the smells of art materials like paint, glue, or paper make my nose wrinkle, and the dozens of finished projects on display at any given time mock my lack of artistic ability. Like the cultural masks we made before Halloween. A bunch of them line the shelves on the back wall, judging me with their empty eyes.

Today, we're supposed to make collages. That's not terrible, I suppose. Collages require cutting and pasting skills, talents I actually have. I head to my seat, avoiding all the drops of paint and smears of glue that always seem to mark the floor in this room. Mr. Anton, our art teacher, starts up the projector and aims a remote at the laptop connected to it.

"Okay, let's examine some examples of pop culture's influence on graphic and digital art." He begins scrolling through some magazine ads. "What jumps out at you?"

A murmur rises up across our class. Laughs and gasps quickly change to full-out whistles, hoots, and cheers.

"Okay, keep it professional. Obviously, you've noticed these images are intentionally trying to be provocative. Why?"

"Because sex sells!" a guy shouts from the back of the room where the shelves of masks watch with total disdain.

"Okay. Sex sells. Why?" Mr. Anton prompts. When no one replies, he advances his slide show. "That's what we're going to investigate today. Each table will spend the next twenty minutes researching provocative advertising. I've got piles of magazines for you to examine. Go through them and tear out the ads that speak to you. We're looking for the psychology here, so if you have tablets or phones, feel free to google all you want, but find me more than what's on Wikipedia."

Ooh. That's fun. Usually, we can't even take out our phones during school.

There are four of us at my table. Me plus Ken, Craig, and Peter. Ken hasn't talked to me since freshman year. His brother is the same age as Derek, so when football got canceled, his family took it personally and naturally blamed me instead of Vic. I don't know Craig at all. This is the only class I've ever had with him. Peter's okay. I've known him almost since kindergarten. He lives down the street from us, but we're not tight or anything.

Mr. Anton drops a stack of publications on our table, and the boys lunge for them. Past issues of *Seventeen, Vogue, Cosmopolitan,* a Bloomingdale's catalog that's several years old, *Sports Illustrated, Car and Driver.* I grab the catalog and start flipping through it while the boys huddle around the *Sports Illustrated* and *Car and Driver* issues and ignore me.

That's okay. I'm used to it.

While I turn pages, bits and pieces of the conversations taking place around me drift into my ears.

"Totally do her. She's so hot."

"What car? I only see the girl in the bikini."

"Great tits."

"Legs."

"Ass."

"Mouth."

It happens slowly, the dread pooling in my belly. Conversation fades to the background. The words become white noise, leaving behind the grunts, sounds of appreciation, and hums of sexual interest that start to morph and blend into memories that lap at the dams and levees I keep erecting.

Ashley, you're so hot. You have the best tits in the entire freshman class. I love to touch them. You like it, don't you? You like it when I touch you.

Oh God. I can smell the sour beer on his breath and the locker room soap on his skin. I scan the room, telling myself I'm wrong, that he's not here and that I'm safe, but it's no good.

"Whoa!" Craig shouts, tearing a page from his magazine. "Look at this one!"

The sound feels like sandpaper against my eardrums, and I clap my hands to my ears, shaking myself out of the past, blinking rapidly, stunned to discover my chest actually hurts from the memory of Vic's hands on me. Ken, Peter, and Craig have a pile of sheets torn from their magazines…images of girls in bikinis, miniskirts, close-ups of pouty lips or curvy butts, each with captions suggesting all manner of innuendo and insult. The tightness in my chest that's become so familiar spikes abruptly, making me gasp. I rub at it, but I can't reach it because it's too deep. It's changed me into something that's more pain than person. I force my attention back to my catalog and stop suddenly at a holiday ad that says, *"Hey! Why not spike your best friend's eggnog?"*

I stare hard at the image. The girl on the left blurs, but the guy on the right snaps into sharp relief, his eyes shifting to meet mine, lips curling into the same lazy smile that Vic wore when he… when he…oh God. The lump that lives in my throat pulses in time with my heart rate and all the bad stuff…the memories, the pain, the betrayal, the shame—it all swirls together like sewage, swelling and rising and overflowing every one of the walls I put up. It sweeps away everything that used to be me until it's all that's left. The classroom spins at the edges. My limbs are numb, dead. I can't move. I can't breathe. I'm drowning.

No.

No, damn it. *No!*

I gasp and watch the guys shoot me the *you-are-so-weird* eyeball. Whatever. They can stare all they want because right now I'm in control.

I am in control. I am in control.

I'm not going to let paging through magazines and catalogs flip me out. They're a bunch of stupid, harmless photos. They shouldn't be able to hurt me.

But they *do*. In fact, they don't simply hurt me. They freaking *torture* me, hammering home a point made over and over again since the first day Vic assaulted me, the same point Derek made in his court testimony.

It's just a game. It's just an advertisement. It's just a joke. It's just guy talk. It's just boys being boys.

Just.

Just!

JUST!

Oh my God, the excuses never stop.

The idea that half formed during lunch abruptly snaps into focus, and I know exactly how to make a statement as powerful as the ones I studied during lunch in the library. The more I think about it, the easier it is to breathe.

I've finally found my weapon for fighting back.

20

DEREK

NOW

LONG ISLAND, NEW YORK

The week before Thanksgiving, I wake up to rain.

Great. No wonder I have a pounding headache. At least there are no classes because of the holiday break.

But there *is* practice for the Rock Bowl tomorrow, and damn, I hate practicing in mud.

I drag my ass out of bed, unsurprised to find Julian's bed empty. He pretty much only uses this room as a closet to hold his clothes.

What sucks is that *my* bed is empty.

I apologized for ditching Brittany at the rally. Of course, I apologized. I was a dick for taking off. She *said* she forgave me. But...here we are. Empty bed. Cold shoulder. I figured she'd have gotten over it by now, but no such luck, and I've got one more thing to fix without any clues.

Just how in the hell do you fix shit after apologizing doesn't work?

The question makes my head pound as I shuffle into the bathroom across the hall.

"Morning, Derek," Tommy Heath says with a jerk of his chin that's all slathered with shaving cream, which is weird because I'm pretty sure Tommy Heath hasn't hit puberty yet. He's got on ancient '80s music on his phone, propped up inside a plastic shower tote. Don Henley's "The End of the Innocence."

I take care of business and head for a shower stall. The water's hot—thank you, God. It helps wake me up and melts some of the tension from my muscles. But the headache just won't quit, and the lyrics to this song are drilling through my tortured heart. I stay in the shower until Tommy disappears, but it doesn't help.

The song remains behind.

My reflection in the mirror looks like some stranger. Pasty skin, red-rimmed eyes, stubble on my face… I look hungover, but I haven't had a drink. I swallow a few Tylenol capsules from the bottle at the bottom of my toiletry case and spend two seconds deciding whether I should shave or not.

I go with *not*.

Just as I stick a toothbrush in my mouth, my phone rings. I glance at the screen and curse.

"Yeah."

"Yeah, yeah, good morning to you, too," Justin snaps. He's been calling or texting me a few times a day for weeks, and I'm tired of him. "Look. We have problems."

Of course we do because what else can we possibly squish inside my pounding head? "What," I say, but with a little less attitude.

"Mom and Dad are in their room having a really loud fight. Again. So I'm giving you a heads-up…you'll hear from Dad any minute."

"About?"

"Mom."

My stomach drops a few feet. "Is she okay?"

"No. She's pissed off. She expects everybody home for Thanksgiving next week."

"I thought you were home already."

He sighs long and loud on his end of the phone. "Been home for weeks, Derek. Now it's your turn. Mom told Dad to buy you a plane ticket. She wants you home *now*."

"I'm not going home."

"Yeah. You are. I just listened to them fight for an hour. I figure you have about two minutes before he calls you."

My phone beeps. Shit. "Less than that. Gotta go."

"Good luck."

I switch over to the second call, and sure enough, it's Dad.

"Derek."

"Hey, Dad."

"I'm buying you a ticket—"

"Don't. I'm not coming home."

"I already did. And you *are*."

"Cancel it."

"Derek, this isn't about Ashley. It's about your mother. She wants you home. She wants all of her children home."

I flinch at the pang of guilt that's now so familiar and then wonder why I'm still flinching. That pang of guilt is almost normal. "Dad, I *can't*."

"Okay, how long are you gonna run away from what you did?"

I double over and fall to the cold, gross tile and stay there. I don't care if I die of flesh-eating staph. "I'm not...I swear I'm not." The words are flat, lifeless.

"You are, and I'm sick of it. I supported you on this in the beginning! Do you remember that? You were entitled to your own life. I held your mom back when she wanted to ground you for being mean to your sister. I let you play ball, but this—no. It's gone way too far now, Derek. Your sister pretends you don't exist, your brother thinks he's some kind of U.N. peacekeeper living in a goddamn demilitarized zone, and your mother blames *me* for this whole mess. I'm minutes away from a total breakdown, and I've had it. Do you hear me? Take some responsibility for your part in the entire shit show. If you are not on that plane on Wednesday, I will take the next flight out to retrieve you lock, stock, and barrel, and that means you can kiss college and football goodbye. Are you hearing me?"

"Yeah." My voice is small.

"Good."

He hangs up, and I'm still on the cold, germ-covered floor in a towel. I shuffle on my knees into a stall just as my stomach turns itself inside out and upside down. Julian wanders in some time later—how long is anybody's guess.

"Aw, hell, Derek. You play, you pay. Didn't anybody teach you that?"

I can't muster up the strength to tell him I'm not hungover.

He gets an arm under me, half carries, half drags me back to our room, and dumps me back in bed. "Don't move." He disappears for a minute and returns, carrying my toiletry bag and my phone. "What's your code?"

I mumble the numbers, and a few seconds later, he's got Brittany on the phone.

"No, it's Julian. He's in bad shape. Can you get over here? I don't know. Sick, I think. Okay."

I stare out the window into the sky. It's gray and bleak. When we were little, we used to go outside and play in the puddles. Ashley had a pink-polka dot umbrella. Justin and I were too cool for umbrellas. We just wore our rain slickers with the hoods up and bright yellow boots. It was a game to see who could make the biggest splash.

I always won.

I'd get Justin soaked and have Ashley in tears.

Who knew that would be so prophetic? A soul-deep sob claws its way out of me. I'm not strong enough to hide it. Julian curses and sits on the bed next to me, hauling me into his arms like I'm a toddler. I'm gone, man, too far gone to give a shit how weird this is, how inappropriate or politically incorrect or whatever-the-hell term you got. All I know is I can't stop, can't fucking stop, and it feels like it's gonna kill me.

"Derek, talk to me, man. What the hell's wrong?"

"Me, Julian. Me. I'm wrong. I'm the monster." I try to tell him, clutching his shirt like it's all that's saving me from finishing the plummet into hell, but it comes out all garbled and incoherent.

"I got ya, pal. Whatever it is, we'll fix it, okay?"

I shake my head. He doesn't get it. Nobody gets it. I *can't* fix this. There's nothing anybody can do to ever fix this, and dammit, goddammit, the weight of that is so fucking heavy, I can't breathe anymore.

I can't breathe.

The air won't move in my lungs. It's stuck behind the weight of my guilt. The edges of my vision go fuzzy, and my heart starts to jackhammer its way through my sternum. I cling tighter to Julian's shirt, but it's no good. It doesn't help. I can't breathe. Jesus, I'm dying, I'm gonna die and part of me stops struggling, stops holding on so tight, because death beats the hell out of trying to carry around all the guilt and pain and shame.

I can't hear Julian's words anymore. I turn my head to the side and give up. The last thing I see is Brittany's anxious face when the world goes dark.

......

The most god-awful odor assaults my nose, and I jerk back to consciousness, only to find my room is full of strangers.

Brittany and Julian are sitting on his bed. She's pale, and he looks worried.

Standing over me are three people—all in uniform. One's

campus security—I recognize him from the Aaron incident. The others? No idea.

"Derek? Hi. I'm Mary Ann. I'm a paramedic. Can you tell me where you are?"

I struggle to sit up and focus on the woman waving an ammonia stick under my nose, but my damn head is still pounding. "Um. My room. My dorm room."

"Good. How about what day it is?" She puts a cold damp towel on my head, and I want to kiss her, it feels so good.

Day. I know this. "Friday."

"Excellent. Did you take anything? Drink anything?"

I shake my head, and fuck, that hurts. "Tylenol when I woke up. Vicious headache."

Mary Ann shines a light in my eyes, and I want to hurl the damn thing into Mount Doom next to the One Ring.

"How does your head feel now?"

"Same."

"I'm told you play football. Any injuries?"

"No."

"No falls, no accidents, no drug or alcohol use?"

"No. None."

She moves the towel to my neck. "Okay. That leaves one more question. Your girlfriend here tells me your family suffered a trauma. Your sister was raped, correct?"

I can't speak. My eyes snap to Britt's, but she won't look at me.

"She also tells me you got upset and took off during the Take Back the Night rally."

I still can't speak.

"Your roommate tells me you were gasping for air, unable to breathe. That ever happened to you before?"

I shake my head as easily and slowly as I can.

"Okay, Derek. I'm thinking you had yourself an anxiety attack."

An anxiety attack. Somewhere inside my brain, I swear I hear Ashley laugh.

"If you head over to the infirmary, we can get you some antianxiety medication, but honestly, there's only one thing that helps this."

I wait, hoping whatever it is won't hurt.

"You need to face it head-on. No holds barred."

So much for hope. I'll just skip off to battle the one person on earth who actually hates me more than I hate myself.

After ten more minutes of instructions and warnings, everybody finally leaves.

Except Brittany. She still sits on Julian's bed, studying me carefully.

"Take off, Britt. I'm fine."

Her face falls, and it hits me again, that stab of guilt.

"Derek, talk to me, please," she says so softly I could hardly hear her. "I know you're in pain."

Pain? I wish. "I'm not in pain. I'm in *disgust*—if that's even a thing. How the fuck can you stand me?"

"You didn't—"

"I *did*, Brittany!" I shout at her and then clutch my pounding head. "I am the reason a fucking rapist is back on the streets. I am the reason my sister can't seem to make it a day without having the same kind of *anxiety attack* that just about killed me, and I'm a hell of a lot stronger than she is." At least, I used to be.

Suddenly, she jumps off Julian's bed, blue eyes snapping. "I am so sick of this." Flinging both hands up, she shouts, "I keep telling you you're not a monster. Why can't you believe it?"

I stare at her, because hello? Isn't it obvious? "Britt, you were at that rally. You heard all those sexist, misogynistic things women like you have to put up with from guys like me." I pound my chest. "I participated in a sexist scavenger hunt with not just enthusiasm but actual excitement. I never saw rape even when it was right in front of me. I *am* all those sexist, misogynistic things! Every one of them, and I can't. Fucking. Stand it."

"Fine." She takes a step closer and leans over to get right into my face. "You know what? Maybe you are the kind of guy who thinks he should be allowed to have whatever fun he wants, no matter who gets hurt." She shakes her head and shrugs. "Now what? I admitted it. You're the bad guy, Derek. The monster. What are you gonna do about it?"

I don't understand. I don't get what she's so pissed off about. I study her, unable to say what she wants me to say.

She makes a sound of disgust.

"Anybody can see all this guilt is eating you up alive—except you, of course." She flicks a hand at me and turns away. "I was patient. I gave you some space, I tried to be here for you, be supportive, but I've done all I can. Now it's your turn." She turns back to face me, jabbing a finger in the air between us. "You heard that paramedic, and I *know* you heard every single word people said at the rally. You've had *years* to figure this out, Derek. Your family is disintegrating, and I am tired of waiting for you to do what you *know* you have to do! You think you're some kind of monster, fine! Now change." She finally stops yelling and stands there, staring at me. When I don't say anything, she rolls her eyes. "You still haven't heard anything I said, have you?"

"Yeah. I heard you. You want me to change."

"Oh my God." She stalks to the door, whips it open, and shoots one more bullet at me. "Your dad bought you a ticket on my flight so we could travel *together*. You better be there, Derek."

As the door slams behind her, I sink deeper into my pillow and squeeze my eyes shut. I don't know what to do.

Christ, I don't know what to do.

21

ASHLEY

I sometimes wonder what he'll do if he sees me. Would he apologize? Would he run the other way? I don't think he would do either of those things. He doesn't see me as a person. When it happened, I was just a way to collect points. After it happened, I was just the girl trying to ruin his life. He doesn't see himself as having any fault or blame or part in this entire ordeal.

—**Ashley E. Lawrence, victim impact statement**

NOW

BELLFORD, OHIO

There's been no sign of Victor, even though we all know he's out of prison. Tara and I have had several classes so far at Street Warriors. It's called "Real-World Self-Defense." There's no bowing and thanking each other or any Zen crap.

This is kill-or-be-killed class.

On our first day, I took a six-foot-tall attacker wearing enough protective gear to turn him into a blob to the ground, and Tara, who stands barely five feet tall, managed to flip him over her shoulder. The instructor is a retired army sergeant who used to teach cadets hand-to-hand combat.

Now he teaches soccer moms and crime victims how to feel safe.

So far, we've learned some basic hold breaks and grappling. I can't wait until we get to pressure points and palm strikes. I've been reading ahead and looking at lots of YouTube videos. Our instructor says the problem with videos is that they don't give you the opportunity to correct bad form, so that's why we spend a good portion of the class sparring, which is really helpful. It gets your body thinking so your brain doesn't have to do all the work. The moves become smooth. Automatic. Someone throws a fist, and my arm comes up in the perfect way to block or deflect it. And the best part? No anxiety episodes. I feel capable. Less afraid. Strong.

So when Sebastian suggests we try that movie date we never got to take, I immediately agree. I am seriously tired of living like a prisoner.

I spend some time dressing up. I put a little lip gloss on, smooth my hair, and find something to wear. Jeans are safe. Boots. I finally decide on a sweater I've never worn. It's blue and kind of sparkly, and when Sebastian's mouth drops open, I figure I must look okay.

"Ready?"

He offers me his hand, and we climb into his mom's car. The theater isn't too far, but the movie doesn't start for a while. "How about some hot chocolate?" he asks.

I grin. He knows I never say no to that. We head to the diner, which is one block south of the theater, holding hands. I really like holding Sebastian's hand. It's just so…normal. We slide into a booth, order, and sit, awkwardly staring and smiling at each other.

"You look nice, Ashley. Really nice."

My smile turns a little less lame. "Thanks, Sebas. Hey, you look nice, too."

He's wearing shoes—actual shoes instead of tennis shoes—with black pants and a button-down shirt. His hair is combed neatly and isn't doing its usual Nike swoosh thing. I miss it, but he looks amazing and smells great, like snuggle-up-close great.

"Hey, thanks for all that Photoshop help."

"No problem." He shrugs. "It's a tough program to learn, but there are tons of tips online that'll show you how to do exactly what you want to do. What's this?" He angles his head to see my phone.

"A Pinterest board I made."

He takes the phone and scrolls down. "This…this is really good stuff." He scrolls through some of my efforts to learn Photoshop. I've been playing around with ads and headlines that offend me, changing them into more honest representations. The first one I changed? Our local newspaper's headline announcing Vic's release.

The original headline reads "Bengals' Running Back Comes Home." The article itself is even more offensive. *Bengals star running back, Victor Patton, 19, was released from prison after serving just thirteen months of a two-year sentence for the sexual assault of a classmate during a scavenger hunt gone awry. Despite the good behavior that resulted in his early release, Victor Patton's name must remain on the sex offense registry for at least eight more years.*

Gone awry. Are they freaking kidding me? The only reason that hunt went *awry* is because boys like Victor perverted it.

I changed the headline to "Victor Patton, Convicted Sex Offender, Released Early." And then I changed the body of the article to explain what really happened. *Convicted sex offender Victor Patton, 19, was released early from prison today. Sentenced to two years for the sexual assault of a classmate, Patton was released after serving only thirteen months of his sentence for good behavior. Nevertheless, his name will remain on the sex offense registry for ten years, as ordered during his trial.*

Then I printed out a bunch of them and started hanging them up and down Blaine and on the school's bulletin boards.

Those have already been taken down.

"Awesome, actually." He looks at me, something that looks a lot like amazement in his eyes. I squirm under the scrutiny.

"What? Do I have something on my face?"

"No. Your face is fine." He smiles.

"What then?"

Lifting a shoulder, he sits back in the booth. "Nothing, it's just…you. You're different."

Great, just what all the girls long to hear. "How am I different?" I ask as the server slides two mugs of hot chocolate in front of us, each with a tower of whipped cream floating on top.

"You're letting your hair grow. You're wearing makeup. And you're here with me. Alone."

I look down and stir my hot chocolate. "Yeah. I got dressed and went outside." I swirl a finger in the air. "Yay, me. I'm a real superhero."

He rocks his head from side to side. "Um, well…you kind of are, you know. First, coming up with that whole Raise the BAR idea? Recording that video? And these headlines? You're like…" He trails off, spreading his hands apart while he searches for the right word. "You're unstoppable."

And then guilt compels me to come clean. "Sebastian, I'm not any of those things. Not unstoppable, not a fighter." I put my cup down and reveal the ugly truth. "I'm scared like literally all the time."

"Yeah, maybe. But you do it all anyway, Ashley. See? Unstoppable." He stands up and pecks me on the cheek. "I'll be right back."

As he heads to the restroom, I think about everything he said. Unstoppable. Shaking my head, I sip my cocoa and look out the window. Blaine Boulevard is busy tonight. There's some traffic and lots of pedestrians.

"Get you anything else, honey?" The server, a pretty woman with her dark hair scraped back in a bun, smiles down at me.

"Um, no. We're fine. Thanks."

Sebastian returns as she slips the check onto our table.

"Thanks." He smiles at the server and slides back into the booth.

I lean over the table and squeeze his hand. "You're pretty awesome. Any other guy would have shrugged me off and gone back to video games by now, but not you. I really love that, Sebastian."

The pink tinge on his neck turns to red and climbs all the way up to his hairline. "It's no big."

"It shouldn't be, but it is. It's a *huge* deal. I hate that it's even a deal at all, but it is. Justin just kind of pats me on the head like it's adorable that I've found a way to cope, and don't even get me started on Derek. I didn't even have to ask you. You just… stepped up. Do you have any idea how *special* that is?" *And how special you are?* I wish I had the guts to say that last part out loud.

He rolls his eyes. "Yeah, I guess. And it kind of pisses me off."

I blink. "Why?"

"Come on, Ashley," Sebastian says, giving me side-eye. "You have to have noticed I'm not exactly popular, you know?"

Oh. My heart contracts painfully. "Do you want that? To be popular?"

He looks out the window for a few seconds and shakes his head. "Nah, not really. But I wish people would just back off, you know?"

So people are hassling him…because of me? Great. I don't say anything for a long time. Neither does he. Another piece of my heart cracks, so I suck in a deep breath and plunge in. "Go home, Sebastian. I'll call my mom to come get me."

His face snaps up at this, eyes stuck on mine, confused and worried. "What? Why?"

"We don't have to do this."

Now his eyes sizzle with annoyance. "Okay, I'm forced to repeat myself. What?"

Sighing dramatically, I struggle to be patient. "It's okay. You're off the hook. We break up, and they'll stop hassling you. It's not like we're in love or anything." There's this moment, a split second, when I swear his eyes flash with the truth, and it hits me hard enough to knock the breath out of me. But it's gone before I can be sure I really saw it. In its place is barely restrained fury.

It takes him a minute, a full minute, to speak, and when he does, his voice is tight and icy enough to send shivers down my back.

"First, I don't want to break up with you. And second, it's *not* okay. It's so far from okay, I don't even know what to say. And third, did I mention I don't want to break up with you?"

I don't reply because I figure it's rhetorical, but when he gives me the hand gesture that says *Say something!*, I realize he really does expect an answer. "I don't want to break up, either." That's pure truth.

But instead of relaxing or laughing it off, he gets madder. "Then what the hell did you bring it up for?" His voice isn't icy anymore. Now it's so hot, I swear I smell sulfur.

Helpless to give him anything but the truth, I blurt it all out. "Because I don't want you punished for being with me. I can't stand seeing you suffer, Sebastian. I've been through it all already.

I know what people say about me. I know what they think, and I'm numb to it now. But I don't want you... I can't stand it if you're hurt—"

"This hurt, Ashley," he cuts in, waving a hand between us. "This, right here, cut like razors."

Oh, hell. "I'm...I'm sorry. I said that to make things easier—"

He throws up one hand. "I get that. But I don't want things easier. I don't want them different. I don't want you gone. You're not some kind of duty. I like *you*. I like hanging out with you. I like being with you. I like *you*," he repeats. "A lot." He glares at me across the table and suddenly curses. "God, Ashley. Don't you get it?" There's that look in his eyes again. The one that takes my breath away.

Holy crap.

"Um. Good. I like you, too. A lot."

After a minute, his anger fades. I like watching his face as his color evens out and his breathing slows. Finally, he smiles at me. "We should go. Movie's starting in fifteen."

I get up and start zipping my jacket, while Sebastian heads to the cashier to pay our bill. I watch somebody walk by, hands stuffed in his pockets, and chin tucked into his jacket for warmth and think, *Him.* I press my face to the window and look again, but it's okay. It's not Vic.

It's not.

"Ashley? You okay? What's wrong?"

I check the window one more time and shake off the thought. "Nothing. Just thought I saw something."

Sebastian offers me his hand, and we leave the diner, the cold dark night somehow feeling not as cold or as dark as long as he's next to me.

......

Inside the theater, we buy tickets and some treats and settle back just in time for the previews. It's cold inside the theater, so I leave my jacket on and sit back. Sebastian leans over and whispers in my ear, "Any time you feel uncomfortable, unsafe, or icky, say the word, and we're outta here."

My lips twitch. "Icky?"

His eyes roll in the low light, looking almost spooky. "You know what I mean." He holds out his hand, so I slip mine inside it and turn my gaze to the screen, feeling warm and safe.

Yeah. Safe.

We munch popcorn, sip from water bottles, and share M&M's while Matt Damon evades some bad guys in one preview, and Chris Pratt flexes in another. I shiver once when the lights go down, but Sebastian's hand tightens on mine. I raise our hands to my lips and kiss the back of his, and I'm rewarded with a sweet smile that glows under the light of the screen.

The movie is good...the latest superhero adventure. There's plenty of action, drama, and impossible decisions to satisfy me. When the house lights come up, Sebastian stands up and suddenly scoops up all our trash, throws an arm around me, and practically shoves me out of our row. "Come on. Let's go."

"Sebas, chill out."

"No. Let's go. Right now."

I turn to study him. His jaw is clenched, and his eyes are hard.

"You wanna tell me why you're so pissed off at me?"

His eyes snap to mine. "I'm not pissed at you. I want us to leave *now*." He pushes me again.

Fine!

I have to jog to keep up with him. He leads me down the stairs that run the sides of the theater, out into the lobby, and back outside to the street. He's still clutching our trash in his other hand, and now we're apparently supposed to jog down the block to where he parked the car.

I don't think so. I dig in my heels and pull back from him. He stops short and whips around, eyes scanning the entire street before landing back on me.

That sets off alarms. My heart starts to pound, and I feel the adrenaline surge. I spin and search for whatever's got him so worked up, but I know.

I already know.

When my gaze snaps to the figure standing by the theater's entrance, the bottom falls out of what's left of my world because it's Victor Patton staring back at me.

22

DEREK

NOW

LONG ISLAND, NEW YORK

I stuff another pair of socks into my bag, zip it shut, and collapse onto my bed with a sigh.

In a rare appearance, Julian lifts his eyes from his laptop and grins at me while he lounges on his bed. "Well, someone's sure happy to be heading home."

"Delirious." Inspiration strikes. "How about you? You heading home? You could join us, you know. If you don't have plans."

"Not a chance in hell, Lawrence." He types for a few seconds, then looks back at me. "Did you decide what you're gonna speak about at that GAR rally?"

Wincing, I shake my head. "Nope. I talked to Ted about it at our last meeting, and he was pretty damn useless."

"Want my advice?"

I nod eagerly. "God, yes."

Julian slides the laptop to the bed and sits up. "Just be you."

"Oh, gee, that's helpful," I say, hoping the sarcasm drips all over his side of the room.

"I'm serious, man. You have lots of stuff you can share, and not all of it's about your sister."

Frowning, I try to think of even one idea, but come up empty.

"Take Tasha, for example."

"Who's Tasha?"

"Tasha's that fine-looking cheerleader who said no to me so she could hang with Brian Kelly."

I shake my head, still blank.

"She's the girl your homie Aaron Dreschler threatened before you shut that shit down."

I snap up straight. "You know her?"

"Do now. Didn't then. She's cool, man. Really sweet. Every time I think about the shit you heard that punk-ass say…" He trails off and shudders. "I say you start there."

Yeah, that's really good. I could show the stats we were given at our first GAR meeting from there. "Julian, you are a genius."

"That's what I'm saying." He flashes another grin.

I grab my laptop and start making some notes.

23

ASHLEY

I also wonder what I'll do if I see him again. Run, freeze where I stand,
lose control of my bladder? I've done all of these things. One of the
worst parts about what Victor Patton did to me is I never know how
I'll react from one day to the next. Little things, things that shouldn't
be a big deal, suddenly are and trigger in me violent reactions that
frighten my family and wreck me. I don't belong to me anymore.

—**Ashley E. Lawrence, victim impact statement**

NOW

BELLFORD, OHIO

My mouth falls open, and I'm paralyzed. All I can do is stand
there, inert, the self-defense classes obliterated from my memory.

He raped me.

And he's standing in front of me.

He raped me.

I did everything I was supposed to do. The rape kit. The trial.

And they let him out of prison, and now, he's at the same place, at the same time as me. Oh my God. Blood roars in my ears, and my heart gallops so hard, every beat feels like a hammer strike. Dimly, I'm just barely aware that Sebastian is still next to me, screaming at me. I can't hear. I can't think. I can't breathe, can't move, can't remember what to do, can't breathe, can't breathe, can't breathe.

"Ashley!"

He's suddenly right in front of me, fingers digging into my shoulders, shaking me. "Look at me. Only at me."

Blinking, I gasp in a deep breath that burns all the way down to my lungs. Bright lights zigzag on the edges of my vision. I recognize the anxiety attack signs, and something inside me snaps.

Not this time.

I beat it back, forcing my lungs not to gulp in air like it's water in a desert and instead do the inhale, hold, exhale, hold, repeat pattern. The bright lights dim, and when I can see clearly again, I open my mouth to tell Sebastian I'm okay, but the most irrational and completely ridiculous urge to giggle bashes me. It's absurd. The whole concept of safety, I mean. I thought I was *safe*, sitting in a dark movie theater with my football-playing boyfriend and a few self-defense classes under my belt, only it turns out that *the guy who raped me* is in the same building, so now I have to convince my boyfriend that I'm okay, except now I know that *safe* is an even bigger lie than *justice*.

And then a new thought shoves that one aside, and instead of wanting to giggle, I want to cry. Sebastian...he'd been acting strange since the movie ended. He...oh God.

He *knew*.

I take a giant step back.

His lips tighten into a line, and he holds up both hands. "Ashley—"

"You knew?" I finally manage to squeak out. "You knew he was here?"

Sebastian shakes his head. "Not until the lights came up at the end."

"Why didn't you tell me?"

He keeps shaking his head. Finally, he says, "God, Ashley. I didn't know what it would do to you—seeing him. I was afraid you'd freeze up, have an anxiety attack, burst into tears, or maybe attack him. I didn't know! I didn't want you to have to go through any of that." Sebastian puts his arm around my shoulder, and as we walk to the car, he keeps looking over his own shoulder. "I wasn't sure how I'd react, either."

I stop walking. "You?"

He urges me to keep moving. "Yeah. I seriously think I could... you know...kill him."

I don't know how to respond to this. Neither of us says nothing until we're in the car. Sebastian hits the door locks, starts the car, and takes the first turn a bit too fast, making the tires squeal. We're silent all the way back to my house, which suits me just fine, because I feel raw, like an overloaded circuit about to pop.

"I'm sorry, Ash. I'm so sorry. I thought we'd be fine. I never expected him...*shit*." He slams a hand on the steering wheel, and I jolt. "I'm sorry. I didn't mean to scare you." He says, frustration clear in his voice.

He *did* scare me. But so did seeing Vic tonight.

And neither of those are the reason I'm upset right now.

It's all those things Sebastian said at the diner, about being unstoppable. What would he say, what would he think if he knew how everything inside me just shut down—shut *off* when I saw Vic? All I want to do is go home, lock the doors, and hide under my covers for the rest of my life. I hate that. I hate that after all this—after Raise the BAR, after the trial, and after everything else that's happened, I'm no better than the first day after it happened.

How the hell am I supposed to do this for the rest of my life?

"Ash, you're scaring me now. Talk to me, please."

I can't. I can't even lie this time. So I say nothing.

24

DEREK

NOW

LONG ISLAND, NEW YORK

I'm standing outside of Brittany's dorm building on Wednesday morning, bags on the ground at my feet, hands shoved into my pockets. I'm cold all over. It's the kind of cold that only comes from dread. I dread seeing Britt, dread going home, dread seeing my parents, and I have no words that come close to describing how much I dread seeing my sister.

"You look like hell."

I lift my eyes and find Britt standing in front of me. I never heard her approach. Her words sting. She looks amazing. She always does. For a tiny fraction of a second, I thaw because she's with me.

And then I remember, I fucked that up, too.

I swing my bags to my shoulders and then grab hers. She gives me a look, but I can't tell if it's gratitude or annoyance. We walk to the train station. It takes about twenty minutes. By the time we get there, I'm sweating, but I'm still cold.

"I'm glad you decided to come with," she says, and I can't stop the surprised look I give her. "What? You think I'm lying?"

"I thought you pretty much hated me," I say, and my voice sounds weird. Like a car that hasn't been driven in weeks, all rusty and slow.

She sighs and grabs my hands in hers. "Your hands are freezing."

She rubs my hands between hers. It actually kind of hurts, but I let her do it because it feels so good to have her touch me again. Suddenly, I can't take it anymore. I grab her and wrap my arms around her, holding her tight and feeling way too close to tears.

"I'm so glad you're here. I am really scared to go home," I admit.

"Derek, you need to talk to her," Brittany says. "I know you've tried, but you have to try harder. You have to convince her to listen this time. This is slowly killing you."

I keep my face pressed against her hair. "Tell me something I don't know."

"It'll be okay."

Maybe.

I've been doing a ton of thinking and finally came up with a plan. But I don't share it with Britt yet. She'd only try to talk me out of it.

The train arrives, and we climb on board. It takes us over an hour to get to Jamaica Station, where we transfer to the AirTrain to JFK Airport.

It's the fastest hour of my life. Britt says little on the train and even less while we endure the security check-in at the airport. The line is ridiculous, and I take a deep breath and prepare to stand here for the rest of my natural life, but like the train ride, it moves faster than I want it to.

We don't talk much at the gate. We don't talk much on the flight. I spend most of the trip making more notes for that GAR talk I volunteered for—the one at Ohio State. If Brittany's reading anything on my screen, she's not mentioning it, and soon, I kind of forget she's even there because I'm so into this. I've got a story now, a really great story.

I hope it works. I hope I can help somebody before their family turns into mine.

FOUR YEARS AGO
BELLFORD, OHIO

Dad orders Justin and me to help get the house all set up for Thanksgiving dinner, so we haul out the expanders for the dining room table.

"Where's the third one?" Ashley demands.

"Downstairs," I tell her, placing the one I carried on my shoulder into the open gap in the table. Justin has a second one. With Dad's help, we get the table secure.

"Mom, what about the third expander?" Ashley whines, but Mom just waves her hand.

"I don't think we need it. This is fine."

"But, Mom, you and Granny will squash me," she whines some more, and I roll my eyes. This is all Ashley does. Whine about stuff instead of just doing it herself. She could go fetch the third expander.

That afternoon, the rest of our family arrives.

"Diane, honey, the table looks beautiful!" Granny gushes while Dad takes her coat and Pop gives Mom a hug. The doorbell rings again, and this time, it's Aunt Debra and Uncle Jim. Uncle Jim is Dad's brother. They have three kids, too. All boys. Yes! We have a team now.

I love Thanksgiving. Even more than Christmas, I love this holiday. Food and football—what else could a guy wish for? Besides having his pesky little sister banished from the field, of course.

While the turkey roasts, we choose teams. Ashley's whining changes from the table expander to the game I'm trying to get started.

She hates my football. She's hidden it from me more than once. One time, I found it in the garbage. She can't understand how much it means to me to have something that's mine alone, something *manly* like football. The more I play, the more annoying she seems to get. But today? This is *parent-approved* football. Dad tells her it's boys only, and her little lip quivers.

For a second, maybe two, I almost cave in. I could show her how to throw a decent spiral, maybe run a few plays.

Could but don't.

If I do, football is only gonna become one more thing we have to share. One more reason to dress us in matching outfits—which

I hate, by the way. I just want that on record. Matching outfits for siblings is the worst idea ever.

So we're playing a great game of Turkey Day football even if Ashley pouts until the pumpkin pie is served.

Aunt Pam arrives with Uncle Phil and their kids, Paige and Logan. Aunt Pam, Granny, and Aunt Debra disappear into the kitchen with Mom. Everybody else heads out to the backyard to play football, even Paige.

"Go inside, Ashley!" Dad orders when she tries to play, too.

She puts her hands on her hips. "How come Paige can play?"

"Because she knows how. You don't," I retort.

She stamps her foot and goes back in the house to complain. Again.

"Let her play, Joe," Uncle Phil tells Dad, but he shakes his head.

"Nope, not the way Dynamo plays," he says with a grin aimed at me. "She'll get hurt. If I were you, I wouldn't let Paige play, either."

Aunt Pam's head popped out of the back door. "Paige." A minute later, Paige stomps back into the house, her face furious.

We play for *hours*.

By the time the turkey's ready, we're filthy, covered in leaves and grass stains. We head inside to clean up, Dad, Uncle Phil, and Uncle Jim all groaning about knees, backs, and a hip hurting. My cousins and I just roll our eyes.

God, they're so *old*.

When we're all gathered around the table, squeaky clean again, Granny tells Mom everything looks delicious. We start passing around dishes, bowls, and plates.

"Ow!" Ashley shrieks, clutching her head.

"Oh, I'm sorry," Granny tells her.

"I'll eat later," Ashley says, standing up with a murderous look aimed at me.

"No, you won't. You will eat now or not at all." Mom points at Ashley's seat.

Slowly, Ashley sits back down.

"Mom, there's—"

"She's just mad nobody would play with her," Paige announces to the entire table.

All eyes turn on Ashley, and they aren't full of love and sympathy.

"There's no room—"

"Just eat, Ashley." Dad says.

I feel sort of bad because she does look a bit squished, but jeez, it's a holiday. We're supposed to be on our best behavior, right?

Ashley pouts, and when she discovers both drumsticks are already claimed, she drops her fork and just sits there, mopey and depressed. Aunt Pam and Aunt Debra exchange a look of disapproval, which never fails to piss off Mom. I cast a worried glance at Dad, who's really gonna hear it later tonight, but he's too busy talking to Uncle Phil about the Buckeyes.

When dinner's done and everybody so stuffed they have to adjust their belts, Ashley sneaks away from the table sometime between the clearing and the dessert. The really sad part is nobody even notices until the coffee finishes brewing and everybody's back in their chairs.

The aunts do another disapproving look, and this time, Mom says something.

"You know, I'm not sure I'd want to eat with any of you either after getting ignored all day."

"Ignored?" Aunt Pam echoes.

"Yes. Ignored. Paige was outside playing football, even though we'd agreed it was too rough for the girls. When you called her inside, she sulked and blamed Ashley, and nobody seemed to mind that at all."

Paige looks ready to shout the house down, but Uncle Phil cuts that off at the knees. "You'll apologize to Ashley, Paige. It wasn't her fault you couldn't play."

"But, Dad—"

"You heard me."

Paige huffs out one of those loud sighs girls must master by the age of ten because Ashley sure performs it as well as Paige does.

Logan snickers next to his sister, earning an elbow in his ribs for it.

Nobody's shocked when they're the first to leave.

Ashley finally reappears later that night, after everybody has gone home. Dad and I are watching a football game, and Justin's working on his computer. Mom's reading a book. Ashley just walks right by us like we're not even here, makes herself a sandwich, and disappears back up the stairs.

I catch Justin's gaze and shrug. Everything with Ashley is always drama, drama, drama.

25

ASHLEY

It's not just my life he ruined. My parents fight all the time. My brothers can hardly look at me. Derek is a senior right now, and because there's no football this year, he's afraid he's not going to get a scholarship to college now. Because of me—not the defendant. Me.

—**Ashley E. Lawrence, victim impact statement**

NOW

BELLFORD, OHIO

Justin left school so Dad hit the roof.

He's in grad school, and the semester isn't over yet. But Justin said he'd finish what was left of the semester online and after that, he'd transfer to a school near home. Mom was ecstatic. It's barely the middle of November, and she's buzzing with preparations to make this the *Best Thanksgiving Ever*. Eye roll.

The only thing I'm buzzed about is having no school. And Sebastian. But Mom thinks it's great the aunts, uncles, cousins, grandparents…and brothers are coming. I don't know why. There's always tension between Mom and one of the aunts…or me and my brother.

She's got out her recipe cards, magazines with cute orange and red and brown decorations to make, and all the good china out of their packing boxes. Even now, she's outside in the yard, a mask over her face, dipping silverware in de-tarnishing solution. Justin's been running around like a minion, fetching boxes, running out to various stores, and moving furniture.

I feel ill.

I don't want this. I don't want any part of this and wish I could just cancel the holidays or take off somewhere and hide until they're over, somewhere secluded where there's no chance I'd run into Vic.

A chime on my phone reminds me it's time to call my therapist. Dr. Joyce is pretty amazing. I see her once a month, and in between, we have phone sessions.

"Hello, Ashley," she says a minute later.

"Hey, Dr. Joyce."

"Are you excited about the holiday?"

I groan.

"I'll take that as a no. Why don't you tell me about it?"

So I do. I tell her how Thanksgiving's good for nothing but testing the effectiveness of my antianxiety meds.

"Ashley, it sounds like you've been bitterly disappointed by your family's inability to anticipate your needs and desires. Have you considered sitting down and talking with them about your expectations for this year?"

Um. No. "Actually, it seemed kind of obvious so..."

"So you haven't. Okay, I want you to try that this year. Start with your mom. Sit down, or better yet, take her out for coffee or ice cream. Calmly and rationally, explain how Thanksgiving has been a source of anxiety for you in the past, and how this year, you'd like her help in avoiding your triggers. Then talk to your dad."

My triggers. Jeez, ice cream won't be enough. I'm gonna need a four-course meal to have that conversation.

"And then, I suggest you ask your mom how you can make the holiday less stressful for her."

She's the one who's going overboard for this holiday. How is that my fault?

"It's a challenging meal to prepare," Dr. Joyce continues like she read my mind. "Add in the stress of having all of your siblings together again, plus your extended family, and your mom is likely feeling the tension of trying to make things perfect, but knowing it's not possible."

Sighing, I agree.

"As for your extended family, that's a perfect time to practice your affirmations."

Dr. Joyce is a big believer in positive self-talk. For months, she's been encouraging me to tell myself, "I'm fine. I'm normal. I'm a-okay." She claims the more I tell myself that, the more I'll believe it.

Lie, lie, lie.

"Your cousins don't know how to behave around you or what to say. That's why they treat you differently. So show them you're not different. You're still you. Do the things the old you liked doing."

"Dr. Joyce, that's the problem. I can't. I'm not allowed. The old me wanted to do whatever Derek was doing. Derek doesn't want me anywhere near him and hasn't since I was ten or eleven years old."

"Ashley, I think that's a big part of the problem. You've always idolized your brother. You've never given yourself time or opportunities to discover what *you* like doing."

I go still because *whoa*. That…that actually makes sense. When Derek shoved me aside, there was nothing else there. Maybe that's why it hurt so much. "I don't know what I like."

"Sure you do. Would you even consider football if your brother wasn't into it?"

I think about that for a moment. "No. Football's boring."

"Okay, so if everything were still the same, what would you be doing?"

"Um, watching movies, I think. We used to do that a lot. Watch movies. Play video games."

"Okay, so why don't you buy a new movie or game to play with your family? It's neutral. It'll give them the excuse they need to avoid the discomfort they feel being around you and give you the opportunity to show your mother you're trying your best to de-stress the day for her."

I guess I could make more of an effort to make the day happy for everybody else. I get that it's not all about *me*.

"Now tell me how school's been going."

I wince. "Um, well, the Raise the BAR program's been a huge success. Pretty much everybody signed the pledge, and there's been no sign of any scavenger hunt activities."

"Ashley, that's wonderful! That's a personal victory."

Personal victory. Yeah, maybe it is. "You know he's out, right? Released early. I...I saw him. He was at the same movie theater."

Dr. Joyce hesitates for just a moment. "That must have been difficult for you. How do you think you handled it?"

I puff out my cheeks. "I froze like a deer in headlights, Dr. Joyce. He could have killed me."

"We'll come back to him in a moment. How did you respond?"

"I just stood there." Damn it, I freaking hate that I did that. "I've had three or four self-defense classes, and didn't remember anything I learned."

"What about your anxiety?"

"Um...I think it was kind of frozen, too. I didn't feel like I was about to fall apart until after."

"After?"

"Yeah. Sebastian got me out of there, and then I started to feel like I couldn't breathe."

"And then what?"

"That's it." I flop down on my bed. "I got really mad and refused, just absolutely refused, to deal with an anxiety attack on top of seeing Vic."

"So you were able to talk yourself down from an anxiety spike."

Yeah, I guess I was.

"Ashley, I think you've made some amazing progress. There's no doubt in my mind that you'll keep making great strides like this. Our time's almost up. Is there anything else you want to talk about?"

"Well, I started this Pinterest board."

"Oh?"

"I got really pissed off at the way the newspaper covered Victor's release. It was all braggy, you know? Like he's this star athlete who got railroaded or framed, and his early release is a victory for the wrongfully convicted."

"You said this pissed you off. So what did you do?"

"I photoshopped corrections in an image of the original article. I changed it to the truth. He's a convicted sex offender. So that's what I put in the headline."

I hear some clicking through the phone and realize it's Dr. Joyce's computer.

"I've found it. My, you've been busy." There's a smile in her voice. "I like the way you presented these images. Before and after."

There are about a dozen or so pictures I've been playing with.

"Ashley, I think this is a great way of channeling your anger into a productive outlet. In fact, I think you should send the newspaper a link to your board and explain why you felt it necessary to correct their slant."

"Yeah. Maybe."

"Ashley, we're almost out of time. Is there anything else we should discuss?"

Yes. "No."

"I see. Okay then, let's schedule our next appointment."

With our next session scheduled, Dr. Joyce and I hang up.

When I head downstairs, Mom's got about eleventy million recipes on cards, torn out of magazines, and printed from the internet spread out on the dining room table, which is a long natural-pine rectangle that Dad refinished when we were little. The chairs are new and don't match, but Mom adores it. Against the short wall, there's a matching cabinet that holds all Mom's nice dishes. Beside it are the expanders wrapped in plastic covers—three of them, not two.

They remembered. My heart gives a little *ping* at this, and I smile.

Mom looks up, waiting.

"Hey, Mom. Need some help?"

Her eyes pop wide, and she shrugs. "Um. Sure. Why not? Why don't you go through this pile and tell me what your favorites are? I'll try to make them."

My favorites? Seriously? Happily, I sit next to her and do exactly that. She's got broiled brussels sprouts with balsamic vinegar.

Ugh.

Next up, stuffed acorn squash stars. I like these. She stuffs them with wild rice.

I skim three different recipes for stuffing and finally pull the one with sausage. And whoa! There are seriously six different ways to cook the turkey. I choose the barbecue one. I go through all the recipes she'd given me and then hold them out.

Mom takes the stack and nods. "Hmm, okay. Yeah, we can do this." She looks at me and smiles. "Thanks, Ashley."

"Sure. So do you maybe feel like going out for ice cream or something?"

If she looked surprised before, her face is downright funny now. "You want to go out for ice cream…with me?"

"Yeah. Can you go?"

She studies me for a minute or two and slowly nods. "Yes. I can go."

It takes us about fifteen minutes to drive over to the diner near Dad's garage and find a place to park. We slip into a booth. Mom orders coffee and a slice of pie. I choose a sundae. We're both quiet and maybe a little uncomfortable. Mom keeps looking at me like she's never met me before.

"So, um, that recipe for barbecuing the turkey. Have you used it before?"

She thinks it over and finally says, "Oh! Yes. The year Justin sprained his ankle."

"Right," I say, nodding and rolling my eyes. My nonathletic brother sprained his ankle taking the trash to the curb.

Mom laughs.

I don't remember the turkey tasting any different. Turkey's turkey. "Which one's your favorite?"

"I really like the way the turkey came out the year we tried frying it. But Dad's afraid of those fryers—says they're too risky."

Nodding, I try being practical. "It would be so much easier if we had two ovens. Hey, maybe we can rent one just for the day?"

Mom's lips twitch. "I have no idea, but that's a really good idea." She pulls her phone out of her bag. "I'm looking it up." A few minutes later, she pats my hand. "Ashley, you are a genius! You *can* rent ovens. Look." She shows me her phone just as our treats arrive.

"Kind of a lot of money for one day," I observe, but Mom shrugs.

"But worth every penny. Imagine getting all the food hot at the same time." She props her chin in her hand and smiles at me. "You're so smart. I've been doing this for how many years now? It's never once occurred to me to rent an extra oven." She stirs some sugar and cream into her coffee and takes a sip.

I pause. I don't think I've ever noticed that Mom likes two sugars and cream in her coffee.

"Mom, I wanted to thank you."

She looks over her cup at me, eyebrows raised. "For?"

"I saw all three of the table expanders out. For remembering how uncomfortable it was, getting knocked in the head every time Granny lifted her fork."

She nods and grins. "Yeah, I guess that was a bit annoying." And then her grin disappears. "I'm sorry I yelled at you that time. And so sorry for everything else. I want—" She breaks off, biting her lip and looking out the window.

I can see tears in her eyes, and I squirm.

"Ashley, I want so badly to make everything okay. To make everything stop hurting you."

"I know, Mom." I lift a shoulder like it's no big deal, even though it is. "I have a favor to ask."

She lowers her cup. "Okay, what's up?"

"Could we please make this year a no-football holiday? It's a trigger of mine that I'd much rather avoid."

At my use of the word *trigger*, Mom instantly nods, recognizing it as one of Dr. Joyce's words.

"Ashley, honey, of course. I'll speak to Dad and your brothers. But what will we find for everybody to do while we're waiting for the meal?"

"I've been thinking about that, too. We could buy a game. Or a movie. Or maybe both."

Mom nods. "Okay. Let's hit the stores after we eat." She glances at the watch on her wrist and gasps. "We should hurry. There's so much to do." She puts her cup back on the saucer and slides toward the end of the booth, but I hesitate.

"Mom, there's something else I want to talk about."

The frown comes back. "Ashley, I promise you, Victor will not bother you. Dad and I are taking every legal step possible to make sure of that."

I nod. "Right. The restraining order."

"Yes. Plus a civil suit."

I nod and decide I should tell her. "Um, Mom. You should know I saw him. Vic." God, even saying his name makes my skin crawl.

The color drains out of Mom's face.

"It's fine. Really. Sebastian got me home."

She pulls in a breath, and her nostrils flare. "Tell me everything."

So I do. I tell her we had hot chocolate right here in this booth and then went to the movies, and Vic was apparently in the same theater, but we didn't know until the lights came back up.

"Ashley, you cannot be alone. Not for a single minute, do you hear me? What if you'd gone to the ladies' room? You could have bumped right into him by yourself."

I wasn't even thinking about stuff like that. But I am now. "It's okay. He didn't approach. And Sebastian was right there."

Mom presses a hand to her mouth and shakes her head. "Baby, you shouldn't have to go through this. I'm so sorry."

I wince. "I just wanted to forget it. The media keep calling him the *former Bengals quarterback*. God, that pisses me off," I admit. "They used his yearbook photo. It's not right, Mom! It's just not right. They should use his mug shot, and they should call him what he is. A convicted sex offender. It should have been convicted *rapist*, but they believed him instead of me."

"Ashley," she whispers, her voice high and choked.

I lift my eyes to hers. They're so blue, like ridiculously blue. I was jealous for so long that the boys inherited her eyes and I didn't, but now I'm kind of happy I don't share this with Derek, too. My eyes are deep brown like Dad's. Sebastian says they remind him of melted chocolate, which is kind of funny because I get soft and gooey every time he says that. But right now, Mom's eyes are worried. Anxious.

Sad.

"And then, all those magazine ads and catalogs… I just kept getting madder and madder."

"What ads?"

I put my cup down. "It was in art class. We were looking through a bunch of old ads and catalogs to see how sex sells and I felt like I was going to vomit. It's like I'm the only person in the whole world who sees them as permission slips, you know? Like, go ahead and rape. It's okay. Dulcet & Marcus said so in this year's holiday collection."

"You're amazing, you know that?"

I blink and shake my head because I'm not amazing. I can't be. If I were, none of this would have happened. I sigh because there's no way to ease into this, no way to make it hurt less. I go with the get-it-over-with approach. "Can I ask you something?"

When she nods, I blurt, "Are you and Dad okay?"

The effect is instant.

She lowers her eyes, hiding from me, and sits back in the booth as far as she can. Her lips tighten into a flat line, and when she opens her mouth, I know it'll be a lie. "Of course we are, honey. Dad's stressing over the business, and I'm stressing over the holiday. We'll get past it. We always do."

I'm not talking about the business or Thanksgiving, and she knows it.

"Mom, I know you guys are fighting. And I know it's because of me and Derek. I'm really sorry."

Her eyes snap up to meet my gaze, and they're still sad, but this time, there's something else there. Something like…hopelessness.

"Ashley," she begins, then stops, bites her lip again, and shakes her head.

"What?"

"Never mind. You won't understand. You can't, not until you have kids of your own."

I lean forward and grab her hand. "Mom, tell me."

Her hand twitches under mine, but she nods. "It's just…I love *both* of you. No matter what."

I pull my hand back, and that's when her first tear falls.

"See? I knew you wouldn't understand. I feel like I'm in the center of this tug-of-war. I know he hurt you, but even I can't understand what you're going through, and I'm your *mom*. I'm supposed to protect you from pain, but how do I do that when it's coming from another child I love as much as I love you?"

"Do you?" The words fall out of my mouth before I can stop them. Mom looks at me, horror blazing in her eyes. "Derek always said *he* was planned, but I was an accident."

Mom's expression wavers somewhere between amusement and outrage. "Did he? God, that explains so much." And then she laughs.

I'm glad one of us finds this funny.

She leans forward and grabs my hand this time. "Ashley, it's true you were a surprise for Dad and me, but you were never unwanted. I was—*am*—so grateful you were born and absolutely ecstatic I got a daughter."

She says the words, but I don't believe them. "Then why didn't you ever take my side? Why did you let Derek treat me like crap all this time?"

Mom reaches out a hand to my face and traces my cheek. "Sweetheart, I've never let Derek treat you like crap. When I knew about it, when I saw it, I stopped him. He was punished a lot for the things he said and did to you."

Doubt that.

"I eased off when it seemed to make him more frustrated with you."

Yeah, right.

"Dad assured me it was a phase. He went through the same thing when he was a kid. He promised me Derek would outgrow it. We never had anything like it with Justin, so I wasn't so sure. But Dad's a middle kid, too, so I figured he knew what he was talking about and went along. At first, I agreed that Derek had a point. He was older than you and should be allowed to do things you weren't. And yes, I agreed he should have his own friends and not be expected to entertain you all the time. I permitted that. But it wasn't enough. The more he pulled away from you, the tighter you clung to him. I tried, Ashley. I tried so hard. I took you to dance classes so you'd have something to do that was just yours. But you didn't seem to like them. And when he started high school, I thought that would finally be the end of the tension between you. I'm sorry, baby. I'm sorry I couldn't fix this for you before—"

"Yeah. *Before.*"

Mom sighs. When she looks up again, her face is dead serious. "Ashley, tell me the truth. Do you honestly believe Derek *knew* what Victor was planning and didn't stop him?"

I slouch back in the booth and press my lips together. For so long, there was nothing—absolutely nothing—too mean for Derek to say or do to me. But that? No. Not even Derek could do that.

I shake my head.

"Then why can't you forgive him?"

"Because he's *not sorry*, Mom."

"He's apologized so many times," she says, spreading her hands out.

I want to forgive him. I really do. I *can't*. "But he doesn't mean it! He's never once meant it. They're just words he says because he knows how to work you and Dad over to his side."

Mom puts up a hand. "Okay, okay. He's coming home soon, and I want him to. I need him home, baby. I know that feels like I'm taking his side, but I'm not. I promise you. I just need *all* my babies. Can you understand that?"

No, I really can't. "I'll try, Mom."

The lies just tumble from my lips these days.

TWO YEARS AGO

BELLFORD, OHIO

Mom tries to pretend everything's fine…that I'm fine. Dad goes along with it and so do Justin and Derek. Nobody mentions the *R* word, and that seriously annoys me, but fine. Whatever.

Granny and Pop arrive right after Aunt Pam and Uncle Phil. Granny hugs me extra long and cries a little, but Paige obviously

SOMEONE I USED TO KNOW

doesn't care what happened to me, because the first words out of her mouth are, "What'd you do to your hair?" Her words are accompanied by an equally offensive sneer that leaves no room for interpretation just what she thinks of my new style.

Mom does damage control. "We decided to cut it after Ashley left the hospital." She puts an arm around me and gives me a squeeze, then shoots Aunt Pam one of those looks Aunt Pam usually exchanges with Aunt Debra.

We did no such thing.

I did it because I woke up one morning after a night of almost constant bad dreams and remembered Vic had wrapped my long hair around his hand. There were a lot of things I couldn't remember during the day. But at night, the memories came out to play.

I got up and cut off as much as I could. By the time Mom got the bathroom door unlocked, it was up to my jawline.

She screamed. Dad came running. They held me and kept promising me I'd be okay, but I didn't believe them.

Here it is, a month later, and I still don't.

Mom gives Aunt Pam side-eye, and Aunt Pam quickly jerks Paige out of earshot and threatens her with—I don't know—a painful death, maybe?

Whatever she said had Paige crossing her arms and muttering, "Fine."

Everybody tiptoes around me. They make sure I'm comfortable and don't need anything, then disappear because it's too uncomfortable to be near me. The aunts and Granny join Mom in the kitchen, and the guys all head outside.

When Derek comes downstairs in a jersey and carrying his football, my anxiety levels hit the redline, and I end up passing out.

These anxiety episodes are getting worse, not better.

After the first one, Mom called one of the numbers the hospital sent us home with and got me a therapist. Her name is Dr. Christine Joyce. I think it's cool…like a pen name. She's pretty cool, too. I have antianxiety medicine now. It makes me feel strange, but the nightmares aren't as bad, so I keep taking it.

After my *attack*, we all just sit in the family room instead, trying to pretend that I wasn't raped a month earlier. I hear Paige whisper something and immediately hear Aunt Pam's loud, "Shhh!"

"But what if—"

"It's not your business."

"But what if she is?"

From my corner of the large sofa, where I'm tucked in with a nice warm blanket, I scream, "I am not pregnant, Paige!"

Mom and Granny come running in from the kitchen, Dad and Uncle Phil look murderous, and Aunt Pam's face goes red. About fifteen minutes later, they're in their car, heading for Aunt Debra's house, this being the same Aunt Debra who claimed she wasn't feeling well and couldn't come this year.

Mom cries, and Granny hugs her, then she takes her back into the kitchen.

Derek glares at me from across the room. "Way to go, Ashley."

I shut my eyes and go to sleep. Thanks to my new medicine, sleep is the only thing I'm good at now.

NOW

BELLFORD, OHIO

When the bell rings on Wednesday, I blow out a long, slow breath, and my shoulders fall a bit. Four whole days of holiday vacation, four whole days of family togetherness.

Yay.

At the sound of the bell, the school is evacuated within five minutes, like someone announced it was summer vacation instead of Thanksgiving. I take my time, strolling through the corridors. Don't get me wrong; I'm psyched I have the long holiday weekend, but...Derek is coming home.

Justin's been home for weeks, and for the most part, he leaves me alone, and I leave him alone. He checks in, makes sure I'm still breathing, and goes off to do Justin stuff, which is apparently being the Perfect Son. He helps Dad at the garage and helps Mom do all sorts of stuff he never wanted to be bothered with in the past.

It's all so phony, I can't stand it.

I haven't seen Derek since August. Three months. That's the longest I've ever gone without seeing my brother, and there's that stupid little pang in my chest at the thought. God, I hate it when my body reacts one way while my mind says something else. I hate him.

Pang.

I loathe him.

Pang. Pang.

Okay! So I love him. Big deal. He still hurt me, and damn it, I'm tired of being hurt.

I wonder where to go. Maybe the library. It's quiet there, and it's not far. I start walking, wondering where else I can go after the library closes because home isn't where my heart is anymore.

......

Tires squeal and a horn blares as I walk along Blaine, kicking my heart rate into the stratosphere. When I look over, I'm not entirely surprised to see Dad's truck at the curb, but I am kind of surprised to see *both* of my brothers climb out of it, wearing twin expressions of rage.

"Where the hell have you been?" Justin reaches me first. "Mom's actually calling hospitals."

Guilt creeps along my skin, along with a hot flush. "Wasn't in a rush to get home today. For obvious reasons," I add with a pointed look at Derek.

"Yeah? Even with Victor Patton out of prison?" Justin shoots back, and all the blood freezes in my veins. He rambles on. "He lives barely half a mile from here, and you're just out strolling, not even a phone call to let anybody know where you are."

"J. Back off," Derek murmurs with a jerk of his chin toward me.

"Ashley, are you trying to get hurt?" Justin demands, and that kick-starts my system.

"No. I just forgot about Vic."

Justin's blue eyes bulge behind his glasses. "You forgot? Jesus, Ashley, Mom almost put out an APB on you. Why didn't you tell her?"

Rolling my eyes, I pull out my phone. "I did."

"That was hours ago!" Justin crosses his arms, and I blink. He looks fierce, like he might take on an army. And, jeez, when did he develop actual biceps? "Could you please get in the damn truck so we can pretend we're a normal happy family?"

Pedestrians walking on both sides of Blaine are staring at us, so with a huff, I climb into the back seat.

Derek doesn't say anything. He looks exactly the same. I don't know why, but I expected him to look different somehow. Less like my brother maybe. There's a blotch of red on his throat—a classic sign that Derek's upset. It gives me a perverse thrill. I like knowing he's anxious about seeing me, too. He starts the truck and merges into traffic.

"Mom's pretty pissed off at you," he finally says.

I shrug. Who isn't pissed off in this family?

"I get that you don't want to see me, but we need to try to get along, for Mom's sake."

I swivel my head to stare at him. "Oh, for Mom's sake. Right."

He makes a left turn, and even in the dark, I can tell his fingers are white on the steering wheel. He drives for a few blocks in silence and then clears his throat.

"So I heard about your BAR rally. That was a, um, really great idea."

I say nothing.

"I signed a pledge form myself."

I resist the urge to swirl my finger in the air.

"I joined this group called GAR at my school. Guys Against Rape. How lame is that?" He laughs, but it's fake and forced, and oh my God, the great Derek Lawrence is actually nervous. I want to keep ignoring him, but he keeps talking. "We meet a few times a week and pledge to do our part to end misogyny and add our voices to protests."

Wow. What a load of crap. "Well, good on you, Derek."

Justin flicks me a look of frustration, but Derek ignores my obvious sarcasm and keeps babbling. "Oh, it really is good. We do stuff like shut down sexist jokes, remind guys they're not owed a damn thing. Oh, and I volunteered to speak."

Is he bragging? Is he actually bragging about what a great non-rapist he is? Fuming, I sit in the back seat, counting the blocks until we're home. By the time Derek pulls into our driveway and turns off the engine, a very angry Mom is waiting on the front steps.

"Wonderful. All three of you are present in the same space. Go inside. Sit at the table."

"Not hungry," I tell her as I get out of the car.

"Then you can sit and watch the rest of us eat. Table. *Now*."

I am *not* sitting at the same table as Derek. But I go in the house and drop my bag at the foot of the steps. Dad's already at the table, slouched in his chair. He glances up when I come in and smiles stiffly. The boys shuffle in and take the seats they've always sat in, Derek next to Dad, Justin next to Mom, leaving me to squeeze in beside Derek.

Not today.

Today, I drag my chair around the table to squeeze next to Justin.

Mom storms into the kitchen and comes back a few seconds later with a huge bowl of pasta that she plops on the table with a heavy bang, only to disappear back into the kitchen. The food smells great. If I shut my eyes, I can remember all the other pasta dinners we've had here.

Wednesday night was family night.

With Justin working his part-time jobs and Derek at some practice or another, weekends were always packed full of schedule conflicts. So Wednesday became the only night the five of us could eat a real dinner together. We settled on pasta because it was easy—boil some water, cook, done.

It evolved into a big thing. Mom progressed from boring spaghetti to homemade manicotti, Derek's favorite, lasagna, which was Justin's, and ravioli, which was mine. We'd eat, we'd tell Mom and Dad about our days, we'd have dessert, and then we'd play a board game or maybe cards.

I was always on Derek's team, if we had teams. We all used to get mad at Dad because he'd play aggressively, and Mom would tell us to deal with it because out in the real world, nobody would ever go easy on us.

I squeeze my eyes shut. *God.* Truer words were never spoken.

Mom slams another dish to the table. Garlic bread this time. Dad jumps up and disappears into the kitchen with her. They return together. He holds the grated parmesan cheese, and she's got the bowl of meatballs.

I notice that tonight's dish is nobody's favorite. Just spaghetti and meatballs.

Mom drags out her chair, plops down on it, and snaps her fingers at me for my plate. Wordlessly, I hold it out to her. It's the good china. She set the table with all the good china we'd need for tomorrow's holiday meal, and now I feel like a brat for trying to blow off this dinner, which makes me hate all of this even more, because seriously, don't I have a right to feel how I feel without the guilt trip?

She scoops out a serving of spaghetti with an angry twist of her arm that splatters sauce all over the table. With a loud curse, she drops her elbows to the table and lets her face fall into her hands. I *am* a brat, and because I know I am, I'm going to wash all these dishes tonight myself.

"Mom, I'm sorry," I squeak out, shooting a nasty look at Derek, but he's looking away, an expression of such sadness on his face that for a moment, I forget that he hates me and I hate him and almost run to him with open arms. When we were little, Derek was almost never sad. Like *never*.

God, I wish we were little again.

Mom doesn't move, but Dad and Justin wear twin looks of annoyance. Dad clears his throat. "Ashley. Derek. The two of you have treated this home and this family like a battleground long enough. It ends now. Is that clear?"

Derek nods immediately.

I sneer. What a kiss-ass. I keep my eyes pinned on Derek, waiting for the usual malicious grin or stuck-out tongue.

"Ashley, you knew your mom was planning a nice family dinner tonight, and you deliberately disappeared. Why would you do that?"

"Because."

Dad knows the answer to this already. I'd told them both enough times.

"Because why, Ashley?" he demands.

We're back to everything being *my* fault. "Because!" I repeat with venom. "Because I saw Victor Patton at the theater! Because *he's* out of prison, and I'm not. I have to live with what happened every second of my life. It's like this festering wound that won't heal because the scab keeps getting torn off. Because I can't stomach the thought of eating while looking at *him*." I shout, that single statement aimed with all my hatred and outrage and sarcasm right at Derek.

He flinches and lowers his head, but he doesn't deny it, doesn't try to deflect and blame me for it.

What strange alternate universe did I fall into?

Nobody says anything for a minute. Mom mops her eyes with a napkin, and my heart sinks. I'm breaking her heart, and I know it, which is why I really need to be away from here. I'm afraid I may actually not be able to help doing it.

"You saw Victor Patton?" Derek asks me but sends a pointed look to Dad.

"We're doing all we can—" Mom starts to say, but Dad's still stuck on his original point.

"Ashley." Dad holds up a hand to Mom, glaring at me. "Has it occurred to you that other members of this family love Derek, want to see him, want to hear how school is? Have you forgotten that Derek is *our child* and we love him as much as we love you?"

I stare at my father and try to breathe around the spike he just drove through my gut. I press both hands to my chest where the pain is so huge, I'm sure it's gonna kill me. I forget all about Mom's feelings because my own boil over. "How, Dad?" I croak. "Vic is out of prison." A shudder of revulsion ripples over me. "And I'm stuck in one!" I shout. Shaking now, I jab a finger in the air toward Derek. "And you still love *him*? Tell me how!" I scream.

Dad's fist hits the table, and everybody jumps. "Because he's my son!" he shouts back, his face dark. "I know you blame him for what happened at the trial, but it's not his fault, Ashley."

I laugh, a bitter sound that holds zero humor. "You think I'm upset about the trial? That's the least of it. No. I know how Derek really feels, and he's not sorry. Not one bit. He got what he always wanted. For his annoying sister to leave him alone."

"No! Jesus, Ashley." Derek shuts his eyes. "You just want to believe it so you can keep hating me."

"No. No more hating anybody." Dad stands up and walks around to me. "I love him like I love you, like I love Justin. Do you hear me, Ashley? Do you understand how you're cutting us to pieces?"

"Joe," Mom tries to interrupt, but he's not having it.

The veins are standing out in his neck now. "None of you are perfect, you know. All of you make mistakes! I forgave Justin for wrecking the car a few years ago. So I can forgive Derek for what he said to the judge just like I can forgive *you* for drinking with that boy in the first place."

The air leaves my lungs in a *whoosh* that freezes me where I sit. A ball of ice sits heavy inside my gut, making me shiver, while those two words echo.

Forgive you.

Mom makes a sound of horror—a loud gasp that echoes around the dining room.

Justin leaps to his feet. "Dad, come on. Let's you and me go take a walk."

Dad shrugs him off.

Then Derek's head snaps up, and for one brief second, I see outrage in Derek's blue eyes, the same outrage that reminds me of that hot day so many years ago when he beat up a playground bully and became my Leo.

And then he's on his feet. "Are you crazy?" he asks quietly, pulling out a folded-up paper from his pocket and all but shoving it under Dad's face. "Did you not read a word of all the literature the hospital sent us home with? Don't blame the victim, Dad! It's the first thing they told us back then. It's the first thing they tell us now in my GAR meetings." Derek's voice is steadily rising, and that icy ball deep inside me just cracked a little.

"It is *not* her fault, Dad. It doesn't matter if she had a beer, it doesn't matter if she said yes and changed her mind later, it doesn't even matter if she slept with him a hundred times in the past. All that matters, the only thing that matters, is she said no, and he didn't listen. He made that choice. Nobody else." Derek flings the paper to the table and looks around. He seems surprised he's on his feet. Slowly, he sits back down, but his face is red from his temper, and a muscle in his jaw twitches. The rest of us watch him, stunned into silence.

Especially me.

My brother just defended me.

Slowly, everybody sits. Derek picks up his fork, his flush deepening. He twirls some spaghetti around it and then drops it with a curse. "You know, I cannot actually believe this. You signed one of Ashley's pledge forms! How can you sit there and judge her?"

"How could you?" Dad fires back, and Derek winces.

"You're right," he admits quietly. "I did then. But not now, Dad. I read every word of that material." He stabs a finger at the brochure next to Dad's plate. "I know all the statistics by heart. I know that recovery depends entirely on a rape survivor's support system. That's us. She needs us to tell her over and over again that it's not her fault, that we love her, that we don't blame her."

"Sitting right here," I remind them, putting up a hand to stop this act, entertaining as it is. I already know what they really think.

Derek turns his head and then lowers his eyes. "Sorry, Ashley."

"Oh, you're sorry," Dad mocks. "Where were you when she screamed in her sleep, Derek? Where were you when she couldn't leave her bedroom for days at a time?"

Derek lifts his eyes to mine. "I couldn't face it then."

"Face *me*, you mean," I correct him.

"Face *me*," he corrects, leaning toward me. "I'm sorry. I'll say it every day for the rest of my life if it'll help. I'm sorry for all of it. The hunt. For ditching you. For teasing you. You have any idea how many nights I spent wondering if this would have happened if I hadn't been such a jerk?"

I stare at him for a moment. Are we really gonna play this game? Get out the ruler and measure whose pain is worse? "Nowhere even close to how many I have."

He jerks and then inclines his head in a single nod. "There is nothing I can do to change it, Ashley. Nothing. All I can do is tell you I'm sorry, tell you I love you, that I believe you. That I'm here for you."

His words are pretty, but I know that's all they are. I know *him*. So I watch and wait, wondering what his endgame is. I study him, waiting for him to reveal the truth. The curl of his lip, the roll of his eyes, maybe a stuck-out tongue—all the signs of the old Derek that always, always follow this sort of performance.

The others watch us, eyes flicking from Derek to me.

"Please, honey," Mom whispers. "Please. Just try to forgive each other."

I wish I could believe him. I want to believe he's serious, want to believe my Leo is still buried somewhere deep inside the stranger at our dining room table. But I remember what he said that night in the hospital.

Every word.

I shift my gaze to Mom, to the raw hope etched into every line on her face. An eerie calm settles over me. An almost supernatural sense of...serenity, I think. It confuses me until I feel the burn in my chest when my lungs constrict. No, not serenity. It was the ebb before the flow, the draining of the ocean before the tsunami surges. Blinking lights fill my vision, and my chest goes tight. The ball of ice in my belly shatters. I gasp, trying to move air past that pain, hoping I'll pass out because at least then, I'd be free of the pressing weight of the guilt and pain that started at homecoming two years ago and just never leaves.

"Breathe, Ashley!" a voice says, but it's too far away to tell whose. I try to inhale, try again and again to suck air into my body, but the gaping wound where my heart used to be is a vacuum.

My vision fades completely, and a split second later, so do I.

26
DEREK

NOW

BELLFORD, OHIO

I'm up and around the table to Ashley's side before she slumps out of her chair. Her eyes are rolled back in her head. Mom's hysterical, and I kick myself for not sticking to my guns. I shouldn't have come home.

I only make it harder for her. I know now that there's no apology big enough for all the shit between us, the shit I put there. There never will be.

I scoop her into my arms, take her to the sofa, and lay her gently against the pillows. "Justin, get a cold cloth or something. Dad, we got any smelling salts?"

They sure worked on me.

He stares at me. Mom's still crying.

"Mom, stop! This isn't about you," I shout.

Pissing off my parents does the trick. Dad's blank look disappears and is replaced with red-faced rage. Mom's sobs stop, and she hurries to the sofa, petting Ashley's hair.

Justin comes back with a damp towel. I press it to Ashley's forehead and neck like Mary Ann, the paramedic, did for me. Her eyelids flutter, and she moans.

"How the hell did you learn this?" Justin wonders.

"Personal experience," I mutter.

"What?" Dad asks, and I sigh.

Now is *so* not the time for this.

"I passed out last week."

"Why? Were you drunk?"

My temper surges. "No, I wasn't drunk. I don't drink because I have an athletic scholarship, remember? I had an anxiety attack."

Justin flings up both arms. "Great. Now we've got a matching set of bookends."

I ignore them and focus on Ashley. Her face is kind of gray. I take her hand and put two fingers on her wrist, not surprised to feel her pulse weak. I tap her cheek.

"Come on, April, snap out of it before Mom has a cow."

Brown eyes blink open and then focus on me. She shrinks farther into the pillows. "Don't call me that."

I hold up both hands in surrender. "Better?"

Her hands flutter up to her chest, and she rubs a circle over the middle. Yep. I remember that pain, too. Felt like my heart had exploded.

She looks around, discovers she's no longer in the dining room, and sighs.

I get it; she's embarrassed.

"How did I get on the sofa?"

"I carried you," I admit.

She shoots me a look that could peel the paint off the walls. "Surprised you didn't let me drown in the spaghetti sauce."

Mom makes a sound of protest, but I laugh. "Drown? Hey, you may be a pain in the ass, but I don't want you dead."

Ashley's face goes red. Good. Getting everybody angry is productive. I can work with anger.

"Look, before you checked out in there," I say, jerking a thumb toward the dining room. "Dad was talking about forgiveness. I was about to tell you something, something I should have said years ago."

Ashley sucks in one cheek and shoves herself up into a sitting position, wincing from the effort. "This should be good. Okay. Let's hear it." She circles her hands.

"I was an asshole—"

"You think?"

I clear my throat and start again. "I was a total jerk to you for a long time, and I'm sorry for that. It wasn't you. I just wanted my own space. Mom wouldn't let me escape." I shake my head with a laugh. "And you were fucking relentless."

"Derek!" Mom gasps.

I, um, kind of forgot we have an audience.

"Sorry, Mom, but she was," I insist. And then I shrug. "And I got desperate. And none of that—absolutely none of it deserved, asked for, or justifies what Vic did to you. I'm sorry for it, Ashley. I meant what I said. I'll apologize every day for the rest of my life if you need that."

Mom squeaks and puts both hands over her mouth. Dad and Justin look to Ashley. I swear I hear everybody take a breath and hold it.

But Ashley's not impressed. Her face gets redder. "You are so full of it, Derek." She swings her legs off the couch. "You aren't sorry at all."

"Ashley, I—"

"Save it!" she screams so loudly the dog next door starts barking. "I know what you really think. I *know*."

What the hell?

"Ashley, Derek is—"

"A liar, that's what he is," she says, cutting off whatever Mom was about to say. "Every word out of his mouth is bullshit! I know how you really feel, Derek. No apology in the universe can ever change what you told me that night in the hospital."

I blink at her.

"Oh my God! You really believe your own bull." Ashley rakes both hands through her hair and grunts in frustration. "They may think the lawyers tripped you up, but I know, Derek. I *know*. I heard every single word from your own lips because I wasn't asleep."

I still don't know what—

Oh my God.

The memory sinks its pointy fangs in me, forcing me to relive every horrible word as it gnashes its jaws. Both of my parents go on the attack.

"What is she talking about?"

"Derek, what does Ashley mean?"

I want to puke, but all I can do is sit there, on the edge of the couch, unable to push words out.

"Tell them, Derek," Ashley jeers. "I'm sure they'll want to hear all about this."

......

I got hit wrong in a game once.

Some kid came at me and hit me helmet to stomach. I don't know who taught him to play football, but I was lucky he was weak, or he'd have ruptured my liver. I felt like I'd been hit by a fast-moving train.

This is worse. Like a hundred times worse. It's like getting hit in the solar plexus, and while you're gasping for air like a fish on land, bam! You get kicked in the nuts.

My whole body goes numb. I don't know if my blood is still circulating. I don't know if my heart's beating. I can't tell if I'm still breathing. I've been blasted outside my body. I can see it—the whole scene—beneath me. Ashley on the couch, Mom hovering over her, and Dad and Justin hanging back, staring at me.

At me.

Oh God, oh God, oh God.

"Tell them, Derek!" Ashley screams at me, and suddenly, I'm sucked back into my body, and I can feel every fucking thing.

My hands shake when I pull them through my hair and sink deep into the sofa by her feet. She snaps them away and curls into her own corner, still spitting in rage. "I was awake, you ass. I *heard* you. You stood there and said why couldn't I just stay home, just stay home like you told me to. You said I was such a pain, and that none of us would ever be the same now because of me."

No! I'm screaming inside. She has it wrong, all wrong. But I can't shove the words out.

"You said you couldn't look at me. I can't believe you have the balls to attack Dad for blaming me after that."

Slowly, I lift my head and look at her now.

I see it.

The answer. The solution. The key to fixing everything that I broke.

It's in her eyes, dark and round and filled with hate. Shivering, I stand up.

"You're right," I tell her quietly. My voice is nothing more than a scrape of sandpaper on wood. "I said all those things."

Mom's groan is so deep, I think we all feel it down to our bones. Dad slumps into a chair, and Justin stands frozen by the dining room entry.

I stumble toward the door and turn back for another look. I make it a good one.

It'll be my last.

"But you're wrong about what I meant. I didn't blame you. Not then, not now. I blamed *me*, Ash. Me." I thump a hand to my chest. "I didn't know how to handle it, how to express it, how to even think about it. So I got mad. And I'm sorry for it. I'll never be able to tell you how much. I love you, and I know you don't believe that, but I do. Always."

I grab the coat and the bags I left near the front door and walk out.

Nobody follows.

......

I have a speech to make in like three hours, but first, I head to Brittany's house and just stand outside for a long time. Damn, I love this girl. Who knew? Shaking my head, I almost laugh. Instead, I dig into my bag and pull out the present I bought her. Britt's birthday is coming up. It's a few days after Thanksgiving.

I put a lot of thought into this gift. I planned to put on nice clothes, take her out for a really great dinner, and give her the words that make every girl smile. Instead, I tuck the small box and card just inside the front door, where she'll be sure to see it. A noise makes me panic, so I hide, melting into the shadows where all the other monsters live.

It's Brittany. She opens the door, sees the gift, and smiles, her teeth shining in the darkness. She almost spots me.

Almost.

"Derek? Derek!" She looks up and down the street, but I'm here, right here, and she can't see me. I think that's been the problem all along. She can't see me for what I really am just like the court couldn't see Victor for what he is. She shakes her head and goes back inside the house, carrying the present.

Inside the house, lights blaze from different windows, a TV is on, and music plays. It's happy here. Happy is good.

"Bye, Britt," I say to the closed door. I turn and head back the way I came because it's so fucking clear I don't belong here. And then I slink away, alone.

Better get used to it.

I need to leave.

I've known it for a while now. Tonight. Leave my family. Leave my life. I can't fix what I broke. I'm not sure anything or anybody can.

But I can give them peace. I can give Ashley space without me in it, constantly reminding her. Hurting her.

I head into town and duck into a Starbucks and use my phone to set up an Uber ride to get me to Columbus for the big GAR speech. Jeez, isn't that ironic. Me? Speaking to families of rape survivors? *Hey, check me out, everybody! I'm the poster child for exactly what not to do.*

I'm next in line when I see a familiar figure bent over a laptop. Alone, at a table in the back corner, a girl drinks from a tall cup, hands wrapped in fingerless gloves. Her hair's different, longer than I remember. But I still know her, even without seeing the name written on the cup.

"Hey, Dakota."

Her head snaps up, and her mouth opens.

"Mind if I sit?"

She doesn't answer me. She just stares.

Old Me would have sat anyway. New Me remains on my tired

and cold feet. "I'm sorry," I blurt out with no prep work. "For what I did two years ago."

Dakota's face shows shock then scorn. "Really."

I open my mouth to defend myself and then reconsider. I can't really blame her, given my priors where she's concerned. I nod and try again. "Yes. Really. I'm going to school in New York. We held a Take Back the Night rally. Ever heard of it?"

The scorn on her face goes back to shock, and I wish I could remember how to laugh because it should be funny how she has only two gears where I'm concerned. "Yeah. I've been to a couple."

"A couple?" Now it's my turn for shock. "I barely survived the one." Before she can skewer me with the response I can see she's dying to give, I plow ahead. "I was a total ass to you. My parents found out about the item on my scavenger hunt list. You know the one with—"

"Yeah. I remember." Her face goes red, and she darts an anxious glance around the shop.

"They pointed out that treating you like that was incredibly offensive."

For the first time, she looks at me with interest. Encouraged, I keep going. "I kept telling them you let me. That you said yes. But they…" I suck in a deep breath and stare her right in the eyes. "It wasn't—*I* wasn't honorable, and for that, I'm sorry."

She watches me carefully, her expression giving nothing away. I shift uncomfortably, but I remain standing.

"Derek, did Ashley put you up to this?" she finally asks. She's a grade ahead of Ashley, and I wonder if they're friends. Probably not, since Ashley isn't exactly social these days.

"No, I—" I shove both hands into my jacket pockets and stare down at the floor. "I treated you like crap. I'm sorry."

She's still staring at me with those dark, unreadable eyes, and then she nods. "Okay."

Okay? That's all she says. She doesn't invite me to join her. Doesn't say a word. After a minute, I nod awkwardly.

"Um. So have a great Thanksgiving." I turn my back to rejoin the line at the counter.

"You must be really proud of Ashley."

I turn back and angle my head.

"She's doing amazing work," she adds, waving a hand.

"Yeah," I agree, happy to talk about something other than my sins. "I heard about BAR."

"BAR's great. But her artwork is getting noticed."

"Artwork?" I echo. I haven't heard a word about any artwork.

Dakota shows me what's on her laptop. It's a Huffington Post page that says "Bellford High School Rape Victim Turns to Pinterest to Combat Rape Culture."

I lean in and study the screen.

"She hasn't told you." Dakota sits back in her chair and takes a sip from her cup. "You should look it up. She, like, just started it, and already it's getting tons of hits." She shoves back from her chair and collects her laptop and cup and her purse. "You can sit now." At the door, she turns back and stares me right in the eye. "Thanks for the apology."

I sink into the chair I've been gripping this entire time while she disappears around the corner. Points. Those damn points, every single one of them, flip in my mind, a virtual Jumbotron scoreboard. I used a girl to try to win a stupid game. There's literally no apology big enough to make that right.

I tug my laptop from my bag and log on to the free Wi-Fi to click over to Ashley's Pinterest board. Once again, I'm blown away by her rock-solid convictions. And once again, I hate myself a little bit more because I never noticed the things she sees.

She named the board "Before & After." It's full of images from ads and commercials, songs, news headlines, and videos. All of them bear the caption, "Instead of That, How About This?"

The work is bold. She doesn't pull any punches but digs right in and circles everywhere the source material insults, offends, and perpetuates the things my GAR group calls rape culture. There are a bunch of pins about Victor's release. I open one where the headline reads "Bengals Football Player Released from Prison in Time for Holidays." Ashley drew a single line through some of the words, changing it to read "Convicted Sex Offender Released from Prison after Serving Only Sixteen Months of a Two-Year Sentence."

The next one I open shows a magazine ad for a department store. The original ad reads "Spike Your Best Friend's Eggnog When They're Not Looking." She changed it to read "Watch Your Best Friend's Eggnog So She Makes It Home Safely."

Oh, God.

I shut my eyes for a minute and then keep reading. She's got a bunch of these pins posted, and they totally *wreck* me not because they're offensive—and they are—but because the Derek I was two years ago never would have noticed.

I click over to my Facebook page and start scrolling through photos—mine, Ashley's, Justin's, and Mom's. There are hundreds. Pictures from holidays, from school, my games, Justin's robotics club competitions—happy family photos from a happy family.

God.

Our whole life story is posted up there. I download a series of pictures. Mom is crazy with family pictures. There are so many to choose from, but I don't need them all. It takes me ages, but I finally narrow down the field to just six.

And then I start editing. I'm pretty good with graphics software and even thought about becoming a video game designer once. One after the other, I edit. It's surprisingly easy to change history.

Just crop.

Erase.

Hide.

Blur.

Delete.

When I'm finally done, I sit back and examine my work, nodding. I add some captions, zip them up, and email them to Ashley for her board. A horn honks outside. My ride's here. Time for me to go convince a bunch of guys that we can undo a couple hundred years of wrongheaded thinking.

27

ASHLEY

I've been seeing a therapist to help me deal with all the guilt and shame I feel every time someone throws a rock through our window or leaves a disgusting message on our answering machine. She tells me to do two things. First, tell myself over and over again that it's not my fault. And second, avoid the things that trigger bad memories and cause anxiety attacks. I always tell her it's hard to do that when the biggest trigger is your own body.

—**Ashley E. Lawrence, victim impact statement**

NOW

BELLFORD, OHIO

Time stops when Derek walks out.

He never looks back. He doesn't even dramatically slam the door.

He just leaves. Nothing but empty space where he stood a second ago.

We all stare at Mom, arms stretched toward the door, hoping that he'll walk back inside and say something stupid like, "Can't get rid of me that easily."

But…

Nothing.

The really messed-up part is that I don't know how I feel about this. I'm still bleeding from Dad's big revelation about forgiving me, still wobbly after passing out during that last anxiety attack—thanks a lot, Derek—and now this. I ache because Mom looks like somebody just died, and Justin looks like he wants to vomit.

I burrow deeper into the sofa and curl my legs under me. Dad stands by the dining room, his eyes shifting from me to the front door and back again. Justin is the first one to move. He walks over to me and smooths the hair back from my face.

"Better?"

I nod.

"Good." He sits on the coffee table to face me. "You need to fix this, Ashley."

"Justin—" Mom turns to him, but he shakes his head.

"No, Mom. This needs to stop. Ash, I'm serious. You've punished him long enough. Let it go."

I stare at him in total disbelief.

"I know what you're thinking," he continues. "Nobody understands. Nobody gets what you've been through. You're right. We don't. We *can't*." He spreads his hands apart and lets them fall with a slap against his legs. "But you don't understand what we've been through, either."

I open my mouth, but he cuts me off before I can argue.

"Ashley, just listen."

Fine. I drop my head back and let him speak.

"You don't understand how it broke us, all of us, to know what happened to you. What was done to you. I kept thinking, maybe if I was home more, it wouldn't have happened. Maybe if you and I were closer, it wouldn't have happened. But it *did*. After, when you came home, we all had to learn how to help you, how to make sure you knew you were safe, knew you were loved, and we've *done* that, Ashley. But you need to try, too."

"Are you kidding me right now?" I demand. "Try? Try what, exactly?" My voice grows louder as I talk. "Try to pretend everything's fine, that I'm fine? Well, I'm not, and I never will be again."

"You can if you want to!" he shouts back. "That's the whole problem. You don't *want* to. You keep looking at the past, trying—no. *Insisting* that we all change it. The trial didn't go your way, the sentence sucked, and you know what? It cannot be changed." He lets that sink in for a minute, and I'm shaking.

"Ashley, the only thing you can change is yourself, but you won't even try. You want to punish Derek for the rest of his life for a couple of mean things he said to you, and I'm sorry, Ashley, but you can't. He's our brother. I'm *not* choosing you over him."

"So you'll choose him over me? Nice, Justin. Real nice."

"Damn it, Ashley, you still don't get it. I'm not choosing at all! I want my *whole* family."

"Yeah, well, I want to be an only child, how's that?"

He recoils like I just kicked him in the teeth. He drops his head into his hands and stands up. "You know what? Maybe that can be arranged." He grabs his coat from the hook near the door and walks out.

When the door clicks shut after him, I am afraid to look at Mom and Dad. Mom just stands in the same place she's been in since I opened my eyes—frozen in shock.

Dad moves first, walking across the room, putting his arms around her, pulling her against him. She shoves him back with a tortured moan and runs up the stairs. Dad's arms, still open, hang there, empty. A minute later, he too grabs his coat and leaves the house.

Three for three.

I pull myself up on shaky legs. I have cleaning to do. Two rooms of it. As I stand, the cool towel Derek pressed to my head falls to the floor in a heap. I pick it up and stare at it for a long time. I feel nothing.

Absolutely nothing.

I should feel bad. Or guilty. Or even angry.

But there's nothing. Just a numb hollowness so vast, I swear there's an echo with each breath.

In the dining room, I grab the bowls of meatballs and spaghetti, wrap them in plastic wrap, and try to shove them in the refrigerator, but there's no room. A giant turkey takes up a ton of space. Sighing, I transfer the leftovers to plastic containers and find room in the freezer instead. I collect all the dishes and flatware and load them into the dishwasher. It takes me close to forty minutes to clean up the dining room and kitchen. When it's finally clean, I step back and examine my work.

Perfect.

There's no evidence, no chalk outline, not even a single drop of spilled blood to tell you a whole family just disintegrated in here.

I slap both hands over my mouth to kill the sob and just let the tears come. I indulge myself for a long time, and then my phone buzzes.

And buzzes.

And buzzes.

Impatient, I tug it out of my pocket. A string of text messages waits for me, most from Brittany and a couple from Sebastian.

Brittany: Ash, I'm worried about Derek. Look what he left for me.

There's a picture attached to the message. Derek's scrawl across a birthday card makes me frown. *Brittany, I bought this when I thought I had something to offer you. I know better now, but I can't return it and can't give it away, so keep it and remember me when my heart was full of love for you. I'm leaving and won't be back. I'm sorry. Goodbye.*

Brittany: Ash, call me! I'm really worried. Is he suicidal?

What? Derek, suicidal? No. No way.

But apprehension skates up my back. Is he?

I sink into one of the dining room chairs and try to think.

You're wrong, he'd said. *I blamed me.*

His face was red, so red he looked like he might stroke out. His eyes, the eyes I used to be so jealous I didn't inherit, held no sparkle, no life. They were flat and empty, except during dinner, when he'd yelled at Dad. Then, they'd been full of rage. *There is nothing to forgive!* he'd yelled at Dad.

I gasp. How did I miss it? I was so friggin' angry at him, I couldn't see it. I *didn't* see it. Derek *meant* it. Growing up, Derek said so many things he never meant. He used to toss around *Sorry, Ashleys* like they were his football and then stick out his tongue or shrug his shoulders the second Mom turned her back.

But this time, he meant it.

And I didn't fucking see it.

I stare at the phone clutched in my hands like it'll tell me where I messed up or how to fix this, but all it does is display an email alert from my brother.

Hi Ashley,

I am sorry. I know you don't believe that, and I also know you never can. So I'm taking off. Thought you might like these for your Pinterest board. It's really good work. Bye, April.

I open the zip file. Inside, there are six images that I recognize. One picture is from a pumpkin picking day trip we took back when I was about ten maybe. Justin, Derek, and I are standing in a huge field surrounded by pumpkins, each of us holding our pick.

But in this version, Derek is gone.

The photo is Justin and me, with more pumpkins between us. I click through all six pictures. It's the same thing. Where we were once three, there are now only two. But it's the last picture that does me in.

The last picture is—was—of the three of us cuddled under a blanket, watching a movie. Now, it's just two of us. Where Derek had been, there's only the huge bowl of popcorn.

There's a caption on this image. "Instead of punishing her rapist, how about punishing the brother who told the court her rapist didn't need to go to prison for one mistake?"

My lip quivers. Oh, God, Derek.

Justin's words replay in my head.

You want to punish Derek for the rest of his life.

No. I put the phone away. No. I stand up and scrub the counter that already gleams.

That is *not* what I'm doing. Derek is a trigger for me. All I'm doing is what I need to do so I can heal, so I can survive. If he can't take it, that's his problem. Maybe if he'd spent less time calling me Ash Tray and ditching me on my first day of school and making me feel unwanted and for making me a target in his stupid scavenger hunt and for abandoning me when I needed him the most, when the sun went down and never came back out, when the bad dreams and anxiety attacks and threats from people we used to know poured in. Maybe if he actually acknowledged the worst thing that happened to me, that could have ever happened to me, and called it what it is instead of *a mistake*—

You're punishing him for not tearing Victor Patton apart for you.

The thought is a gut punch and steals my breath away.

I clench my hands into fists so I don't have to think it again, don't have to face it. Derek deserves the guilt he feels. He should suffer the way he made me suffer for the past...how many years now?

You're punishing him for not tearing Victor Patton apart for you.

"No! I'm not."

The dishwasher clicks over to the end of the cycle, and I remember what today is. What tomorrow is. Mom said she wanted all of her babies together. And now she's upstairs sobbing because Derek had to be a jerk. I stalk out of the kitchen and pace the living room.

You're punishing him.

Justin's words are like an itch I can't help but scratch. As soon as I do, it blooms to a rash that spreads fast and far, and the more I scratch, the more I itch, and damn it, damn it, damn it, okay!

I *am* punishing Derek. I'm punishing him because he didn't defend me and because he didn't do a single thing to help me. In fact, he did the opposite of help.

You're punishing him.

"Ashley."

I lift my head and find Mom on the bottom step, mascara streaks down her too-pale face, and her entire body shakes likes she's being torn into pieces, and oh my God, she *is*.

Dr. Joyce's words haunt me. She said I need to avoid the things that trigger me. And then Sebastian's words join in. He said I'm unstoppable, but I'm not. I'm...

It hits me then, with all the force of an atom splitting, exactly what I am.

I'm scared.

I've been scared for years now. Scared all the way down to my bones but *not* of Victor Patton. I've been scared of this, *exactly* this…of my family blaming *me* for the rape, of taking Derek's side instead of mine, of hearing him say it was my fault, that every snub, every harassing phone call, every nasty look and whispered remark…all of it was my fault. Only Derek didn't do that. My father did.

Derek defended me. Derek, the brother who calls me Ash Tray and ditches me any chance he gets and…volunteers with a sexual assault awareness group. He *defended* me.

And I made him leave.

Justin is right. I *am* holding on to the past. But Sebastian's right, too. I *am* unstoppable. For the first time in more than two years, I know what I have to do.

I have to *choose* what to fight for. I thought I was supposed to fight for justice, and I did that. But justice wasn't enough, not for me. I need more.

Now, I'm choosing my family.

I stand up, walk to the steps, and hold out my hand. "Mom. Let's go find Derek."

She stares at me for a minute and then she shakes off her expression the way a dog sheds water. She grabs our coats, and we are out the front door before I can take another breath.

......

"You're sure he's not here?" Mom asks as we pull up in front of Brittany's house.

"Yes. She said he left the gift on the doorstep." I shoot Britt a fast text message, and seconds later, she's in the back of the car. I twist around so I can see her.

"I'm really worried," she says with an anxious glance at my mother. "He's been quiet. Too quiet. I think he's been planning to leave for good for a while now, and I… God, I didn't pick up on it."

"But where would he go? He doesn't have money to just… take off like this."

"I don't know!" Britt shakes her head. "He was supposed to speak at Ohio State. There's a GAR event there tonight."

I wave that away. "He won't be there. Derek hates public speaking."

But Brittany shakes her head. "He *volunteered* for this, so I don't think he'd blow it off."

"Volunteered for what?" Mom echoes. "And what is GAR, anyway?"

"It stands for Guys Against Rape. Derek's been involved in our school's chapter since September."

Mom glances over at me in the passenger seat. "Did you know about this?"

I shrug. He may have mentioned it in that bragging sort of way. That's Derek…doing whatever he can for the points.

"Text Justin and Dad. Tell them what's up and that we're driving to Columbus now," Mom orders.

Sighing, I do. Neither one responds. The ride is tense and long. Traffic is ridiculous, as it always is before a holiday. By the time we arrive and park, it's after nine.

"We missed it. I know it," Mom says, her voice choked.

"No, I don't think so. At our school, these events go on for a while," Brittany says. "Come on." She takes off at a jog, heading for one of those you-are-here maps under lighted glass in the center of a footpath.

We follow the signs and eventually find the building where the GAR event is being held. The room is on the first floor. It's a large theater-style classroom, filled to capacity, which is about a hundred and fifty people. We sneak in, slowly closing the heavy steel door so it doesn't make a sound, and find ourselves at the rear of the huge lecture hall, where it's dark. Below us, a man in a suit speaks at a podium, his head facing the slides displayed on a screen behind him. People take notes and look bored. The room smells like industrial cleaner and just the barest hint of male sweat. I roll my shoulders and put that thought firmly out of mind.

"Okay, that's it for me. I hope you'll seriously consider joining GAR and standing up for those who have been hurt."

Polite applause rings out across the large hall.

Mom's frantic. "He's not here. Maybe we should—"

"Mom." I point to the podium. She gasps, but I grab her hand and hold her back. Derek is walking toward it like a man about to be executed. I want to see what he's going to do. He shakes the man's hand and spends a minute hooking up his computer to the projector. When he's ready, Derek clears his throat and shoves his hands into his pockets. He leans into the podium's mic and over the reverb introduces himself.

"My name is Derek Lawrence. I've been a GAR member for a couple of months now. I joined because somebody close to me got raped."

Mom's hand, still clasped in mine, squeezes before I can even react to that.

"No. That's not entirely true," Derek continues. "That may have been the reason I went to my first meeting, but I signed up because I finally realized rape was *my* problem, too." He spreads his arms apart. "I mean, look at me. I'm six-foot-three and two hundred pounds. Rape isn't something I worry about. I walk outside at night. I park my car anywhere I want. It doesn't bother me who gets on the elevator after me. I've never had a date demand services after she spent money on me. I go through life feeling relatively safe. The women I know? They go through life scared…and the part that sucks the most? It never occurred to me to help them."

A ripple of discomfort skates over the crowd. Derek adjusts the mic's flexible neck.

"My girlfriend," he begins, and immediately stops like someone just kicked him in the groin. "Well. We're not exactly together right now."

Next to me, Brittany covers her mouth with both hands. Mom wraps an arm around her.

"This really great girl I know told me to check out these

Twitter hashtags. Maybe you've heard of them. *Me Too* and *Yes All Women*."

Derek clicks a few keys on the computer, and when Twitter appears on the screen, he displays the current tweets from the hashtag, scrolling down. The tweets are horrifying. Derek stops scrolling and reads one out loud. "Every woman I know has a *Me Too* story. Every single one, even my mom."

I stare at my mother. "You do?"

"Shh." She flips what I said away, her eyes glued to Derek.

He turns back to his audience. "Guys, I know what you're thinking. I thought it, too. Trust me. They're not exaggerating. The more tweets and stories I read, the more I understand that this rape culture thing? It's *everybody's* problem."

"That's just bull. Not everybody rapes, man. Not every guy is a pig," someone down in the front row calls out. "I'm a nice guy. I don't treat girls like that."

Still on the stage, Derek walks away from the podium and asks him, "So you're not that guy?"

"Yeah. Exactly."

"Great!"

I take a step forward and lean over a half wall that circles the top of the theater, dying to hear what he says next.

"Show of hands—how many of you are nice guys?"

Unsurprisingly, all the hands go up.

"Keep your hands up. If you've ever said nothing while one of your pals harasses a girl walking by, put your hand down."

A bunch of hands go down, but not without more grumbling.

"Hold up. I'll explain in a minute. If you've ever said 'She's lying' after an athlete or celebrity you admire got accused of rape, put your hand down."

More hands disappear.

"If the first thing you said after hearing the news about a rape was something like 'Why was she jogging there by herself?' or 'Why was she wearing that outfit?' put your hand down. If you've ever used feminine words as insults, like calling your friends a pussy or saying they fight like a girl, put your hands down."

When there are only five or six hands still in the air, Derek lifts his own. "You seeing the pattern now?"

Nobody answers him, and Derek holds up one finger. "Okay, guys, put your hands down. The point I'm trying to make is I didn't get it, either, not for a long time." He moves back to the computer and clicks a couple of keys. He shows an image that dumps acid into my gut.

"Anybody recognize this?" he asks, jerking a thumb to the screen behind him. It's his scavenger hunt list. "I'll give you a hint. Two years ago, I played football for the Bellford Bengals."

This time, the sound is no ripple. It's a collective gasp.

"Yeah. *Those* Bengals. The ones who played a scavenger hunt that got our coach fired, our football program canceled...and my sister raped."

Another gasp. Someone calls out, "The Bellford High School rape victim is your sister?"

"Yeah." Derek nods, and I feel a wave of shame wash over me. That title has become my name now.

"Two years ago, when I was a high school junior, there was one guy on our team who said he wouldn't play in the scavenger hunt because it scared the girls."

Sebastian. My heart flips over.

"I wish I could tell you I was that guy, but…no, I played and scored over a hundred points, completing my card. Some cards had stuff on them like sex in public, sex on a moving vehicle, sex with a virgin. That's the one that led to my sister's rape. Over the past two years, I've replayed the day I chose my card, that moment, a few million times. If I'd stood next to the guy who said no and backed him up, I'm convinced a few of my buddies would have stood up with me. And maybe a few more guys with them. If I'd done that, I think my teammate wouldn't have picked my sister to target, and if he hadn't raped her, I'm dead-set sure my family wouldn't be falling apart."

Beside me, Mom lets out a broken breath and stretches out a hand to Derek. But he can't see us way up here. He clicks some more keys, and the screen refreshes. This time, it's a picture of us. Justin, him, and me. Big cheesy smiles, Derek in the center, as always.

"This is us before."

Click.

"And this is us after." Great chasms of distance with Justin on one end of the sofa, me on the other, and Derek on a chair. He's the only one attempting a grin. "My sister can't…" His voice cracks, and so does my heart. "She can't tolerate my presence, which is funny in a way, because this before-and-after idea? I got it from her."

From my Pinterest board. Derek saw my Pinterest board. I lift a hand to my face because it aches. I'm…I think I'm actually smiling.

At my brother.

"It doesn't matter how sorry I am, and believe me, I am. I used to be a superhero to her. My roommate and my girl are both psych majors, so I've learned from them that I'm kind of a walking, talking trigger for Ashley. The tension is massive," he says, holding his hands apart as if to measure it. "And it's hurting everybody. My parents are on the brink of divorce. My chess-club brother has taken up bare-knuckle fighting."

What? What? I whip around to my mother, but she drops her head and won't meet my gaze. I asked her, and she said everything was fine. I should have known. How could I not see any of this?

Because you never wanted to look too closely.

"It all goes back to that moment, in the locker room, when I picked that stupid card and decided to play a dishonorable game instead of saying no, instead of standing up to the guys who think this is how you prove you're a man."

Derek wipes his face and…God, he's crying. The last time he cried…it was in my hospital room.

He clicks another key, and suddenly, it's there. My Pinterest board. "Here's the work my sister's been doing. Every day, there are moments like these," he says, stabbing a finger toward the screen. "No big deal, right? They're funny. They're not meant to be taken seriously. What's the big deal? Well, if you look at the tweets under those hashtags, you'll see. Better yet, ask. Go home tonight and ask the women you know—moms, sisters, friends. Ask them if they have a *Me Too* or *Yes All Women* story. I guarantee they will. In fact, they'll have more than one. Because every day, while we're busy pretending it's not happening, the women we know are facing questionable, creepy, and outright threatening behavior from guys. What I'm saying is it doesn't matter if you're not *that guy*. What matters is we're the guys who keep ignoring this crappy behavior because we're afraid we'll look like wusses."

Derek pauses.

I lean forward.

He waits and scans the faces he can see.

"We've ignored and pretended for way too long. The reason men like Ariel Castro and Elliot Rodger and Aaron Persky exist is because men like us never called them out on their bullshit the first time they showed it." One by one, Derek clicks through newspaper accounts of the man who kept women imprisoned in his house for a decade, of the man who went on a shooting spree because women didn't pay attention to him, and of the man who sentenced a rapist to only six months in prison.

I swipe a hand over my face, shocked to find it wet from tears. There's this warmth in my chest...a comfortable, soothing warmth right under my heart, and I swear it's actual pride. All this time, I thought Derek was bullshitting me, going through the motions to placate Mom and Dad, but he wasn't. He gets it. He truly gets it, and oh, God, that's worth more to me than infinite apologies.

Derek moves out from the podium to the center of the stage. "I'm here because we need you. Not GAR, but women. Humanity. We need men like you, men who don't need to prove anything to anybody. Men who do what needs doing because it's right. So what do you say, guys? If you're not that guy, are you strong enough to call out the guys who are? Will you speak up when you witness misogyny and sexism and shut that shit down?"

The room erupts in applause and cheers that rattle my brain. A few of the guys stand and approach Derek to shake his hand.

I'm on the top step, moving down. I'm not even thinking about it. Just moving.

One step.

Another step.

Another.

I'm on the floor now, surrounded by men I don't know...so close, I can feel their heat. They could hurt me, but there's no fear, no anxiety. All I feel is relief...this huge satisfaction, this immense joy. It's like I finally found that thing I'd been missing, hidden in the shadows of ourselves.

April and Leo.

Me...and my brother.

"Leo," I say, and my voice is nothing more than a rasp.

Heads swivel my way. I hear Derek's sharp breath, and the crowd separating us moves aside. Our eyes meet, and his mouth falls open, and he goes so completely still, I swear even his heart stops beating. There's this seismic shift that realigns all my broken, scattered, and missing pieces, and suddenly, we're crying and laughing at the same time, and he's hugging me so hard, I may snap, but I don't care a bit.

"I'm sorry. I'm so sorry, Ashley. God, please, please, please tell me you believe me."

I do. I do believe him.

"It's okay now, Derek. It'll be okay now."

I believe me, too.

EPILOGUE

I know drinking beer at my age is wrong. I think ignoring me when I tell you I'm dizzy and sick is also wrong. I think stripping my clothes off and putting a hand over my mouth because I'm screaming for help is wrong. I think forcing me down into the dirt and garbage to take points in a scavenger hunt that never should have been started is wrong. The defendant did all those things, Your Honor. He should be punished to the fullest extent of the law because doing anything less tells him he wasn't wrong, that what he did to me, what he took from me, is okay, and it's not. I'm a person, not a trophy, not a game. I deserve justice.

—**Ashley E. Lawrence, victim impact statement**

NOW
ASHLEY

"I am so full," Justin groans from my left. He's sprawled in the corner of the sofa, belt loosened and feet propped up on the coffee table.

"Me too," Derek adds from my right in pretty much the same position.

My lips twitch. "Maybe you guys shouldn't have bogarted the drumsticks."

"Oh my God, Ash, you didn't starve, did you?" Justin reminds me.

"No, but I did want a drumstick."

"Yeah, well, turkeys only come with two, and there are three of us."

"Don't remind me."

A finger drills me in the ribs, and I squeal, slapping Derek's hand away. The three of us are huddled under a blanket, and bowls of popcorn—untouched—sit on the coffee table in front of us. Aunt Pam, Aunt Debra, our cousins, and grandparents have all gone home—finally. Mom is already asleep on the far end of the huge sectional sofa. Dad's asleep in his chair.

I swear they're both smiling.

It's just like those sappy pictures Mom took of us when we were little. Except this time, I'm in the middle.

I actually kind of like it.

Thanksgiving had been quiet this year. Real quiet. Calm, maybe. Yeah. That's it. Calm. Derek woke up me early, said he was heading out to meet Brittany for breakfast, and asked if I wanted him to bring me back a bagel. When I made it downstairs, I found Dad sitting at the table with a cup of coffee, waiting.

For me.

"Ashley, I know I don't deserve it, but I would love if you

could just forget every word I said last night. I didn't mean it. I was angry at all of you. Had been for a very long time."

Dad's words reminded me of Derek's at last night's GAR meeting. I'd never noticed how that tension had impacted everybody else in this family. I may have been the one who'd been raped. But I was never in this alone. I wish I'd seen that. I wish I hadn't been so blinded by my own torment.

"The truth is, I'm proud of you. Proud of the fearless way you've approached life since the assault and proud of the way you saved us all last night."

I stared at his profile while he sipped coffee. *Proud, fearless* and *saved*? I didn't know if any of those words applied to me. "Dad, I'm not fearless at all."

He shook his head. "You *are*. Do you think I haven't noticed the way you tense up when you have to leave the house, but do it anyway? I've been watching you carefully, Ashley. I wasn't careful before, but I am now. I watched your video. I've talked to the principal at your school and know how many signatures you got for Raise the BAR. I read the letter you sent to the judge, to the newspapers. And the stuff on your Pinterest page is brilliant. I'm damn proud of Derek, too. He was willing to remove himself from our lives to give you the space you needed. Did you know he was thinking of enlisting?"

A wave of nausea swelled, and I bit my lip. I hadn't known that, and the thought of him fighting a thousand miles away does me in. Dad reaches across the table and squeezes my hand.

"Ashley, I promise—no matter how angry one of you three makes me, I will never say something as cruel as I did last night. I hope you can forgive me."

It occurred to me in that moment that forgiveness was one of those concepts that everybody thought they understood but didn't. It was so easy to say, "Sure! I forgive you." But meaning it? That was a whole other story. *Forgiveness* is rarely this once-and-done thing. It's an ongoing battle, a struggle to remember that love is worth more than pain, and that fighting for it matters more than a grudge.

"Okay, what are we watching?" Justin grabs the remote, jerking me back to the here and now.

Derek's cell phone buzzes.

"Is that Brittany?" I ask when he tugs it from his pocket.

"Mmm-hmm." He taps out a reply and puts the phone away.

"Derek, you talked to her, right? Apologized? She was seriously worried about you." So was I.

"Yeah, yeah, relax, *Mom*. I went over there this morning and took her out to breakfast. Everything's cool. She just wanted to make sure you haven't poisoned my pumpkin pie or anything."

"You noticed I didn't have a piece, right?"

His eyes snap to mine, and it takes him a second before he grins. "Touché." He settles deeper into the sofa. "I told Brittany something this morning that I guess you guys should know because…well, you'll hopefully be seeing a lot more of her."

"Yeah? What?" Justin asked in a sleepy voice.

"I told her I love her. You know. Like, *in love* with her."

Justin and I exchange surprised looks. "Holy crap, bro."

"Did she say it back?" I demand to know.

Derek's face splits into the biggest smile I've ever seen. "Yeah. Don't ask me why, but she did."

A warm tingle spreads over me. I know why.

And then Justin opens his mouth. "Dude, you're such a girl."

Derek reaches over me and punches Justin in the arm. "We've talked about this, J. That's sexist and misogynistic."

I offer Derek my fist to bump. Justin manfully doesn't let out a peep. But he rubs that arm for the next twenty minutes.

The credits are just starting to roll on *National Lampoon's Christmas Vacation* when a knock on the door makes us all jerk.

"I'll get it," Justin offers since he's closest to the door.

A few seconds later, Sebastian walks into the living room. When he sees the blanket covering Derek, me, and the spot where Justin had been sitting, he smiles.

"Hey, Sebas. Did you have a good Thanksgiving?"

Shrugging, he jerks his head to the side, flipping his hair. "Not bad. I just wanted to see how you're doing."

"Good," I tell him.

And yeah, I really mean it.

"We're about to watch a sappy Christmas movie. Want in on that?" Justin asks.

Sebastian laughs. "Which one?"

Derek ticks them off his fingers. "Uh, we've got *Home Alone* and *Home Alone 2*—anything after that doesn't really count— and *Elf.*"

Sebastian shakes his head. "Nah, I just wanted to check up on my girl."

His girl.

Derek and Justin exchange a look that's so evil, I immediately brace for impact.

"Awww," they say in perfect unison, complete with matching levels of sarcasm, and it's so normal, so incredibly typical, I just smile and let them have their fun.

I can always get even later.

"Give us a few minutes." I detangle myself from the blanket and tug Sebastian into the kitchen. I grab two forks and cut us a piece of leftover apple pie to share. When I hand Sebastian his fork, he's staring at the oven we rented for the day.

"What's this?"

"Rental oven," I tell him proudly. "It's a de-stresser, trust me."

This time, he looks at me, angling his head to study me carefully.

"You look good, Ashley."

I'm wearing pajama bottoms and an old ratty flannel shirt. "Um, seriously?"

"No, not the outfit. I mean, you're…" He trails off, circling his hands to find the right words. "You're like really relaxed and happy."

I am.

He grabs a chair and leans forward. "So what happened last night? When you didn't text me back, I got scared."

Yeah. I was scared, too. "Derek took off, but we went after him, and we talked."

"So everything's okay now?"

"It got…pretty intense." I pull out the chair beside him and sit. "Derek said he'd see Dr. Joyce with me and maybe separately, too," I tell him. "Oh, and Justin, too. He's tired of punching people."

Sebastian's eyes bulge. "Punching who?"

I shrug. "Apparently, anybody who talks shit about me."

"Well, hell."

"Yeah."

I guess it's true that still waters go deep. I was weirdly touched by Justin's attempts to defend my honor and horrified that I'd become so furious with one brother for not defending me, I never noticed the other brother had been doing exactly that.

"And your dad?" He takes my hand, and I look up at him, smiling.

"Everything's not quite okay yet. But it can be. It will be."

His eyes, those beautiful hazel eyes, crinkle at the corners. "Yeah. It will be." He reaches over and cups my face in both hands…and waits for me to decide if I'll choose fear or love.

I lean in and touch his lips with mine, and it's this perfect moment when there's no pain, no scar tissue, no shame or guilt or grief—just a girl who's a little bit in love with a boy with Nike swoosh hair and magic eyes who maybe loves her back and is willing to let her set the pace. His lips are warm and firm, and his hands gently caress my face, my hair, my neck, making me feel like something valuable, something treasured, something that matters. We angle our heads, move closer, and let the kiss go on for a long time. I'm warm, soothed, and stirred up and can feel all these dark and hidden parts of me ignite, parts I was sure had been drowned in hurt and anger.

Every last bit of the pain and shame and guilt and grief I've carried since my freshman year drips from my soul, collecting in a reservoir. They're not gone for good though, and I know they'll leak out sometimes.

But my dam is stronger now. Higher walls. Reinforced not with concrete and steel, but with unbreakable family ties.

RESOURCES

The statistics in *Someone I Used to Know* are frighteningly true. Sexualized violence is more prevalent at colleges as compared to other crimes. But *you* can help. If you're interested in creating a rally at your school similar to the ones depicted in this novel, please contact these organizations. They're happy to help you get a program off the ground.

- **Take Back the Night**: Visit takebackthenight.org to learn how you can organize rallies, glow runs, and other events to encourage activism in your area, as well as support healing and end sexualized violence.
- **End Rape on Campus (EROC)**: Visit endrapeoncampus .org and learn how you can help change the sexual assault policy at your school. This organization directly supports students as well as their communities.

- **Students Active For Ending Rape (SAFER)**: Visit www .nsvrc.org/organizations/3521 and learn how to draft a campus policy for your school including information about federal law, training programs, and mentoring that brings about change through community mobilization.
- **National Sexual Violence Resource Center**: Visit www .nsvrc.org for access to a national library of resources related to sexual violence and its prevention including publications, projects, and organizations committed to eliminating such violence.

If you or someone close to you experienced sexualized violence including molestation, assault, or rape, I urge you to seek help from organizations like the following, where team members are skilled in helping you cope with the crime committed against you, no matter when or how it occurred:

- **Rape, Abuse, and Incest National Network (RAINN)**: This organization is the United States's largest anti-sexual-violence organization and operator of the National Sexual Assault Hotline (1-800-656-HOPE). RAINN can help you find medical treatment, help family members learn how to support your recovery, and help you navigate the legal system. Visit rainn.org for more information.
- **National Sexual Violence Resource Center (NSVRC)**: This organization can help you find a local chapter if you or someone you love is a survivor of sexual violence.

If you'd like information about Ashley's pledge form and want to create your own, start here:

- **It's On Us**: Visit itsonus.org to take the pledge.
- **Men Can Stop Rape**: Visit mencanstoprape.org to take the pledge against domestic violence.
- **Men's Involvement**: Visit the National Center on Domestic and Sexual Violence's links page at www.ncdsv.org/ncd _linksmaleadvoc.html for a list of ways men can help prevent sexualized violence.
- **#HowIWillChange**: Follow this Twitter conversation, along with **#MeToo** and **#YesAllWomen** and listen to the stories.

If you're a relative or friend of someone who's survived sexual violence, understand that you are also a victim and need help. Don't try to go it alone. These wonderful organizations are staffed with experts and volunteers who know exactly what you're going through. They can help. Please let them.

You are not alone. I believe you.

ACKNOWLEDGMENTS

Usually, this is where an author thanks the people without whom a book could not have been written. Well, in this case, this book *truly* would not exist without Annie Berger, Evan Gregory, and Annette Pollert-Morgan. For most authors, ideas abound and are so plentiful, they fret over not having the time to write them all. For me, ideas are scarce...a feast during a famine. When I find an idea, I write that book and then starve until another one grows. It was during one of these idea famines when the four of us hopped on a conference call to discuss a possible *Some Boys* sequel. Out of this discussion, Ashley and Derek were born. Originally titled *Boys Will Be Boys*, this story explores the toxic masculinity we've been seeing unfold in Hollywood, in Washington, DC, and in various other segments of society. We later changed it to *Someone I Used to Know* for several reasons. First, the idea of a sibling fallout intrigued me. Blood's supposed to be thicker than water, so the idea of exploring issues so divisive they actually break up a family became something I needed to explore. Second, we thought the original title might turn male readers away from the story. Third, because so many sexual assaults are perpetrated not by strangers, but by friends, relatives, or acquaintances, this new title took on more than one meaning.

Thank you to my son, Chris, whose experiences at a local state university fueled many of Derek's chapters.

Special thanks to Katie K. and my friends Laura Cassini, Geoff Symon, and Deb Z. All provided essential realism to significant sections of this story. Katie, from the Take Back the Night organization, helped me obtain permission to use the organization's name in this story. Laura, an attorney, explained trial process and rape sentencing. Geoff, a forensic investigator, described the purpose and procedure of collecting evidence during a sexual assault examination, better known as a rape kit. Deb, a rape survivor, shared the painfully personal details of her assault to help me inform Ashley's healing process. Any inaccuracies in my portrayals of the Rocky Hill University Take Back the Night rally, Victor's rape trial, and Ashley's experiences are my mistakes.

Thank you to all the members of RWA, especially the LIRW, CTRWA, and YARWA chapters, whose blogs and emails provided support and the knowledge that though it may often feel otherwise, I'm never alone on this journey.

Thank you to every reader who sent messages thanking me for writing a strong heroine like Grace Collier. I hope you'll find Ashley Lawrence a worthy successor.

Finally, a personal note of thanks to every survivor who shared a #MeToo story.

I hear you. I believe you. And I'm fighting for you.

ABOUT THE AUTHOR

Powered by way too much chocolate, award-winning author Patty Blount loves to write and has written everything from technical manuals to poetry. A 2015 CLMP Firecracker Award winner as well as Rita finalist, Patty writes issue-based novels for teens and is currently working on a romantic thriller. Her editor claims she writes her best work when she's mad, so if you happen to upset Patty and don't have any chocolate on hand to throw at her, prepare to be the subject of an upcoming novel. Patty lives on Long Island with her family in a house that sadly doesn't have anywhere near enough bookshelves...or chocolate.

SOME BOYS GO TOO FAR.

SOME BOYS WILL BREAK YOUR HEART.

BUT ONE BOY CAN MEND IT.

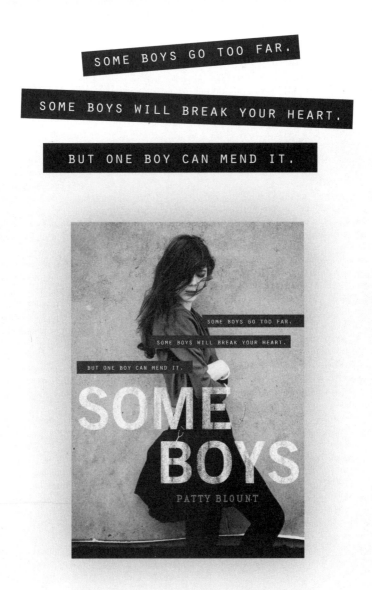

"A bold and necessary look at an important, and
very real, topic. Everyone should read this book."
— Jennifer Brown, author of
Thousand Words and *Hate List*

Chapter 1

GRACE

No Monday in history has ever sucked more than this one.

I'm kind of an expert on sucky days. It's been thirty-two of them since the party in the woods that started the battle I fight every day. I step onto the bus to school, wearing my armor and pretending nothing's wrong, nothing happened, nothing changed when it's pretty obvious nothing will ever be the same again. Alyssa Martin, a girl I've known since first grade, smirks and stretches her leg across the empty seat next to hers.

I approach slowly, hoping nobody can see my knees knocking. A couple of weeks ago during a school newspaper staff meeting, Alyssa vowed her support, and today I'm pond scum.

"Find a seat!" Mrs. Gannon, the bus driver, shouts.

I meet Alyssa's eyes, silently beg her for sympathy—even a little pity. She raises a middle finger. It's a show of loyalty to someone who doesn't deserve it, a challenge to see how far I'll go.

My dad keeps telling me to stand up to all of Zac's defenders, but it's the entire bus—the entire *school*—versus me.

I gulp hard, and the bus lurches forward. I try to grab a seat back but lose my balance and topple into the seat Alyssa's blocking with her leg. She lets out a screech of pain.

"Bitch," she sneers. "You nearly broke my leg."

I'm about to apologize when I notice the people sitting around us stare with wide eyes and hands over their open mouths. When my eyes meet theirs, they turn away, but nobody *does* anything.

This is weird.

Alyssa folds herself against the window and shoves earbuds into her ears and ignores me for the duration of the ride.

The rest of the trip passes without incident—except for two girls whispering over a video playing on a phone they both clutch in their hands. One of them murmurs, "Six hundred and eighteen hits," and shoots me a dirty look.

I know exactly what she means and don't want to think about it. I look away. As soon as the bus stops, I'm off. On my way to my locker, most people just ignore me, although a few still think they've come up with a clever new insult. An elbow or the occasional extended foot still needs dodging, but it's really not that bad. I can deal. I can do this. I can make it through school unless I see—

"Woof! Woof!"

My feet root themselves to the floor, and the breath clogs in my lungs. And I know without turning who barked at me. I force myself to keep walking instead of running for home, running for the next town. I want to turn to look at him, look him dead in the eye, and twist my face into something that shows contempt instead of the terror that too often wins whenever I hear his name so he sees—so he *knows*—he didn't beat me. But that doesn't happen. A foot appears from nowhere, and I can't dodge it in time. I fall to my hands and knees, and two more familiar faces step out of the crowd to laugh down at me.

"Hear you like it on your knees," Kyle Moran shouts, and everybody laughs. At least Matt Roberts helps me up, but when Kyle smacks his head, he takes off before I can thank him. They're two of *his* best buds. Nausea boils inside me, and I scramble back to my feet. I grab my backpack, pray that the school's expensive digital camera tucked inside it isn't damaged, and duck into the girls' bathroom, locking myself into a stall.

When my hands are steady, eyes are dry, stomach's no longer threatening to send back breakfast, I open the stall.

Miranda and Lindsay, my two best friends, stand in front of the mirrors.

Make that *former* best friends.

We stare at one another through the mirrors. Lindsay leans against a sink but doesn't say anything. Miranda runs a hand down her smooth blond hair, pretends I'm not there, and talks to Lindsay. "So I've decided to have a party and invite Zac and the rest of the lacrosse team. It's going to be epic."

No. Not him. The blood freezes in my veins. "Miranda. Don't. Please."

Miranda's hand freezes on her hair. "Don't, please?" She

shakes her head in disgust. "You know, he could get kicked off the lacrosse team because of you."

"Good!" I scream, suddenly furious.

Miranda whips back around to face me, hair blurring like a fan blade. At the sink, Lindsay's jaw drops. "God! I can't believe you! Did you do all of this, say all this just to get back at me?"

My jaw drops. "What? Of course not. I—"

"You *know* I like him. If you didn't want me to go out with him, all you had to do was say so—"

"Miranda, this isn't about you. Trust me, Zac is—"

"Oh my God, listen to yourself. He breaks up with you, and you fall apart and then—"

"That is *not* what happened. I broke up with him! I was upset that night because of Kristie, and you know it."

She spins around, arms flung high. "Kristie! Seriously? You played him. You wanted everybody to feel sorry for you, so you turned on the tears and got Zac to—"

"Me? Are you insane? He—"

"Oh, don't even." Miranda holds up a hand. "I know exactly what happened. I was there. I know what you said. I figured you were lying, and now there's no doubt."

Lindsay nods and tosses her bag over her shoulder, and they stalk to the door. At the door, Miranda fires off one more shot. "You're a lying slut, and I'll make sure the whole school knows it."

The door slams behind them, echoing off the lavatory stalls. I'm standing in the center of the room, wondering what's holding me up because I can't feel my feet...or my hands. I raise them to make sure I still have hands, and before my eyes, they shake. But I don't feel that either. All I feel is pressure in my chest like someone just plunged my head underwater and I tried to breathe. My mouth goes dry, but I can't swallow. The pressure builds and grows and knocks down walls and won't let up. I press my hands to my chest and rub, but it doesn't help. Oh, God, it doesn't help. My heart lurches into overdrive like it's trying to stage a prison break. I fall to the cold bathroom floor, gasping, choking for breath, but I can't get any. I can't find any. There's no air left to breathe. I'm the lit match in front of a pair of lips puckered up, ready to blow.

Minutes pass, but they feel like centuries. I fumble for my phone—my mom's phone since she made me switch with her—and call her.

"Grace, what's wrong?"

"Can't breathe, Mom. Hurts," I push out the words on gasps of air.

"Okay, honey, I want you to take a breath and hold it. One, two, three, and let it out."

I follow her instructions, surprised I have any breath in my lungs to hold for three seconds. The next breath is easier.

"Keep going. Deep breath, hold it, let it out."

It takes me a few tries, but finally I can breathe without the barrier. "Oh, God."

"Better?"

"Yeah. It doesn't hurt now."

"Want me to take you home?"

Oh, *home*. Where there are no laughing classmates pointing at me, whispering behind their hands. Where there are no ex-friends calling me a bitch or a liar. Where I could curl up, throw a blanket over my head, and pretend nothing happened. *Yes, take me home. Take me home right now as fast as you can.*

I want to say that. But when I glance in the mirror over the row of sinks, something makes me say, "No. I have to stay."

"Grace—"

"Mom, I have to stay."

There's a loud sigh. "Oh, honey. You don't have to be brave."

Brave.

The word hangs in the air for a moment and then falls away, almost like even it knows it has no business being used to describe me. I'm not brave. I'm scared. I'm so freakin' scared, I can't see straight, and I can't see straight because I'm too scared to look very far. I'm a train wreck. All I'm doing is trying to hold on to what I have left. Only I'm not sure what that is. When I say nothing, she laughs too loudly. "Well, you're wearing your father's favorite outfit, so just pretend it's a superhero costume."

That makes me laugh. I glance down at my favorite boots— black leather covered in metal studs. My ass-kicking boots. Ever since Dad married Kristie, Mom lets me get away with anything that pisses him off, and wow does he hate how I dress.

"Grace, if you feel the pressure in your chest again, take a deep breath, hold it, and count. Concentrating on counting helps keep your mind from spiraling into panic."

"Yeah. Okay." But I'm not at all convinced. "I missed most of first period."

"Skip it. Don't worry about getting in trouble. Where are you now?"

"Bathroom."

"Why don't you go to the library? Relax and regroup, you know?"

Regroup. Sure. Okay. "Yeah. I'll do that."

"If you need me to get you, I'll come. Okay?"

I meet my own gaze in the mirror, disgusted to see them fill with tears. Jeez, you'd think I'd be empty by now. "Thanks, Mom." I end the call, tuck the phone in my pocket, and head for the library.

The library is my favorite spot in the whole school. Two floors of books, rows of computers, soft chairs to slouch in. I head for the nonfiction section and find the 770s. This is where the photography books live—my stack. I run a finger along the spines and find the first book I ever opened on the subject—*A History of Photography*.

I pull the book off its shelf, curl up with it in a chair near a window, and flip open the back cover. My signature is scrawled on the checkout card so many times now that we're old friends. I know how this book smells—a little like cut grass. How it feels—the pages are thick and glossy. And even where every one of its scars lives— the coffee ring on page 213 and the dog-eared corner in chapter 11. This is the book that said, "Grace, you *are* a photographer."

I flip through the pages, reread the section on high-key technique—I love how that sounds. *High-key.* So professional. It's really just great big fields of bright white filled with a splash of color or sometimes only shadow. I took hundreds of pictures this way—of Miranda, of Lindsay, of me. I practiced adjusting aperture settings and shutter speeds and overexposing backgrounds. It's cool how even the simplest subjects look calm and cheerful. It's like the extra light forces us to see the beauty and the flaws we never noticed.

I unzip my backpack and take out the school's digital camera. It's assigned to me—official student newspaper photographer. I scroll through the images stored on the card—selfies I shot over the last few weeks. Why can't everybody see what I see? My eyes don't sparkle. My lips don't curve anymore. Why don't they *see*?

I shove the camera back in my bag. With a sigh, I close the book, and a slip of paper floats to the floor. I pick it up, unfold it, and my stomach twists when I read the words printed on it. A noise startles me, and I look up to see Tyler Embery standing at one of the computers. Did he slip this paper into my favorite book? He's had a painfully obvious crush on me forever. Every time he gets within five feet of me, his face flushes and sweat beads at his hairline. Tyler volunteers at the library during his free periods and always flags me over to give me the latest issue of *Shutterbug* that he sets aside for me as soon as it arrives. He grabs something off the desk and walks over to me. I smile, thankful there's still one person left in this world that doesn't think Zac McMahon is the second coming of Christ. But Tyler's not holding a magazine. He's holding his phone.

"Six-eighty-three." There's no blush, no sweat—only disgust.

I jerk like he just punched me. I guess in a way he has. He turns, heads to the magazine rack, and places this month's issue, in its clear plastic cover, face out, in a subtle *fuck you* only I'd notice. I stuff the paper into my backpack and hurry to the exit just as the bell rings.

I make it to the end of the day. At dismissal I make damn sure I'm early for the bus ride home so I can snag an empty row. I plug in my earbuds to drown out the taunts. *It's not so bad*, I tell myself repeatedly, the taste of tears at the back of my throat familiar now. I don't believe me.

Once safely back in my house, I let my shoulders sag and take my first easy breath of the day. The house is empty and eerie, and I wonder how to fill the hours until Mom gets home. Thirty-two days ago I'd have been hanging out after school with Miranda and Lindsay or shopping at the mall or trying to find the perfect action photo at one of the games. In my room, I stare at the mirror over my dresser, where dozens of photos are taped—photos of me with my friends, me with my dad, me at dance class. I'm not welcome at any of these places, by any of these people anymore. I don't have a damn thing because Zac McMahon took it all. I think about Mom killing all of my online accounts and switching phones *just until things settle*. But now that the video of me that Zac posted on Facebook has 683 Likes, it's pretty clear that waiting for *things to settle* is a fantasy.

I rip all the pictures off the mirror, tear them into tiny pieces, and swipe them into the trash bin next to my desk. Then I pull out the slip of paper I found in the photography book, and after a few minutes of staring at it, I dial the number with shaking hands.

"Rape Crisis Hotline, this is Diane. Let me help you."